"Build a wall about your heart."

Riordan Wollstonecraft labors under the heavy burden of his forebears. For generations, a curse has followed the dashing young men of his family, guaranteeing the women they love an untimely death. The youngest grandson of the Earl of Wollstonecraft Hall, charismatic Riordan is quietly resigned to his fate, an educator who devotes his life to good works, and ignores any longing for something more . . .

Widowed and penniless, Lady Sabrina Lakeside is desperate to avoid a second forced betrothal—this time to an aged marquess. Her chance encounter with Riordan leads her to an impulsive offer: a temporary marriage of convenience that could benefit them both. His agreement is as surprising as it is welcome. Before long, Riordan's keen intellect and kind words have Sabrina rethinking her plans of a union in name only. But her new husband is holding something back. Will giving in to their tantalizing passion lead her only to further heartache . . . or could it be the first step toward healing them both?

Books by Karyn Gerrard

The Hornsby Brothers
The Vicar's Frozen Heart
Bold Seduction

The Ravenswood Chronicles
Beloved Beast
Beloved Monster

The Men Of Wollstonecraft Hall
Marriage With A Proper Stanger

Published by Kensington Publishing Corporation

To my teacher husband, who is not only the inspiration for the hero of this book, but my rock and support. Love you. Always.

Acknowledgments

Many thanks to Martin Biro, editor, at Kensington Publishing, my editor, Amanda Siemen, and my agent, Elaine Spencer from The Knight Agency. What a support you all are!

Prologue

Wollstonecraft Hall, Kent
Autumn, 1831

Taking a stroll through a gloomy graveyard was the last thing thirteen-year-old Riordan wished to do on this dismal, overcast autumn day. But he and his twin brother, Aidan, followed dutifully behind their grandfather as he led them to the private area on the edge of the vast estate of Wollstonecraft Hall.

Ravens cawed loudly overhead as they swooped and circled above the rows of tombstones. Gnarled trees stood around the perimeter of the cemetery, as if guarding the dead. Riordan swore he could see screaming faces in the patterns of the bark. A breeze rustled the remaining leaves, creating an eerie sound, causing a chill to curl about Riordan's spine. Aidan, however, was not affected by their gothic surroundings; he gave Riordan a shove, almost knocking him from his feet.

"Stop it," Riordan whispered fiercely.

Aidan gave him a smug smile and shoved him again. It was tempting to wrestle his annoying brother to the ground, but he decided against it when their grandfather stopped before a polished marble tombstone. "It is time you lads learned of the curse."

That brought Riordan up short. He'd heard whisperings, from other boys in town and between the servants, but had never given the story another thought. To him, it was a fairy tale, and he was far too old for fairy tales.

"See all these graves? They belong to women who dared to love the men of Wollstonecraft Hall. Many of the men married young, had their first child before the age of twenty, and all buried their wives only a few years into their marriages. Most of the unfortunate women have died in childbirth. Generations of women who either married or were born into the family. Your own mother survived your birth only to succumb four years later to a heart ailment called carditis." His grandfather laid a hand on top of the stone.

Fiona Fannon Black Wollstonecraft.

Riordan and Aidan's Irish mother. Sadly, he had no memories of her. He glanced at his brother; Aidan's expression was as serious as his own. He turned his attention to their grandfather.

"She was a rare beauty, your mother. Your father met her while on a business trip. He'd gone to meet with her father, a rich Irish merchant, as we wished to expand trade. At least, as far as the Corn Laws would allow." This was the most Riordan had ever heard about his mother and her family—his father refused to speak of her. "A whirlwind romance. I advised him before he left to guard his heart. But he did not listen to me."

"Why is it we've never met our Irish grandfather?" Aidan asked.

"Ah. When informed of your mother's death, he was quite distraught. Blamed your father. Claimed he wanted nothing to do with him or his sons. It's his loss that he does not wish to know you boys." He pointed to a tombstone in the aisle behind them. Riordan and Aidan turned and found a crow perched on the stone, giving them a defiant look. It was a disturbing vision, and it caused another shiver to trickle through him.

"There rests my first wife, your grandmother, Lady Patricia Ackerly, daughter to the Earl of Clapham. Not exactly a love match, but a solid one in society's eyes. She gave me a fine son, your father. However, she never recovered from the trauma of his birth, contracted a bed fever, and died a month later. I swore my next wife would be of heartier stock. I would defy the Wollstonecraft curse and bring it to a swift end."

Their grandfather moved along the row and laid his hand on top of another gravestone. A wistful sigh escaped his throat.

Moira Mackinnon Wollstonecraft.

Uncle Garrett's Scottish mother. "God, how I loved Moira," he whispered mournfully. "But it wasn't enough to shield her from the curse."

Riordan did not like the sounds of this. He and Aidan exchanged worried looks.

"I met Moira in Edinburgh, about twelve years after your grandmother died. She was the epitome of a bonnie lass, with her fiery red hair and passionate nature. Does your father ever speak of her?"

Riordan nodded. "He said he remembered her always smiling."

"She embraced this family. Became a mother to Julian. Always had a song in her heart. When Garrett was born, my happiness was complete. I didn't give a hang what society thought about my choice of bride. For once in my life, I was content and in love. At peace." A lone tear trickled down his cheek. "But it was not to be," he whispered. "I wish you could have known her. She died when Garrett was five years of age. The year before you lads were born."

"I thought the curse was broken if a Wollstonecraft man found true love?" Aidan asked. It was the first Riordan had heard of this. How did Aidan know about it?

Their grandfather barked out a cynical laugh. "Apparently not, for what I had with Moira was all that and more. Your father thought he'd found it. Yet here our wives lie, taken from us far too young. The doctor claims Moira died of a cancer that lay dormant for years, long before we met. Who is to know what to believe?" He shook his head.

"I dismissed the curse and refused to allow it to rule my life. Your Uncle Garrett needed a mother. Three years later, I remarried. A complete miscalculation, as we were not compatible. Yet I managed to get her with child the three or four times I visited her cold bed."

Riordan was not used to such frank talk from his grandfather, and his cheeks flushed with embarrassment. A wave of apprehension rolled through him.

"She died giving birth to a girl, who died three weeks later. They are buried together there." He pointed to a small stone farther along the row. "Heed me, lads. The proof is before you. Ultimately, it will be your decision to involve yourself with a young woman when you're older, but you would be better off guarding your heart. Let no female close, for it will end in tragedy. Do you understand?"

"Yes, Grandfather," they answered in unison.

All at once, the dead-leafed trees appeared to be skeletal and more terrifying. Riordan couldn't suppress the shiver that ran through him. A terrible sense of foreboding took hold. Death, tragedy. All of this took place before he was born, or he was too young to have it impact him. But it did now. His family was cursed. *He* was cursed. He would not forget this day.

Not ever.

Chapter 1

Wollstonecraft Hall, Kent
August 1844

Growing up in an ancient, medieval hall filled with powerful men had not been without its issues, especially when tragedy and loss hung over the place like a heavy, melancholy mist on the moors. Today, however, Riordan was ready to embark on a new chapter of his young life.

Since sleep had been sporadic the previous night, he arrived in the dining room for breakfast and the first-Monday-of-the-month family meeting before the rest of his family. Rubbing his hands together to elicit a little warmth as he entered the room, the enticing aromas of bacon, ham, and coffee filled his senses. Murmuring "good morning" to the phalanx of footmen standing by, Riordan lifted the covers of the silver chafing dishes and commenced loading his plate with food.

Martin, the butler, already well-versed in Riordan's beverage preference, prepared his tea the way he liked it, with two teaspoons of sugar and the milk added first. He set the cup and saucer on the table next to Riordan. "Cook made cinnamon scones, sir. Would you care for one? I know how you enjoy them."

"After I tackle this rasher of bacon, I will. Thank you, Martin." Popping a forkful of curried eggs in his mouth, he nodded to his father, Julian Wollstonecraft, Viscount Tensbridge, as he strode into the room. All the Wollstonecraft men were tall and dark-haired, save his Uncle Garrett, his father's thirty-two-year-old half brother. At the age of forty-five, his father had threads of gray at his temples but was often mistaken for someone younger. His detached, distinguished air bespoke of their venerated lineage.

"Already tucking in, I see." His father gave him an amused smile as he took his seat, content to allow Martin to serve him.

"I'm blasted hungry this morning. Perhaps it is the change in temperature," Riordan said between bites.

"Coffee this morning, my lord?" Martin asked.

"Yes. Coffee it is. And ham instead of bacon." Julian snapped open the linen napkin and laid it on his lap. "Riordan, where is your older brother?"

Older by fifteen minutes, Aidan was the heir apparent and Riordan was fine with it. His paternal twin had stumbled in at three in the morning; he couldn't help but hear his brother's cursing and bumping into furniture from across the hall. "Still asleep, I believe."

His father sighed. "Martin, send one of the footmen to rouse my slugabed son."

"At once, my lord." The butler inclined his head toward one of the footmen, who exited the dining area.

Garrett walked into the room dressed as if he had come straight from the barn, which he had, seeing he spent all his time with horses. His uncle had inherited his red hair, pale skin, and freckles from his Scottish mother. Close to six and a half feet in height, his barrel chest and massive shoulders were a stark contrast to the leaner musculature of the rest of the men. *Much like a medieval Highlander*, Riordan mused.

"Before you ask, brother, I wiped my muddy boots," Garrett said as he moved to the sideboard. His uncle managed to pile more food on his plate than Riordan had. Sitting across the table, Garrett immediately started to eat as the footmen brought toast and poured his tea.

"How's Starlight doing?" Julian asked while cutting his ham into meticulous bite-sized pieces.

"She hasn't foaled yet," Garrett replied. "Going to be a long siege, I imagine. The stable lads are keeping watch and will inform me if there are any developments."

Aidan happened into the room with a short, unsteady gait, looking the worse for wear. He plopped down next to Garrett. "Coffee, Martin, and lots of it. Bring me nothing else or I shall puke, for certain."

Julian curled his lip in obvious distaste. "Out gambling and whoring again? Best not let your grandfather see the state of you. Sit up straight." Aidan sneered, but did as he was told. "Martin, bring the heir toast and cheese. You will eat and get that insolent expression off your face. Look at the state of you, unkempt, eyes bloodshot. We will be speaking about this at great length after the meeting concludes."

Riordan did not envy his brother. *He's in the soup now.* But when had he not been with their father? It was as if Aidan acted in such a way to rile him on purpose.

As always, Oliver Wollstonecraft entered last. Tall and regal, his grandfather defied Father Time, standing as straight and tall as his sons and grandsons. He was a sterling example of exemplary hereditary vim and vigor and amazing good health. Riordan's great-grandfather, the old earl, passed away five years ago, and he'd remained a striking figure well into his eighties. Of all the maladies to cause death, it was a winter chill that took him.

"Ah, all here. Excellent." The earl took his seat at the head of the table while Martin and the footmen laid tea, coffee, and various food items in front of him—and Aidan, who turned a sickening shade of green at the sight of it. Riordan smirked. Having his brother cast up his accounts would certainly add drama to the gathering.

Attendance was mandatory at these family meetings. The earl would brook no argument or accept any excuses for not being present. What was discussed at these compulsory summits? Ways to further the family's progressive agenda. Though distantly related to Mary Wollstonecraft, the late-eighteenth-century scholar, philosopher, and advocate of women's rights, and to her daughter, Mary Wollstonecraft Shelley, essayist and the novelist of the gothic tale *Frankenstein*, the men of Wollstonecraft Hall were no less involved in liberal causes.

When he finished serving, Martin sat next to the earl, pen, ink, and parchment at the ready to record the minutes. The footmen moved efficiently around the table, bringing the scones, cheese turnovers, and fruit, and refilling beverages as the men conversed.

"I've received word that our eccentric neighbor, Sir Walter Keenan, has passed away," the earl stated.

Riordan's mouth quirked with amusement. Not at the news of Sir Walter's death, but at the fact his grandfather found him eccentric, considering what society thought of the Wollstonecrafts. Sir Walter was an ex-soldier, granted knighthood for his bravery in the Peninsular War at Salamanca in 1808. Since returning home from the army in 1819, he had lived as a hermit.

"Since he is unmarried, the property is passing to his next of kin," his grandfather continued. "His niece, a widow, I don't know her name, is the beneficiary. He's been our neighbor for more than thirty-five years. Someone should put in an appearance at his funeral."

Julian shook his head. "The widow will be inheriting a run-down manor, to say the least. I will not be able to attend. I am heading to London, the autumn session of parliament, as I've meetings with Lord Ashley." Since his father had a courtesy title, he didn't sit in the House of Lords. He served as a member of parliament for this region of Kent, though he often worked with the upper chamber on many bills.

Riordan would not be able to attend the funeral either, but he decided he would leave his announcement for the end of the gathering. Why stir up the hornet's nest at this juncture?

"How go the discussions for restricting the number of work hours?" Garrett asked as he sipped his tea. All the other men gave him incredulous looks. "What? I read the papers, and I am a member of this family. I have broadminded views."

"I'm working with Lord Ashley to reduce the workweek to sixty hours for women and children," Julian replied. "We are being fought tooth and nail. I predict a compromise somewhere between sixty and seventy."

The earl harrumphed. "Still too long."

Julian buttered his cinnamon scone. "I agree, but most peers strongly believe women and children are an integral part of a family's earning power, and under the man of the house's command. Most do not want any regulations at all."

Riordan glanced across the table at his brother. Aidan's expression held a combination of nausea and boredom. "I've read that one out of every three citizens is under the age of fifteen, which is the reason many children labor in textile mills and coal mines," Riordan said.

Julian nodded. "True. There should be regulations in place to protect the innocent. Another touchy subject is repealing the Corn Laws."

"Blasted protectionism. I was against it from the first," the earl boomed. "By imposing restrictions on imported wheat, which in turn inflates grain prices, all it has done is managed to further deepen and expand the wretched poverty infecting this country."

"I agree, Father. It is going to be a nasty fight. I predict it will shake the foundations of the British government." Julian popped a piece of scone into his mouth and swallowed. "You should go with me to London instead of waiting until the middle of next month. There are many battles to be fought, and we need every progressive voice we can muster."

"Yes, perhaps I will," the earl replied.

Riordan's heart swelled with pride as he listened to his father's impassioned words. The subject changed to the running of the estate, and

Garrett brought everyone up to date on the horse breeding, farming, and the surrounding tenants.

Aidan remained silent, slowly picking away at his toast and cheese.

"Aidan," Julian said, his voice tight with annoyance. "You are the heir. You will be carrying our progressive torch into the future. Have you nothing to offer?"

Aidan looked up, a bored expression on his face. "Not this morning, Father."

The rumblings of a heated argument simmered near the surface, and because of it, Riordan decided to make his announcement to divert away from a family spat. At least, he hoped it would. "I have news. I have accepted a position as schoolmaster in the town of Carrbury, in East Sussex."

The table grew quiet and all eyes turned to him. Well, he'd shocked them into silence. Might as well continue. "One of our main concerns is neglected, exploited, and abused children. Trying to pass compulsory education is defeated at every turn for the exact reason you mentioned, Father. The notion that children be kept uneducated and ignorant so that it makes them better workers is inherently heinous."

The men all grumbled, nodding and agreeing with his assessment. Even Aidan reacted with a brisk nod. Riordan pushed on. "Education reform is achingly slow. We all know it will take decades of small, incremental changes before education for all becomes enforced. But there *are* changes being made. The Ragged School Union was set up this past spring. Schools are opening all across Great Britain, but not only charity schools. There's a new concept: board schools."

He had their complete attention. Even the butler listened in. "Fee-paying schools have been around for centuries, but only available to those in the upper class, who can afford them. Board schools would charge landowners and businesses a small fee, to be administered by an elected board of local officials. One of these schools has been set up in Carrbury. I applied for the position of schoolmaster, was interviewed and accepted. I did not go by Wollstonecraft. I applied as Mr. Riordan Black." Black was his middle name, his mother's surname. "One of the board members knows my true identity, as I had to prove my education credentials, but he agreed to keep it secret so that it would not draw too much attention to the school. I will be able to gather information, implement my own reforms, and observe if they take root."

"I am exceedingly proud of you, Son," Julian said, the words spoken with warmth. A erisive snort came from Aidan, but their father ignored it.

"As am I, Riordan. All the information you gather will only strengthen our cause. How far away is Carrbury?" his grandfather asked.

"About twenty-two miles south of here, less than a day's ride. I'm to report there in five days' time. The small township and surrounding area covers a population of about seven hundred, and I'm told I may have upward of thirty-five children of various ages in the classroom."

"Shrewd of you to conceal the name. Come and walk with me, Riordan, and we will discuss this development further. If there is no other business?" He glanced around the table. "I adjourn the meeting," the earl stated.

Aidan stood, but Julian shot him a thunderous look. "Sit. We have much to talk about."

"On that ominous note, I will return to the horses." Garrett took one last sip of tea, wiped his mouth, and stood. He strode over to Riordan and the earl, clasping Riordan on the shoulder. "Well done. You do this family proud." Not used to such gracious words from his self-contained uncle, he was genuinely touched. With a nod, Garrett left the room.

* * * *

The late August morning had a slight chill to the air, a hint of the cooler autumn weather to come. Riordan and his grandfather strolled in silence for several minutes. As they entered the garden, the earl returned greetings to the gardeners, answering them by name. The well-manicured shrubs, hedgerows, rosebushes, and wildflowers added to the pleasantness. The slight breeze rustled the birch leaves, acting as nature's fan.

"For all our progressive views and reform work, we do live a life of privilege. This will be a good opportunity for you, Riordan. To see how others live, how they struggle. Do you plan to stay in the position long?"

"At least one year. I have always wanted to do it. To teach, make a difference in others' lives. To introduce children to a world of books, learning, and imagination."

"A noble calling," the earl murmured.

"I hope one day to start my own progressive school. Employ only the best educators. But I cannot move forward until I'm able to prove my reforms will work in a classroom setting."

"I agree completely. Take extensive notes, as if you were a scientist conducting an experiment, which, in fact, you are. I pledge I will do all I can to see your dream comes to fruition. As will your father."

"Thank you, Grandfather."

Taking a turn on the stone path, Riordan frowned. They were heading to the private family cemetery. The men rarely came here, as it was a place of unspeakable tragedy. He hadn't been to this dreary place since his grandfather brought him and Aidan here when they were thirteen. Thankfully, they stopped well short of the gated entrance.

"This is as good a time as any to discuss the curse once again," the earl stated.

Oh, God. Riordan struggled not to react, but with one glance at his grandfather, at the obvious pain and grief on his face, he decided to keep his opinion to himself. Through the years, he dismissed the fable. Time often lessened the impact of frightful episodes, and his grandfather telling him of the curse was one of them. But here lay the proof. Row after row of graves. It was enough to give him pause. Generations of women. His own mother and grandmother. An aunt who died in infancy.

While his father, uncle, and grandfather had certainly indulged in a few brief affairs through the years, the different generations of men allowed no women close. In truth, many ladies of society were wary of any long-lasting romantic ties to such a storied and tragic clan. The curse followed the men like a hovering black cloud. It was one of the reasons Riordan had hidden his name when applying for the teaching assignment: he did not want the scrutiny or the attention.

"You are about to go out into the world. Make your own way. You will meet young ladies," the earl said.

"Grandfather, I am hardly a monk. I've been in the company of ladies before." A couple of dalliances. Nothing significant, and he certainly didn't have the carnal experience Aidan possessed. His twin had cut a wide swath through London society and beyond in the past six years.

"You would be wise to follow your Uncle Garrett and remain free of any romantic entanglements. Build a wall about your heart, lock it away, and let no one in. I know I told you all this years ago, but a reminder is warranted."

The earl laid his hands on Riordan's shoulders and looked him in the eye. "I have come to learn it is better not to feel anything at all in order to avoid heartbreak. You turned twenty-six last month; you are young and impressionable. Remain aloof, even remote, in your dealings with women. I would not see you hurt for the world."

His grandfather spoke with great emotion, and Riordan took the warning to heart. He would be wise to follow the advice. *Remember the curse.* Though he did not believe it as intensely as other members of his family, it would be prudent to keep it at the forefront of his mind.

There was much he wished to accomplish in this world, and love was a diversion he neither wanted nor needed.

Chapter 2

As she watched her father slice his morning kippers, Sabrina Durning Lakeside, Lady Pepperdon and widow to the late, ancient, and not-the-least-bit-missed Charles Lakeside, Earl of Pepperdon, visibly shuddered. Not because of the kippers, though she'd never liked them. It was more to do with her loathsome father than his choice of breakfast food.

Snapping his newspaper as he chewed noisily, he grunted as he read, his cruel mouth twisting in distaste.

Biting into her toast, Sabrina waved to George the footman and pointed to her empty teacup. The young man moved to her side and filled it, stepping away silently when he'd completed his task.

"It has been nearly a year," her father loudly stated, which caused her to start. "A year since that earl of yours had the bad taste to up and die."

Not only die, but leave her in financial straits, with no choice but to return to her recently widowed father. They both looked ridiculous, sitting at the table in mourning clothes when neither of them truly grieved for those who'd passed. Sabrina had spent the past eleven years in a cold and loveless marriage with a man thirty-eight years her senior, a marriage her father had insisted upon when she turned eighteen. About the same time the old earl expired, her father buried his second wife, a frail creature who died in childbirth.

"What is your point?" she sniffed as she spread blackberry jam on her toast.

"The point is you cannot stay here any longer. The required period of mourning has come and gone. You must marry again." He laid the paper on the table and cut into his kippers again. "And so must I. Any woman I bring into this house will not want my widowed, aging daughter skulking about in the corner like a spider."

Aging? She'd turned thirty last month, not old in her book. "It is not my fault my thoughtless husband did not provide for me in his will. Or that his heir, his slimy nephew, would turn me out without a cent. When you negotiated my dowry, there should have been lawful assurances I would receive something out of this disaster." Sabrina sipped her tea. "A small house, a stipend." *Happiness. Love.* But why would she expect in her marriage what she never had growing up in this bleak house?

"Blame me, will you? I do not care much for your tone." His eyes narrowed. "When a baron marries his daughter to an earl, it is expected that the blasted man will do the honorable thing. Well, I shall not make the same mistake again. I will aim higher and take all legal steps necessary to ensure I will not be responsible for your upkeep. You still have your looks, although the fact that you're barren means you will have to settle for a peer who already has a grown family and no desire for another."

Sabrina's blood froze in her veins. Not again. She would not allow her wretched father to marry her off to an old reprobate. Death would be preferable. A bit extreme, but she would rather die than be used and tossed aside by another man old enough to be her grandfather. "No."

His fist slammed against the table, rattling the dishes. He turned toward the footman. "Leave us, and see we are not disturbed."

George bowed. "Yes, my lord." He scurried from the room.

Slowly and with purpose, she closed her hand over the knife and pulled it to her lap while her father was distracted. It had been many years since he'd struck her, but she would not give him the chance to lay a hand on her ever again. It always started the same way: dismissing the servants. No doubt his second wife endured his temper, as did Sabrina's mother, from what she could recall. Though her mother died many years ago, Sabrina remembered the pleas, and the sound of an open hand making contact with skin.

"Listen to me, you ungrateful slattern. By Tuesday next, you will present yourself in the parlor, wearing a gown showing your décolletage, and will greet the Marquess of Sutherhorne with a smile on your face and a gracious tone in your voice."

Marquess of Sutherhorne? Her mind raced as if flipping through the pages of Debrett's *The New Peerage*. Her heart sank. Another wizened, elderly man. Seventy if he was a day. She'd met him once, during a rare occasion in which her late husband had escorted her to a ball. If memory served, he had missing teeth and clumps of hair in his ears. And smelled of horse. "Why would he want to marry again?" she whispered.

"Why does any man marry? At his age, he no doubt wants you as a bed warmer. I have it on good authority that he has a weakened heart; he will not live long. I will ensure you are left with the means to live a comfortable life when he meets his maker."

The urge to rage and scream nearly overcame her. Instead, she tried to keep her voice steady. "Father, do not marry me off to an old man. Not again."

"You *will* obey me in this. I've waited long enough. I must marry, as I will be fifty-two in four months. I need to find a young woman and breed an heir. You will only be in the way." He crossed his arms. "In fact, I have a young woman in mind and will have to act swiftly, before she is snapped up by a young buck."

Sabrina stared at her father incredulously. Granted, for a man of his age, he was still handsome, in his cold, cruel way, and she suddenly felt sorry for any young, impressionable woman who would be taken in by his fake manners and smooth words.

"If you were not such a failure as a woman, I could shop you about the younger peers, but none would have you," he continued, oblivious to the fact that his words landed across her heart like slices from a blade. "It is the doddering old fools, or you make your own way in the world."

My own way? Sabrina didn't have a blessed clue how to go about it. Regardless of her unhappiness growing up and during her marriage, she wanted for nothing. Why, she never had to do anything for herself, especially when married to the earl since he was rich beyond measure. There were maids and footmen aplenty to do her bidding. In truth, she *liked* being well-off, and reveled in the comfort and luxury. Hot tears stung her eyes, but she blinked them away and swallowed hard. Be damned if she would show the baron any reaction.

"Why not allow me to meet men close to my own age? At least give me the chance before shuffling me off to another aged stranger. We will both be coming out of mourning. We can attend social functions together and assess the market—"

Her father held up his hand. "No, Daughter. I want you gone from this house before I narrow in on my selection."

Sabrina clenched her teeth. "I am of age, a widow. I don't have to obey you in this."

The baron shrugged. "Quite true. Then pack what you came with and leave by the end of the week."

"You would turn out your own daughter?" Her voice quivered on the last couple of words. There was no hiding her distress now.

He leaned forward, his expression hardened. "If you had been a boy, as you should have been, there would be no need for this discussion at all. Daughters are completely useless, except to give other men a son."

Sabrina stood as a potent roll of anger moved through her. She slammed the knife on the table. "Yes, a calamity for both of us."

"I will have your answer at breakfast the day after tomorrow." Picking up the paper, he sat up straight and continued to read, effectively ignoring her.

She indulged in a bout of self-pity for a brief moment. The baron had never loved her. No one had ever loved her. Sabrina stared at her father. Why was he apathetic and unfeeling? Because she wasn't a son? Or was he merely born this way? Or both? From what she'd observed, he treated everyone with cold disdain, from the lowest of servants to his fellow peers. *Hateful man.* She swept from the room and made her way upstairs, determined with every step to thwart her father's miserable plan.

She would find a husband. A man with all his teeth, who did not have one foot in the grave. Surely there must be an unmarried male person in the vicinity willing to take her on.

A plan began to form in her mind. Her father was anxious to be rid of her. For that fact alone, he would be willing to make a monetary settlement to her husband-to-be. All Sabrina had to do was locate an honest man with a modicum of honor to agree to her scheme.

Desperate times called for desperate measures. She must make haste. Seven days was hardly enough time to find such a man. She'd not been to town in months, had not lived in this area for eleven years. She had no earthly idea what type of man she would find.

The middle class swelled in numbers with each passing year. There were always those in trade or public service. A professional of some sort. A solicitor. A doctor. Besides, this arrangement would not be for a lifetime.

"Mary," she called out to her maid as she entered her bedchamber. "Lay out my dark green walking dress. I am heading to town."

* * * *

Lord, how Sabrina wished she'd used the carriage. The mile walk proved how soft and lazy she'd become the past several years. She could send Mary back to the estate and have her bring the carriage for her return trip. The hot late summer sun caused beads of perspiration to trail along the valley of her spine. Tendrils of hair came loose from her upswept style, sticking to her flushed cheeks.

Emerging through a cluster of junipers, Sabrina spotted a fair-sized structure that appeared to be in a state of renovation. A wooden bench along the wall caught her eye. Thank God she could rest for a moment and catch her breath. Funny, she didn't remember this building being here before.

"Mary, let us sit." She motioned to the bench.

"Are you well, my lady? You're red in the face and short of breath," her maid asked, worry etched into her brow.

"I believe once we rest, I will send you for the carriage in order for us to continue our journey. I'm more fatigued than I thought I would be." Sabrina sat and exhaled in relief, resting her head against the wall. Voices drifted out from the building and caught her attention. The window was open, and one voice stood out from the rest. Male, deep, melodic—and mesmerizing.

"It does not matter what you plan to do with your life. Do you wish to be a farmer like your father? Read books. Learn all you can about agriculture, animal husbandry, and excel at your chosen profession. But never stop reading; learn all you can about everyone and everything, if not to learn, then to allow your imagination to fly. How many remember what the imagination is?" Multiple overlapping and enthusiastic replies drifted from the window, drawing her attention even further.

"Good. With the imagination you can see ancient Egypt, the building of the Sphinx, construction of the pyramids, and adorn yourself with pharaoh's gold. Or you may visit what Shakespeare called—"

"Was his name William?" a child's voice called out.

"Yes. Correct. William Shakespeare called the imagination the 'undiscovered country.' What did he mean by it? Immerse yourself in another world. Escape. For what is imagination? The ability to form a picture in your mind of that which you have never experienced."

Sabrina was completely enthralled, not only by the man's enthusiasm, but by his gentle tone.

"Mr. Black, my da can't afford to buy books," a young lad said.

"Ah. That is why we will be starting a library right here in our schoolroom. Does anyone know what a library is?"

"A place you borrow books?" a girl answered.

"Exactly, Becky. Well done. I have brought five books to start us off, and hopefully once we get the word out, we will garner donations to permit the library to grow and flourish. It will be a school library. See the empty bookcase against the far wall? We'll start there. You will sign out a book with the promise to return it in two weeks."

A harmony of happy young voices all talked at once. Curious, Sabrina stood and turned toward the window, but the top of her head barely reached the sill. Standing on the bench would be too obvious. Instead, she stood on the tips of her toes. Quite a few children of various ages were sitting at tables, their bright faces all riveted to the front of the room. Unfortunately, from her angle, she could not see the honey-voiced schoolmaster who held her spellbound.

She imagined him middle-aged, wearing spectacles, with a receding hairline and a prominent nose. A kindly gentleman, educated, decent. One who might listen to her scheme?

"The first book is *Grimm's Fairy Tales*. Who shall be the first to borrow it?"

The children all called out, save one boy sitting near the window. He looked down at his hands. "James? Would you not like to read this book?" the schoolmaster asked in a gracious tone. Blast, she still couldn't see the man.

"I don't read good, sir," the boy replied in a quiet voice.

"Come here."

The boy disappeared from her line of sight. Sabrina was wholly captivated by the doings in the room. The schoolmaster had complete control of the children, not with strict discipline and the threat of a caning, but with compassion, respect, and eagerness.

"Improving your reading skills is accomplished with plenty of practice. I am here to assist you. We will all help you, will we not, class?" the schoolmaster asked.

The children all nodded and answered yes.

"Shall we allow James to be the first to sign out a library book?" A cheerful chorus of affirmatives filled the room. "Well done. I see it's luncheon break. Be off home and return in two hours sharp. Remember; take an apple from the basket on your way out the door. Alice, take one for your little sister."

The room emptied out and grew silent. The door was on the opposite wall, thankfully, or the children would have caught her spying on them.

"Would you like to come into the schoolroom and have a look around?"

The schoolmaster's close-in-proximity voice startled her, and she gasped. He stood at the window, but thanks to the midday sun, she could not make out his features.

"Yes. Of course," she muttered in reply.

Clasping Mary's arm, Sabrina pulled her along with her as she made her way to the front entrance. "Head to the manor and fetch the carriage. I will wait here for your return and then we'll continue into town."

Mary had been with her during her marriage, and had chosen to come with her when Sabrina returned to her father's house. She was a steady presence in Sabrina's life, had helped her through some of the darkest days of her desolate life with Pepperdon. It struck her that her loyal maid's fate was now irrevocably tied to hers. If her father turned her out, what would become of Mary? It made her situation all the more urgent.

Mary raised an eyebrow. "Leave you alone with a strange man? I think not, my lady."

"I am hardly a green girl in need of a chaperone. I can handle a meek schoolmaster. I'll be fine, I assure you. Perhaps he will give me an apple."

Mary smiled and headed off toward the line of trees. She waved, and Sabrina returned the gesture. Sighing, she walked around the perimeter of the building and, as she looked up, stopped dead in her tracks.

The schoolmaster was not a docile, plain man of middling years, but a tall, handsome young man who took her breath away. She'd never seen such virility before, never mind been in such close proximity to it. Her heart fluttered, and Sabrina was shocked at her response, for it was strange and foreign.

He dressed plainly, wearing a black frock coat stretched across broad shoulders, with a simply tied black cravat. No spectacles; all the better to see his piercing light blue eyes. His wavy black hair gleamed in the bright sunlight. Good Lord, he barely looked out of the schoolroom himself.

"Good afternoon. My name is Riordan Black. How may I help you?"

His voice, like melted butter, smooth and delicious. Could he assist her? She should leave immediately, keep her mad machinations to herself. But her feet would not move. Yes, the sight of a handsome man made her heart skip a beat—it still stuttered with an uneven cadence. Sabrina was surprised she even had a heart. All nonsense. The last gasp of long-lost, never-to-return emotions. They had no place here. Straightening her shoulders, she gave him a brisk nod. "Help me? That remains to be seen."

Chapter 3

Riordan's smile twitched in amusement at her brusque tone. James had whispered to him that a lady was peering in the window when the boy stood before his desk. Since Riordan's arrival three weeks past, he'd remained an object of curiosity. Not only for his youth, but for the major changes he implemented right out of the gate. And, he supposed, his dark hair and blue eyes sparked an interest with the young ladies in the nearby town. He wasn't conceited, but he'd been lucky when it came to inheriting certain family features.

This lady was no blushing maiden, could be his age or older. He would guess older, as she possessed an air of maturity. Casually, he glanced at her hand, looking for a ring, but she wore gloves. Riordan let his gaze linger on her trim form, guessing her height was six inches over five feet. Her attire was fashionable, and, shamefully, he quite enjoyed observing how the buttons of her short jacket strained across an impressive bosom.

Moving upward, he made a study of her face. Fine, pale, porcelain skin, and a light brown shade of hair that shimmered gold in the sunlight. She wore a fashionable hat with green plumes sitting atop her stylishly arranged hair. Pretty features and a pert nose. Her hazel eyes met his, boldly holding his gaze. The coldness he saw in their depths startled him. To be unhappy and weary at such a young age, what could have caused it? "And you are…?"

"Sabrina Durning Lakeside, widow to the late Earl of Pepperdon. My father is Baron Durning. Our small estate is beyond those trees."

A widow. The news caused his smile to widen, he wasn't sure why. But, being the gentleman he was brought up to be, he took her gloved hand and bent over it, skimming his lips across her knuckles. "My distinct pleasure, Lady Pepperdon." He dropped her hand and met her gaze once again. "How may I assist you?"

"May we speak inside?"

He held out his arm, bidding her to enter first. She stepped across the threshold and looked about the spartan room. "Forgive the state of the place. The school was built over the summer months, and I'm overseeing various alterations. These windows are a perfect example." They both walked to the opposite side.

"I do not hold with the idea of children learning in a windowless, cold room," he continued. "It's done in order for them not to be distracted from their lessons, but I believe large windows should allow sun and fresh air into the learning environment. If a child is to be here most of the day, they should not be cut off from nature and the out-of-doors. They should smell the flowers, feel the heat from the sun, listen to the birds sing."

"And in the winter?"

"The wood stove there will provide heat, while gently falling snow will cast a tranquil, magical mood," he replied in a light, teasing tone.

Lady Pepperdon turned, studying him closely, though for what reason, Riordan had no idea. She strode over to the tables, her fingers brushing across the slates. "It must be difficult to teach children of different ages and learning levels. Do they all use slates?"

He followed her, clasping his hands behind his back. "No, the older children use pen, ink, and paper. I have not found it difficult. I treat them all the same, regardless of age or stage of knowledge. I find children respond better when you do not talk down to them."

"From what I heard you had them in thrall, in the very palm of your hand. There is no need for discipline, then?" she asked, still sauntering leisurely between the tables.

"I've only been here three weeks, but I am not a believer in the concept of the old adage 'spare the rod, spoil the child.' Children in this day and age have hard enough lives; they do not need me screeching at them or beating them with a cane or ruler in order for them to behave. I don't mind if children become boisterous once in a while. Learning should be fun."

Lady Pepperdon swung about and gave him a brief smile. "You are unlike any schoolmaster I've ever heard of. Your views are…refreshing."

He smiled in return. "Good. Then, my lady, you will not be averse to donating to our school library fund."

"My, you do not waste an instant."

"No, I do not. I wish to start an arts program. Music and painting, for example. Children should not spend hours hunched over their slates taking endless, repetitive notes. I'm in the process of convincing the board to approve the purchase of paints, brushes, and sugar paper."

She arched a perfectly shaped brow. "Sugar paper? And what is a board?"

Riordan crossed his arms. "Sugar paper is the heavy brown paper used for sugar bags. If we buy a large roll, we can tear off pieces for the children to paint pictures on. The board is a group of local officials and prominent persons who oversee the collection of fees to run this school. When you told me your name, I assumed your father wished to become involved. I was told he initially turned down a position on the board."

"I'm not surprised."

"Ah. Then you are not here to inspect the school on behalf of your father, my lady?"

Lady Pepperdon bit her lower lip, and he found it fascinating, as it drew his attention to how lusciously plump they were. She gave off a cool, haughty aura, but he'd observed heated interest flare briefly in her eyes when she first rounded the corner of building. Perhaps he'd imagined it.

"No. Not in any official manner. I was out for a walk and took a rest on the bench. I became quite caught up in your lesson." She sighed. "I wanted to converse with you for another reason, though now it seems flighty and silly. What is your age?"

The question threw him, as he did not expect it. "I recently turned twenty-six. Why, do you believe me too young for such a position?"

"No. Perhaps too young for me," she muttered.

He stepped closer. "I beg your pardon, my lady?"

"I am in a bit of a fix, Mr. Black. A dire situation needing immediate attention." She wrung her gloved hands together in agitation. "Oh, bother. There is my maid, Mary, with the carriage. When may we speak in private?"

His curiosity was piqued, to say the least. "Why not come again at the same time tomorrow, my lady? The children return to their homes for a two-hour luncheon break. Is that sufficient time to have a private conversation?"

She waved her hand dismissively. "Yes, yes. That will do. Good afternoon, Mr. Black."

Riordan gave her a brief bow, but she had already swept from the room, leaving an enticing scent of lemon and orange blossoms in her wake. *Easy, lad.* His grandfather's stark warning came to mind. This was no place for finding any woman attractive, especially a widow to an earl. A schoolmaster could not afford to become entangled with any lady; he must be above reproach with no whiff of scandal.

Then why in hell did he arrange a clandestine meeting with her tomorrow?

* * * *

Sabrina had hardly slept at all. The trip to town turned out to be a complete waste, as the men she managed to seek out could not hold a candle to the appealing schoolmaster. Such a motive as his good looks should not matter in the least for her plan. But from their brief conversation, she had the distinct feeling that Mr. Black could be trusted to keep his word.

What if she was wrong? Many men, regardless of station, presented their best face forward when dealing with women. It was only after they gained possession of you that their true natures appeared. Cruel bullies. Heartless authoritarians. Disgusting reprobates. Sabrina shook away her disturbing thoughts.

Could this plot work? It was not as if she longed for a real marriage, as in physical relations. The idea was abhorrent to her. All she needed was to stay married long enough to apply for an annulment. She knew little of the subject, and asking the solicitor, who she discovered was in her father's employ, would arouse suspicion. Couples were able to obtain annulments, weren't they?

Whatever the response, Sabrina had to give her father an answer tomorrow morning regarding her marriage to the moldering marquess. The conversation with Mr. Black could not be delayed, no matter how uncomfortable the topic.

Before breakfast, Sabrina made a visit to the kitchen, instructing the cook, Mrs. Kempson, to pack a small hamper for luncheon, enough for two, and to make a goodly amount of ginger biscuits for the children. Though the older woman frowned, by the time Sabrina was ready to depart, everything had been prepared as ordered.

At the last minute, she decided to leave her maid behind, taking George the footman instead. As the carriage emerged from the woods, her nerves started to spark. The children were already pouring out of the school and heading toward the town proper. For the sake of propriety, she should return to the estate and accept her fate of sitting in a dark room on a deathwatch, waiting for the old marquess to pass on.

The thought of wrinkled, cold hands touching her caused her insides to lurch—she could not endure it again. Thankfully, after five years and no pregnancy in sight, Pepperdon had left her alone. At least, the physical torture had ended—but not the verbal. She would not allow any man to mistreat her a second time.

The carriage came to a stop. George opened the door, assisted her out, then lifted the large hamper to his shoulder and followed her into the school. Mr. Black sat at his desk, scribbling energetically. He looked up and gave her a genuine, warm smile, and it caused her heart to flutter once again. Sabrina dismissed the reaction immediately.

"My lady. Good to see you."

"And you, Mr. Black. George, please set the hamper on the desk and wait for me in the carriage."

"Of course, my lady." George bowed and left the room, closing the door behind him.

"What have we here?" Mr. Black asked, his blue eyes twinkling with amusement.

"Luncheon. Please, open it and help yourself."

Mr. Black got to his feet, picked up a nearby chair, and carried it to the front of his desk. "Have a seat, my lady."

As she made herself comfortable, Mr. Black unpacked the lunch. "Cold salmon sandwiches. A rare treat. Cheese, biscuits, sliced strawberries." He held up a jar. "And lemonade. Shall I serve?"

Sabrina nodded, and Mr. Black quickly loaded food onto the stoneware plates, passing one to her along with a paper napkin. He took his seat, bit into the sandwich, and smiled. "Very tasty."

"I believe Mrs. Kempson adds dill weed to the salmon mixture. There are four dozen ginger biscuits for the children. For teatime this afternoon."

"No teatime, I'm afraid. The children work until five." Mr. Black finished his sandwich and reached for another wedge. Goodness, she should have brought more food.

"There should be a break, at least in my opinion, to rest or play for ten minutes. Or to have a biscuit. Or an apple." Sabrina pointed to the basket of fruit by his desk. "Do you provide them yourself, or does this board you spoke of?"

"I paid for this, but am hoping it will become part of the budget. Many of the children have little enough to eat, and an apple can provide many needed nutrients." He poured them glasses of lemonade. "I must say, I like your idea of a break. Ten minutes. It would be a recess from learning, to allow for play or quiet time, or to eat a ginger biscuit. Thank you for bringing them." His words were cordially spoken, and despite her determination not to react to this man, her cheeks flushed. "Now that we're settled in, what do you wish to discuss with me?" he asked.

Lord, where to begin? Finishing her sandwich, she dabbed the corners of her mouth and laid the napkin on the plate. "I recently came out of mourning.

My late husband, the earl, did not provide for me in his will. His heir and nephew tossed me out, and I had no choice but to return to my father."

Mr. Black frowned. "I am sorry this happened to you. It's a travesty that women do not have any rights, whether inside of marriage or out."

"No, we do not. None at all. My hateful father no longer wishes to provide for me, as he has his own plans to remarry. To paraphrase, he does not wish his widowed, ancient daughter lurking about the house."

Mr. Black's mouth quirked with amusement. "You're hardly doddering, my lady."

"According to society, I am. I'm thirty years of age. My father believes I'm only fit for old men. Pepperdon was more than thirty-five years older. I will not be forced into such a union again." Sabrina exhaled. She had come this far. Might as well lay it all out. "The baron has given me an ultimatum: marry another prehistoric peer, or find my own way in the world."

Mr. Black's friendly smile turned into a frown. "Damn. Pardon, my lady. I am sorry to hear this."

"Good. Then you can aid me by marrying me. Right away."

Chapter 4

Riordan could not be more shocked if Lady Pepperdon had stripped off her layers of clothes and danced the fandango on his desk. Was the woman insane?

"Hear me out," she said. "It would be a temporary situation. My father would settle a sum of money to be rid of me, I am sure of it. Six months later, or whatever time is required, we can obtain an annulment and go our separate ways. I will pay you out of the settlement for your trouble. Say, twenty percent?"

Jesus, she *was* insane. "Lady Pepperdon…"

"When we are alone you may call me Sabrina."

"My lady, it's not easy to obtain an annulment. It is even more difficult to obtain a divorce, which in itself must be an Act of Parliament. Have you spoken to a solicitor about this?"

A furrow appeared between her brows. "Well, no. The solicitor in town is employed by my father."

"Is there no other family member you can live with, besides your father?"

"I have a great aunt in Manchester, but I hardly know her. She will not take me in; we're complete strangers. Where does it leave me? Become a paid companion to a peer's widow? I was married to an earl, I am the daughter of a baron. I have no idea how to be a companion. Or a governess. Nor do I wish to become one. It is not to be borne," she sniffed scornfully.

A pampered lady of society with no means to look after herself. In one way he pitied her for her hopeless situation, but in another he resented her snooty tone. She had no idea what it was like to truly struggle. But then, neither did he. "And you think being married to a penniless schoolmaster will be a step above a paid companion?" He didn't keep the contempt out of his voice. Let her hear it, for his opinion of her had dropped several notches. "You wish for me to enter into a scheme to swindle money out of your father in order for you to continue to live the life to which you have become accustomed."

Riordan could never stand the spoiled, pampered young women of the upper class. They couldn't even open a door for themselves, let alone pour their own tea. And here sat a perfect example of all he disdained, thinking she could bend people to do her bidding.

Lady Pepperdon at least looked contrite. "Well, since you put it in such stark, mercenary terms, I thank you for your time." She stood, her lower lip quivering. Tears hovered on the surface, and it caused him to soften slightly. After all, she was in a bit of a fix.

"My lady, please take a seat. I know a little about annulments. Let me explain as frankly as I can." She sat, then met his gaze. "Women have no rights. Once married, you become the property of your husband. Any dowry or settlement becomes your husband's. You cannot even open a bank account in your own name. The laws are abhorrent, and in desperate need of reform." Riordan took a breath and exhaled. "For an annulment to take place, you would have to claim the marriage was not consummated."

"We don't have to consummate it. In fact, I would prefer it if we do not."

"Indeed?" Her words stung. Was he repulsive to her? "Regardless, it cannot be proven, as you've been married before. You see, the proof the ecclesiastical court requires is an examination to ascertain if your maidenhead was breached."

"Oh, my Lord. How barbaric," she gasped. "How perfectly medieval."

"I completely agree. The next reason is as humiliating. Forgive me for speaking plainly. I would have to claim I'm impotent. Stand up in court and declare that I could not perform sexually. That I was less than a man. I, too, would be subjected to an examination from a court-appointed doctor."

"Examination? What kind?" she whispered.

The conversation was growing more embarrassing by the minute, but he must make her understand how impossible this entire situation was. "To see if I would become hard under stimulation."

Her hand flew to her mouth in shock. "Oh, dear heaven."

"No amount of money would induce me to subject myself to such humiliation. My career would be at an end. I would be a laughingstock. It would cast aspersions on you, since I would have to state that you were such an abominable creature in bed I could not fulfill my husbandly duties. All this would be laid out for public consumption. You would become a pariah, and a source of amusement for society."

"I...I had no idea." Her tone bordered on horrified.

"The third option is for me to label you a wanton whore, one who cheated on me with several men. You have no legal right to make the same claim of me. Again, hardly fair. As I stated, once married, you become your husband's property. He has every legal right to do with you as he pleases. Take your property. Take your money. Beat you. Rape you."

A lone tear snaked its way down her pale cheek. "I have already endured it. All of it." Her voice was hoarse.

The desolate admission shocked him. It explained why she was driven to such a desperate act, asking a stranger to marry her. It also explained why she did not want to consummate the supposed marriage. A surge of protectiveness moved through him. The thought of this lovely woman beaten and raped churned his insides.

"No woman should be treated as you were. But how do you know I will not behave in the same vile manner? I'm a complete stranger. If I married you, lawfully, I could do as I wished, including keeping all the money for myself. You would be taking a hell of a risk—begging your pardon, my lady."

Lady Pepperdon opened the small reticule dangling from her delicate wrist, pulled out a handkerchief, and dabbed at the corner of her eyes. "You *are* a complete stranger. But I believe a man who would treat children with respect and kindness would extend the same courtesy to a woman in dire need. At least, that is what I'd hoped. Lord, I *am* naïve. And a fool."

He poured her a glass of lemonade and refilled his own. Blast it all, he needed a whiskey, not this sugary, sickening beverage. "Here, drink." She reached for the glass and took a large gulp. Exhaling, she placed the glass on the desk and hiccupped. Riordan bit back a smile; he found her hiccups endearing. It made her far less haughty and more...human. At least, for a moment. "What other options do you have?" he asked.

"Marry my father's choice, the Marquess of Sutherhorne, and subject myself to another repugnant marriage as I wait for the dotty old debaucher to die." Her eyes again showed the weariness of a woman who'd seen and experienced much, all of it reprehensible.

His progressive soul soared with fury. It tore him to shreds to see how the damned laws did not protect the innocent. What recourse was a woman left with but to enter another "repugnant marriage," as she called it?

"My father claims that this time he will ensure there is a provision for me when the marquess dies."

"He should have ensured such was in place with your first marriage," Riordan growled.

"Yes. I'd assumed it had been. What did I know? I was barely eighteen. As I said, naïve."

Riordan laid his hand on top of hers. "You were naïve because of youth and inexperience, hardly any fault of yours. Why wouldn't a daughter trust her father to see to all the appropriate arrangements?"

A small gasp left her throat as she wrenched her hand away from his as if she'd been burned. A look of fright shadowed her lovely face. Dear God, the touch of a man scared her? Another wave of empathy rolled through him. But he couldn't allow it to cause him to make a hasty decision. Again, his grandfather's warning tolled in his mind like a pealing church bell: *lock away your heart.*

Yet he found he wished to assist her. How, exactly, and why...*Scotland.* The rules for matrimony were different there than in England—at least, he thought they were. He would have to investigate it further. For now, he would keep this kernel of an idea to himself.

"I must tell my father my decision tomorrow at breakfast. If I do not agree to marry the marquess, he will turn me out on the street to make my own way, and I have no idea how to go about it."

The damned bastard. "Tell him you agree in order to buy more time."

"For what?" she whispered. "If I agree, I'll meet the marquess next Tuesday. Which leaves no time at all." She stood, flustered. "I should not lay my burdens at your door. Apparently I should accept my fate, as many women before me have done. But as melodramatic as it sounds, I would rather die."

Riordan immediately rose to his feet, sprinted around his desk, and gathered her in an embrace. An impulsive act, but he was a compassionate man, there was no denying it. Her ladyship stiffened in his arms as if she were about to pull away. Then the most extraordinary thing happened: she softened all around him and encircled his waist with her arms, pulling him tight against her. The effect on him was sudden and swift, and her enticing citrus scent filled his senses. He became aroused.

He tried to pull away slightly, but she clutched him tighter, as if he were a lifeline to a drowning woman. The feather from her fashionable hat brushed his cheek, and Riordan had the sudden urge to tear it from her head and tunnel his hands through her golden-brown hair.

A ragged sob escaped from her throat and tore at his heart. *Right. Lock it away. Easier said than actually done.* He gently rubbed her back. "There, do not despair, my lady. I'm not sure what I can do to assist you, but I will give it some consideration." Damn it all, he should not be making such pronouncements. Her ample breasts mashed against his chest, causing his shaft to stiffen. If her ladyship was aware of his arousal, she did not react.

Several minutes passed. Then, as if in slow motion, Lady Pepperdon detached herself from him, and the loss of having her in his embrace struck him like a forcible blow. "Forgive me," she said. "I...I should not have...I must go." She scurried from the room before he could stop her. As tempted as he was to chase after her, his aroused state convinced him to stay inside until his lust subsided.

George the footman entered the room, and Riordan quickly moved behind his desk and took his seat. "Lady Pepperdon wishes you to have this," the footman said. He passed Riordan a heavy brown paper-wrapped package and gathered up the dishes, placing them in the basket. "Her ladyship says keep the food." The footman turned and exited the room.

Riordan untied the string, pulling the paper aside. A note, along with four books.

Please accept this donation for your school library.

Best Regards, Lady Pepperdon

The books were of the highest quality, leather bound with gold-tipped pages. *The Life and Adventures of Robinson Crusoe*, *Oliver Twist*, *The Pickwick Papers*, and *Histories or Tales of Past Times, as told by Mother Goose.*

If there was a path leading to his supposed locked-away heart, Lady Pepperdon had found it. And Riordan had no clue what to do about the surprising development.

* * * *

Another night of restless sleep. Sabrina headed toward the dining room for breakfast like a criminal walking toward the gallows. The thought of eating and watching her father devour kippers made her stomach reel—as did the fact that she would have to give her answer regarding the marquess.

That alone would be enough to disturb one's slumber, but what kept her wide-eyed until the late hours was the fact that she'd thrown herself at the handsome young schoolmaster. Granted, he'd come to embrace her first, to offer comfort, but she'd grabbed him brazenly, pulling him tight against her—and the sensation was like nothing she'd experienced before.

He must be over six feet by a couple of inches, as the top of her head fit neatly under his chin. The warmth and comfort he exuded was addictive, and she ached for more. His body was hard, unyielding, and she could not stop her hands from exploring his torso and trailing up his back. Muscle flexed under her fingertips. The fact that the hardest part of him did not make her flinch and run from him in fright shocked her to her toes.

Yes, she understood what part of male anatomy pressed insistently against her thigh. The fact that she'd aroused him simultaneously pleased and worried her. The most logical explanation? He's a young man in his prime and would react to any woman embracing him. The shameful episode convinced her she would have to keep her distance. It should rule out Mr. Black as a potential partner in her scheme.

During the early years of her marriage, Sabrina came to the conclusion she did not possess the physical urges she'd read about in books. To discover now that she did was confusing, to say the least. Perhaps she merely longed for the warmth of his embrace and nothing else. The schoolmaster was as tempting as a plate of sweet, frosted cakes, and she had sworn off sweets long ago. Dejectedly, she sat at the table. "Tea and a raisin bun, George," she muttered to the footman. "And be quick about it."

Her father continued to ignore her, reading his paper as if she did not exist. Sabrina tore the bun apart and glumly nibbled on it.

"Well?" Her father lowered his paper. "What is your decision?"

Oh, good heavens. "At least grant me a few months to try and find an alternative? I can reach out to my friends." *What friends?* The girls she grew up with had married and moved away and she'd lost all contact with them. Pepperdon would not allow her to entertain nor correspond with anyone. Not that she knew where any of them lived. But she could try and locate them. Perhaps one of them could take her in temporarily.

"I have wasted enough time and money this past year keeping you fed and clothed. And paying the salary for your servant," he snapped irritably.

Clothed? She wore the same two mourning dresses. "Would you entertain another choice? Before next Tuesday, if I found someone who would agree to marry me, would you make a settlement on me?"

The baron regarded her shrewdly. "What are you cooking up, you devious piece of baggage?"

"An alternate plan is all, Father."

Tapping his fingers on the table, he kept his hard gaze on her. "You think to trick me? To bring in an imbecile you snatched off the streets, only to leave him after you sink your claws in my money?"

The fact that he'd managed to hone in on a variation of her plan made Sabrina gulp deeply, but she kept her expression neutral. "It depends how much you want to be clear of me. What amount would you settle?"

"That is between me and the man in question and is none of your business. You can march every eligible man before me from a hundred-mile radius; the fact remains, I would have to approve of the match." A smug smile curved about his lips. "And he would have to meet the terms."

What terms? She sipped her tea. "What does it matter? I cannot leave my husband, can I? Obtaining an annulment is next to impossible and a divorce even more so."

"At least you understand that much. Very well, Daughter. If you find a desperate man who will agree to marry you, by all means, have him come see me." Her father's cruel smile widened. "I will be sure to inform him of all your many faults. Pepperdon kept me apprised through the years. The fact that you are a barren, frigid bitch will give any man pause."

Again, his words sliced across her heart. How she wished she were frigid and unfeeling, then his hurtful words would be a glancing blow, nothing more. Were all men as malicious and spiteful as her father and late husband? She had no other men in her life to compare them to; perhaps all men *were* hateful creatures.

The image of Mr. Riordan Black formed in her mind. *No, not all men.* However, she would not take advantage of his kind, compassionate nature and draw him into this messy mire. There must be another solution, but what?

He deserved better than her, a broken shell of a woman.

Chapter 5

Not ten minutes after Lady Pepperdon departed, Riordan penned a letter to the law firm in London that the Wollstonecrafts had used for years. One of his mates from Cambridge worked there as a solicitor, and Riordan laid out the woman's dilemma (without mentioning her name), asking if there were any precedents for dissolving a marriage, and was Scotland an option? He asked for William Chambers's complete discretion in the matter. Lady Pepperdon—Sabrina—haunted his thoughts as he made his way home at six o'clock in the evening. He felt compelled to help her—why, he hadn't quite worked out. But her desolate declaration of being subjected to horrors from her husband played over and over in his mind.

His residence came into view. The board provided him with a small, partially furnished cottage not a half a mile from the school. They employed a housekeeper/cook, who came four days a week for general cleaning, laundry, and meal preparation. Often Mrs. Ingersoll, the wife of a laborer at the flour mill, made enough to last for days.

Since he'd been brought up with servants to see to his needs, and given every luxury one could imagine, it was an arduous process to learn how to prepare his own tea, fry an egg, and reheat Mrs. Ingersoll's meals. Thinking about it, he could hardly fault Sabrina for wishing to maintain her comfortable living. He may have been hasty to exact a harsh judgment on her when he too had been pampered his entire life.

Becoming used to such a small area in which to live also proved to be difficult. The entire cottage could fit into his dressing room at Wollstonecraft Hall. Yet he understood he still had an easier time of it than the many families in and around Carrbury.

Never had he been so alone. Damn it all, he was homesick. Preparing lessons for the next day took up most of his evening, but he was used to lively conversations and the presence of his family. Sometimes in this small abode, the silence was deafening. The ticking of the wall clock sounded like pistols firing, and the slightest breeze whistling through the shutters mimicked a banshee wail. All this did lessen in intensity whilst he prepared his lessons.

After unlocking the door, he entered the cottage. The bits of furniture were not in the best condition, obviously donations from various residences in town. There would be a brief break next week on the first of October, in conjunction with the harvest moon, an agreement reached by the farmers and board members to allow children to help with the harvest and prepare for winter. Riordan would head home, borrow a wagon and horse from Garrett, and return with a few choice pieces of furniture, like a more comfortable mattress. He sighed as he lit the oil lamp. He missed a great many things. But even in his maudlin bouts of homesickness he found a sense of accomplishment in the fact that he was earning his keep. When he'd accepted this position, he decided to live within his means for the year. It had been sobering and humbling.

Teaching exceeded all his expectations. Never did he believe he would derive such inner contentment. Turns out he enjoyed the experience, and already it had moved beyond research for his educational reforms. He began to foster plans, like building the progressive school he'd spoken to his grandfather about. Perhaps he would make himself headmaster. Until then, he soldiered on with his work.

He'd instituted Sabrina's suggestion of a brief cessation of study, and it had been a complete success. The children gobbled down the ginger biscuits, and after their respite appeared brighter and more alert for the remaining day. Riordan made a mental note to bring up the subject at the next board meeting. There was no reason why the children could not break for a short recess and play outside for ten minutes, weather permitting.

Laying his satchel on the table, he exhaled with relief when he spotted meat pie and fresh bread on the counter. Moving efficiently about the small kitchen area, he lit the wood stove and placed the kettle on it, then slid the plate into the oven to warm up the pie. A knock sounded at his door. He'd already removed his frock coat and rolled up his sleeves—should he answer the door in such a casual state? Riordan strode to the front door and opened it.

Sabrina. At least, he guessed—the lady in question wore a wool cloak with a large, fur-trimmed hood that obscured her face. But the enticing scent gave her away. "Do come in, Lady Pepperdon."

She scurried across the threshold and he closed the door after her.

"May I take your cloak?"

"No. I'm not staying."

"How did you know where to find me?"

"My maid inquired for me."

Her words were clipped. She would not meet his gaze, remaining hidden under the hood. Gently, he lowered it, and she gasped. Grasping her chin, he made her look at him. "Why have you come?"

Her lower lip trembled. "Let go of me."

Sabrina's harsh tone was covered in frost. This from the woman who'd desperately clung to him a mere couple of days past. Riordan did as she asked. "Answer my question."

She looked about the small room, and in finding a chair, sat upon it. He could see the distaste in her eyes as she observed his sparse and simply furnished cottage. She was the same as those pretentious young ladies he'd come across at balls. Her haughty tone and look dismissed his earlier sympathetic thoughts toward her. Annoyed, he crossed his arms and waited for her to respond.

Clasping her gloved hands tightly in her lap, Sabrina finally met his gaze. Her harsh expression relaxed, her eyes glistened. "First, allow me to apologize for being forward in asking you to marry me. I haven't been myself of late. I have nowhere to turn, and the feeling of being lost and desperate makes me cross and annoyed with myself. I do not like being helpless, I abhor it, and yet I have been from the moment I was born." She laughed cynically. "I have had no say in any aspect of my life. My mother died when I was young. All I have known is cold disregard from my father, even hatred, for I was a daughter, not the son he wanted. The first chance he could be shunt of me, he took it, would not even allow me a season to find a suitable husband near my own age. Instead, I was handed off to an old man—sold to the highest bidder, so to speak."

Sabrina looked away, her eyelids blinking rapidly. "Forgive me. I've been indulging in bouts of self-pity. I suppose I could surrender and allow my father to dictate whom I marry. But I cannot. I must fight in any way I'm able, do you see?" She met his gaze once again, her eyes full of unshed tears. She spoke with such heartrending emotion, his annoyance fled. And to think he thought her chilly and snobbish.

"Yes, I see. As a man, I cannot begin to comprehend how powerless a woman must feel. You're right; from the moment of birth she is dependent upon men to see to her comforts, her very survival."

"Precisely. My father threatens to turn me out to find my own way. Where? How? What is a woman to do? I don't want to be a kept woman, but I'm not trained for any kind of occupation. There is the companion path, but those positions are few and far between. This is the best option I can come up with to work my way toward the independence I crave. I need to formulate my plan without haste." Sabrina hesitated, and sniffed the air. "Is something burning?"

Damn it. He sprinted to the kitchen and, using a tea towel, reached into the oven for his meat pie. The edges of the crust had started to burn, but the rest was salvageable. Caught up in her narrative, he'd forgotten about his meal. Placing the dish on the counter, he rolled down his sleeves and buttoned the cuffs. He should put on a jacket, but to hell with it.

Riordan returned to the small parlor. "Merely my dinner. I caught it before serious damage was done."

She stood. "I should leave and allow you to eat…."

"It will keep. Please, sit and continue." As she did, he clasped the chair from the dining table and set it near her, but not close enough to crowd her.

"I spoke with my father; he will meet with you to discuss a possible marriage. That is, if you have decided to participate in my mad scheme." She frowned. "You were correct at the first; I'm committing fraud, but I do not care. My father owes me for my miserable childhood and miserable marriage. And if it sounds like a rationalization for the underhanded plan I'm about to embark on, I can live with the consequences. What I *cannot* live with any longer is not being in control of my life. I am taking the reins."

Sabrina spoke with courage and determination. On the whole, she *was* perpetrating a fraudulent plot. But her reasons smacked of truth, with a smattering of revenge. Did he wish to be part of it? "Let us say I meet with the baron. He could still insist that you marry the marquess regardless."

Her lower lip thrust out. "Yes. He could. My father said, 'You can march every eligible male before me from a hundred mile radius; the fact remains, I would have to approve of the match and the man would have to meet the terms.' I have no idea what he means. He would not tell me the amount of the settlement."

"How much did he pay the earl?" Riordan asked.

"I'm not sure, as Pepperdon would never speak of his negotiations with my father. He did mention a sum of fifteen thousand pounds once, saying

I was not worth the amount. It was meant as an insult; he often claimed I was useless and worth nothing."

He frowned. The earl had been a miserable cur. And hell, was her father that well-off? "Do you believe he would offer as much again?"

"Perhaps. He is eager for me to be gone from his house. Even ten thousand would set me up in a small cottage far from here; the income from the settlement would be enough for me to live on for many years, surely." She gave him a shaky smile. "See? Independence. Life on my terms."

Riordan crossed his arms. "You wouldn't be able to afford a place much bigger than this. Look about. My cottage is probably not as large as your bedchambers. If we agree to move forward with this, you will have to live here with me in these close quarters. We'd have to make at least some effort to show we're married."

The look of horrified surprise on her lovely face amused him. "Here? With you? But I thought to take rooms at the inn in town until we can apply for an annulment."

"It's not feasible, Sabrina. Can you afford such an expense? I cannot. Besides, if we're living apart from the beginning, it will state to the court that we made no attempt to make the marriage work. It could go against us. Speaking of annulments, I've explained what would have to be done to dissolve the marriage. None of those options are ideal for either of us. I've written a solicitor friend of mine in London."

Sabrina gasped.

"Easy, I did not mention any names, merely asked hypothetical questions regarding possible options. I expect a reply any day. In the meantime, refresh my memory: when are you supposed to meet with Sutherhorne?"

"Tuesday next. Why?" Her eyebrow arched in question.

"Does the marquess live nearby or in London?" Riordan asked.

"I believe he is in London at the moment. I assume he attends parliament."

Riordan stood and held out his hand. Hesitating, she finally slipped her gloved hand in his. He assisted her to her feet and took a step closer. She blinked rapidly and her entire body tensed. As he lifted her hand to his mouth, he kept his gaze firm on her. The enticing scent of citrus invaded his nostrils. Her nearness made him aware of her as a woman. An astonishing development.

Brushing his lips across her knuckles, he moved his thumb under the glove and found her pulse. The touch of her bare skin caused his heart to stutter and blood to rush to his nether regions. In response to him caressing her wrist, her pulse quickened. She was affected by his touch. Gratifying, yet alarm bells sounded in his fevered mind. If they steamed ahead with this harebrained scheme, they would be under the same roof. Temptation incarnate.

The overwhelming need to pull her close and kiss her senseless brought him up quick. His fingertips leisurely skimmed across her upturned palm. She didn't pull her hand away. In response, he caressed the tips of her fingers with his, and the heat between them seared, even through her glove.

Riordan stepped away. "Go home, Sabrina." His voice was hoarse. "Meet me at the school Monday during luncheon break. I'll have more information. And my answer. Until then, act as though you're meeting Sutherhorne."

"I do not understand...."

"Go now," he rasped. *Before I pull you into my embrace. Before I touch you all over.*

She must have read the raw desire on his face, for she pulled up her hood and fled through the front door without looking back.

Slowly, he walked toward the door and closed it, sliding the bolt. He rested his hand flat against the door and waited until his racing heart and rampant arousal calmed. What in hell was happening here? Obviously he'd taken leave of his senses if he was even considering this madness.

Her courageous words stirred him. The tragic look in her eyes moved him. Mix in the fact that he found her appealing and this could be a recipe for disaster. With a sigh, he headed toward the kitchen and his burnt meat pie. Could he keep his heart from getting singed?

Chapter 6

Surprisingly, Sabrina slept well after her nocturnal visit to Mr. Black. Correct that—*Riordan.* She couldn't bring herself to address him as such, at least not to his face, even though he'd called her Sabrina. She never should have suggested they use first names. What had possessed her?

However, her inner thoughts used his given name. It was Irish in origin, and certainly fit with his black-as-midnight hair and startling light blue eyes. His pale skin was creamy and flawless—Celtic, to be sure. His speech was elegant, but she assumed it had come more from his training than his actual background.

The schoolmaster had told her nothing of his life. Perhaps he came from the middle class? What did it matter; she would not be bound to him for life. Sabrina didn't like the idea of him contacting a solicitor, but it was one way to be sure of the options. She pulled the blankets up to her chin, closed her eyes, and started drifting to sleep.

Mary entered the room and bustled to the window, tearing open the silver drapes, allowing sun to pour into the room. "It is nigh on eleven o'clock, my lady. You never sleep this late. I'll bring you toast and tea immediately. Are you well?"

Mary hurried to her bedside and plumped the pillows as Sabrina yawned and sat upright, blinking at the bright autumn sun. "I must have needed the sleep. Toast and tea sound lovely. I suppose my father did not miss me at breakfast?"

"I doubt it, my lady. He left around eight this morning. I hear he's off to London for two days, paying a visit to a certain young lady. Would you like me to find out the name?"

A good thing Mary kept her apprised of the comings and goings and other activities of the house, or Sabrina would have no idea what was going on. Her father told her nothing. "Yes, be subtle about it." A maid from downstairs entered the room carrying a tray and Mary took it from her. The girl gave an awkward curtsy and left the room.

"Here we are," Mary murmured, laying the tray on Sabrina's lap. "Toast, tea, and fresh blackberry jam, just how you like it."

Her devoted lady's maid was about fifty-five years of age, the daughter of a sailor. When Mary's father was lost at sea in her early twenties, she'd no choice but to enter service to keep a roof over her head and look after her widowed mother.

By the time Sabrina had arrived at the Pepperdon estate, Mary was already there as a parlor maid, and since she'd served as a lady's maid to the former Lady Pepperdon, Sabrina chose Mary to do the same for her. With her no-nonsense manner, twinkling brown eyes, and kind nature, Mary was precisely what Sabrina needed. Though her chestnut-brown hair had threads of gray at her temples, her pleasant face remained remarkably unlined.

Mary spoiled her terribly, but Sabrina reveled in it. It was the first time in her life anyone had paid attention to her in a positive way. How many nights did her kind maid offer soothing solace after a horrific episode with Pepperdon? At the lowest points of her life, it comforted Sabrina to think of Mary as a kindly aunt. Servants were not supposed to be thought of in such a way, but Sabrina couldn't help it. Mary was all she had.

Swallowing down the ball of emotion lodged in her throat, she gave Mary a warm smile. "I do not tell you enough how much I appreciate you. You mean a great deal to me. Have a seat, Mary. I must tell you about our status in this house. It is rather precarious."

Mary sat in the chair next to the bed. "I've an idea what you're about to say. The servants do gossip, I'm afraid. Your father wishes to marry you off to another elderly peer."

Sabrina arched an eyebrow as she sipped her tea.

"George is worse than an old washer woman for gossiping. He needs a talking to. Mentioned you met the schoolmaster for luncheon. *Alone.* Although he did believe your tale about it being a business-type meeting, contributions for the school and the like. But it wasn't, was it, my lady?"

Spreading jam on her toast, she shook her head. "No, Mary. It was not about the school."

"I heard from the twittering maids that the new schoolmaster is a virile young man, with black hair and sparkling blue eyes to rival the summer sky above. I'm quoting the foolish young things, mind you."

What an apt description. "He is as you describe. When I tell you why I went to see him, you will be shocked."

In between eating her toast and sipping her tea, she told Mary everything—even of her clandestine visit of last night.

Mary sat back in her chair, her mouth slightly agape. "You astound me, my lady."

"I astound myself. Never believed I had it in me to be audacious. But if I can enter this sham of a marriage, obtain a quick and quiet annulment, and collect the settlement agreed upon, then you and I will move far from here. I'll be able to purchase a small cottage by the sea, large enough for the two of us." Sabrina frowned into her half empty cup. "Perhaps at last I will find a modicum of peace." The last words ended on a whisper.

Mary patted her hand. "If anyone deserves it, it's you, my lady. But how can you trust this schoolmaster? He's a stranger, only been in the area barely a month."

Sabrina recalled listening to his lesson outside the window. She'd been enthralled by the mere resonance of his deep, hypnotizing voice. In the rich tones she'd heard consideration, civility, and intelligence. At that point, she did not care a bit what he looked like, he sounded…honest. Sincere. Then, when she had seen him…Lord, what a vision. She nearly sighed aloud thinking of him standing there, the wind ruffling his thick, black hair. The afternoon sun framing him in a golden halo.

Enough daydreaming. "He *is* a complete stranger, but I believe he is a proper one. I heard something in his voice, the way he spoke to the children, treated them with respect. He may not even agree to any of this. Perhaps I'm mad."

"Let me see what I can find out about him. Mr. Riordan Black, you say his name is?" Sabrina nodded. "I'll venture to town this afternoon, for your embroidery thread, and make subtle inquiries."

"I don't like to embroider, as you well know." Sabrina smiled sardonically.

"True, but the baron doesn't know it." Mary stood. "Now, we should get you dressed and ready for the day." Opening the nearby wardrobe, Mary held up the black bombazine dress.

"Discard the mourning garments, Mary. I am done with them. The black bonnets as well." Mary tossed the dress to the bed and instead held up a green and yellow walking dress. Two years out of date, but who would notice?

Confusing feelings swirled about in her mind. This was to be a business arrangement, nothing more. However, she found Riordan attractive. Sabrina would never act on it. Her course of abstinence was set. Never again would a man lay a hand on her for *any* purpose.

* * * *

With the harvest break upon him, Riordan headed to Wollstonecraft Hall. Since his family estate was located near Sevenoaks in Kent and a mere twenty-one miles from London, he was sorely tempted to head to town and locate Sutherhorne. A visit to Barley, Kenworth, and Davis, Barristers and Solicitors, should be at the top of his list. Sitting at the dining room table, he pulled William Chambers's letter from the side pocket of his coat and snapped it open.

Dear Riordan,

Smashing to hear from you! It has been too long. You, a schoolmaster? Knowing your progressive thoughts and beliefs, I suppose I am not surprised. Well done.

To address your inquires: Scotland is not a viable option. It is too far away and with many complicated rules, such as a permanent residency. There are other options for an annulment besides the ones you mentioned in your letter. One of you could claim the other insane and state that you did not know what you were doing when you entered into the marriage. There is also the underage option, or claiming force was used to ensure the marriage took place.

Or, one of you could claim fraudulent reasons. That one deceived the other into a marriage by using a false name, for example.

I can do nothing to assist with an annulment, as the cases are heard before the ecclesiastical court of the Church of England, and only proctors or advocates from the Doctors Common can oversee the proceedings. It is a drawn-out process, and the length of time before the annulment is granted varies case by case. Though most annulments are approved, there are a number that are refused. A person would be stuck with the other for the rest of their lives. It is a hell of a gamble.

I am almost afraid to inquire as to why you are asking these questions. While I sympathize with the unknown lady in question and her "hypothetical" dilemma, I beseech you to come see me here, at the office in London, or at my residence before you do anything rash.

Rescuing a damsel in distress, while an honorable cause, could have life-changing consequences.

Your concerned friend,

William

The passage about fraudulent reasons stood out like a lighthouse beacon. If he married her at a registrar's office using the name Riordan Black, would it be considered fraud on his part? Grounds for an annulment? He scanned the rest of the letter. What honorable man did not desire to rescue a damsel in distress? Though he doubted Sabrina would wish to be thought of as such. As if he knew her at all.

Garrett strode into the room, heading straight for the sideboard. When most of the family was away, meals were informal. "Martin told me you arrived about thirty minutes past. Homesick already?"

Considering there were only six years' difference in their ages, he thought of Garrett more as an older brother than an uncle. He slipped the letter into his pocket, then sipped his tea.

Garrett had hit the nail on the head: he was homesick, but he would never admit it. "Hardly. There is a short break for the autumn harvest. The children are expected to help out, free labor and the like."

Garrett set his overloaded plate of sliced roast pork and assorted vegetables on the table, then sat across from Riordan. "Ah yes, the exploitation of children in the labor market. It is only right they assist with the running of a farm, it keeps them housed and fed."

"I should have expected as such from you, seeing you have hay on your shirt and smell of horse," Riordan teased.

Garrett laughed good-naturedly. "Come now, I do agree education is important. But so is the running of a family farm. At the least, the labor is honest and for the greater good of the family, unlike those poor youngsters who toil twelve hours a day in factories in wretched conditions, receiving no education whatsoever."

Riordan gave his uncle a nod. "You've got me there. Speaking of farms and such, how is Starlight faring?"

His uncle's face lit up at the mention of his prize mare. "Swimmingly. She came through the birth in fine fettle. The foal? He's an excellent specimen, will be a welcome addition to the stable. And Grayson?"

Grayson was Riordan's horse, a six-year-old gelding he'd ridden exclusively for the past several years. "Stabled at a nearby farm. I ride him when I can, usually on Saturday and Sunday. He's being well looked after. You can see for yourself; he's being fed in the stable as we speak."

"I will check on him later."

"I had hoped to borrow a wagon and take pieces of furniture with me to Carrbury. We do have older pieces in storage, do we not? Is there a mattress?"

Garrett shrugged in between bites. "There are some choice bits in the attic of the barn. As for a mattress, we will have to ask Mrs. Barnes. She could no doubt scrounge up proper bedding as well."

"Where is Aidan? Not coming down for dinner?"

Garrett grunted. "Since the blow with Julian, he scampered off to Bath, to lick his wounds and indulge in his various vices."

Bath was a favorite haunt of his brother's, a place of escape when his father and grandfather were in London. In Bath Aidan could attend as many brothels as he chose, or have a scandalous fling with an actress from one of the city's many theaters without fear of censure. How could twin brothers be as different as they were? Since they were paternal twins they did not look exactly alike, and from their cribs they could not have been more dissimilar.

From his early youth, Aidan was always involved in mischief, leading the governess and nurse on a merry chase. Only Mrs. Barnes, the housekeeper, could put Aidan in his place with a stern look and a wag of her finger. Riordan decided not to follow his brother down such a mischievous path, and instead became a sober and studious young lad. The praise he earned managed to inflame his brother's disobedient behavior and increase it a hundredfold.

Finally, Julian had had enough and sent Aidan away to school at age ten, two years before Riordan joined him. Perhaps that is when the resentment took root between father and son. The more their father reprimanded Aidan, the worse he acted. No amount of admonishment from the earl or the kindly Mrs. Barnes had any effect.

There was a serious clash coming, Riordan could sense it: irreparable harm causing a permanent rupture between Aidan and the rest of the family. Harsh words would be spoken, never to be taken back, Aidan sinking to even lower depths, losing himself in debauchery. If only there was a way he could broker peace between his father and brother. If only…

"Thinking of Aidan?" Garrett asked.

"How can you tell?"

Garrett pointed his fork in Riordan's direction. "You always get a particular worried look, like your eyebrows are knotted. Leave Aidan to his devices. He will tire of them soon enough." Riordan wasn't as sure. "I'll come with you to Carrbury. That way I can assist you with the furniture and shortly thereafter return home. I believe I will use Juno for the trip; he's strong enough to pull a wagon full of furniture. Besides, I want to see your setup. Are you enjoying teaching?"

Riordan reached for a fresh piece of bread and buttered it generously. "More than I ever imagined. To be able to mold and shape young minds, open them to worlds they never knew existed. To see the awe on their faces as they learn something new or accomplish a goal. To know you are making a difference in their lives, expanding their imaginations, to show them life holds many and all possibilities."

"A noble calling," Garrett murmured. "You make me feel guilty for not doing more regarding the family's varied causes."

"Nonsense. You do plenty for the tenants and surrounding farms. Did you not assist Mr. Jacobi in repairing his roof last month, not only with your labor, but by buying many of the supplies needed as well?"

"Bah. The man had a hard year, it was the least I could do. I'm hiring a few men to help repair Sir Walter Keenan's fences. I attended the funeral on behalf of the family, and met the niece who is to take possession of the place. The property is in worse condition than I originally thought. Alberta Eaton, the benefactor of the will, is a widow living with a young man I first thought to be her son, but is in fact her brother-in-law." Garrett tapped his temple. "The lad is simple, and I assume not able to oversee any renovations."

Riordan gave Garrett a teasing wink. "A widow, you say?"

Garrett scoffed. "Though attractive enough, she is too old for me. Around Julian's age, I would guess. Besides, you're well aware I have no interest in romantic entanglements, especially with a neighbor. Blasted awkward." Garrett shoved another forkful of pork and vegetables in his mouth.

Speaking of entanglements. Riordan was tempted to inform Garrett about what had happened since he'd arrived at Carrbury, but caution stilled his tongue. First, he must meet with William and ascertain the lay of the land before deciding what to do about Lady Sabrina.

Chapter 7

William Chambers looked at him aghast. "You cannot be serious. Marriage with a stranger?" He rubbed his temples in irritation. "There are many ways I imagine this going, and all of them end in disaster. Not to mention, if the baron finds out the marriage is a complete charade, there could be charges of fraud, a chaotic court case…dear God."

Riordan had had the same thoughts over the past several days. "I will need your assistance to ensure no harm or consequence can damage either one of us. Of all the options available for annulment, I wish to discuss the fraud aspect. I'm using the name Riordan Black for my teaching position."

William raised an eyebrow. "What on earth for?"

"My family is well-known, infamous even. There is the blasted curse hanging over me wherever I go. I didn't want the townspeople and the students to be intimidated by the fact that I'm rich and my father is a viscount and my grandfather an earl. It was of paramount importance I stand on even ground in order to be accepted into the community."

"Does this Lady Pepperdon know your true identity? Does anyone in the vicinity?"

"No, she does not, though one member on the board, Mr. Beatty, is aware and agreed with my well-meaning deception. He will keep quiet, I'm sure," Riordan replied.

William stood and strode to the sideboard. "Good bloody hell, I need a drink." He clasped the whiskey decanter and waved it toward him. "You?"

"Yes, please."

Running his hand through his sandy-blond hair, he poured the whiskey, murmuring under his breath. Riordan smiled. They had shared a room at Cambridge, and William often did this when irritated or under stress.

After passing the tumbler to Riordan, William sat and huffed out a short breath. "Listen to me, my friend: In order for the fraud option to be viable, you cannot tell Lady Pepperdon your real name. The reveal has to be authentic, based in some sort of truth. Do you understand?"

Riordan crossed his legs and regarded his friend. "You mean lie? She is sure to ask me about my background…."

"Tell her nothing. It is not as if you will be carrying on conversations on personal matters anyway." William took a long pull on his whiskey.

"I can hardly avoid it, the cottage is small."

"What do you tell the townspeople?" William asked.

"That I'm half Irish, my mother came from Dublin, and my father is involved in factory work. None of it is a lie, though it is vague. Father is involved with factory reform work with Lord Ashley, but people assumed otherwise. I let it stand."

"There's your answer. Tell her that and nothing more if she asks." William threw back another generous swallow, gritting his teeth. "I cannot believe I am going to be a party to this barmy plot. Have you spoken to her father yet?"

"No. I will when I return to Carrbury. I want a legal and binding agreement drawn up, stating the money is hers free and clear on the date of the annulment. She offered me a percentage—I will not collect. Until then, keep the amount in trust. You look after all my holdings; this will be one more item. I also want a contract for the baron to sign. The money is to be paid to this firm *before* the marriage takes place. Ten thousand pounds. No more, no less. The marriage will not go forward without payment."

William made notes on his legal pad. "The baron can pay this money to the old marquess with the same result. Why would he choose you?"

Riordan smiled. "Because I am going to ensure Sutherhorne is out of the running."

William shook his head. "I shall not ask."

"It is wise you do not. Here is a question: how long do we keep up the pretense of a marriage?"

William laid his pen on his desk and met his gaze. "Before I answer, I want you to think about the ramifications of what you are doing. This will be a stain on your reputation. You have plans to open a progressive school. Do you truly believe people will want to send their children to a school run by a swindler? For that is what they will call you." William paused, his expression turned sympathetic. "Annulments are part of the public record. When your true name is revealed, it will make the papers. Granted, scandals are fleeting in most cases—it well could fade from memory over time—but it could damage you, and your family, in the interim."

Riordan had already considered it. He and his family could weather a temporary storm of scandal. They'd already endured Aidan's antics and the constant scrutiny regarding the curse. "My family will be behind me. We stand for progressive causes. The plight of women needs attention. What better way than this? It is past time women are allowed to have property and rights."

William gave him an indulgent look. "There is more to life than causes."

"Perhaps. But at the moment, not in mine."

"There must be other reasons besides women's rights compelling you forward," William stated.

Were there? To be honest, he hadn't quite made up his mind. He wanted to hear all the options. Perhaps it was her late-night visit and the way she spoke of her plight with such honesty and emotion. She'd spoken to his heart. "I haven't worked out the rest as of yet."

"What of Lady Pepperdon? Is she willing to expose herself to scandal and censure?"

"She's informed me that once the money is in her possession she plans to move far away."

"And leave you to bear the brunt of gossip." William shook his head. "Very well. I will do as you ask. You should be married at a registrar's office. Not in the church. It is an easier process. I know it is blasted hypocrisy that you can marry civilly but must seek an annulment through the church." William waved his hand. "More laws that must be changed. If and when the laws are amended, it will give those of us in the legal field additional clients if divorce and annulments are obtainable through the regular courts."

Riordan smiled. "Always the charitable one."

"To answer your earlier question, I would stay married three months at most. It's enough time to give the marriage a little credence." William paused. "As your solicitor I must beg you rethink this. As your friend, I know you have already made up your mind and will plow ahead regardless. I will do all I can to ensure this goes as smoothly and quietly as possible."

Riordan reached across the desk and held out his hand. William took it and shook it. "Thank you, William."

"I want to meet Lady Pepperdon. Let me know the approximate date, and I will make arrangements at a registrar's office nearby. You both come here first and sign the papers. I will accompany you, to act as witness and attest to the fact that you signed your name Riordan Black."

"Will I have to sign the legal paper as Riordan Black?"

"No, use your real name. We will have her sign it first. We can say you signed Riordan Black at the registrar's office in error, since it is the name you're using at the moment. I may be disbarred for this, but we might get away with it."

"And the motivation for not telling Lady Pepperdon my true name?"

"The truth: you wanted to keep your background a secret because it would interfere with your teaching assignment. The man on the school board can verify. Gad, I need another drink."

"You are a true friend."

"I'm only doing this to protect you, because, as I said, you would plow ahead and damn the circumstances. This way, it may lessen the scandal."

Riordan frowned. "Perhaps I'm making a mistake. This is all becoming convoluted."

"You can try another avenue. Maybe you forced one or the other into the marriage." William leaned forward. "Or, here is a novel idea: do not go through with it at all. Lend her money, it would be less cumbersome."

Riordan shook his head. "She would not take it. Lady Pepperdon is adamant that her father owes her for her misery and is determined to collect recompense. I cannot say I blame her. Besides, how would I explain that I'm rich without revealing my true identity?"

"God, what a tangle."

Riordan dismissed the warning bells ringing in his head. Much could go wrong, or, as William succinctly put it, all could end in disaster. Sitting in the law office, he made up his mind: he would assist Sabrina to gain her independence. The fact he found her attractive could not play a role in this scenario. Damn it, she *was* pretty, and he was growing to like her besides. The path was set, and since stubbornness and determination made up part of his character, he would see this complicated arrangement through to its inevitable conclusion.

* * * *

Sabrina was beside herself with worry as each day passed. Riordan sent a short note stating that he'd departed for home—wherever that was—then to London to see his solicitor friend. The blasted man still had not given her a firm answer regarding her plan.

"Sabrina, I am speaking to you." Her father's cold voice cut through her disquieted thoughts.

Looking up from her barely touched dinner, she met her father's disdainful gaze. "Yes?"

"I have received word from Sutherhorne. He will be here Tuesday afternoon for a short visit. You're to be gracious and attentive, and when he asks you to consider his suit, you are to say yes."

"Have you made progress with whatever poor young woman you have set your lurid sights on?" she snapped in reply.

Her father's neutral expression turned dangerous. She should not be poking the bear with a stick, but she neared the end of her rope. "You are becoming far too bold and outspoken. As it happens, I *have* made progress. A few more visits and the chit will agree to marriage, I am sure of it. I want you gone, and you're to take that nosey maid of yours when you leave." Her father sliced his roast beef. "Sutherhorne assures me he will be obtaining a special license in order for the marriage to take place immediately."

Oh, no. Sabrina stood, nearly knocking the chair to the floor. "I believe I will take a breath of air before the sun sets." She did not wait for her father to dismiss her or even comment before she hurried to her room.

Mary was there, placing clean undergarments in one of the bureau drawers. "Make haste, gather my cloak. I must see if Mr. Black has returned from his journey."

"Yes, of course, my lady." Mary hurried to the wardrobe and fetched the gray wool cloak. "I did find out a little about the schoolmaster. I'm not exactly sure where he hails from, but his late mother was Irish, and his father works in a factory. If he owns the factory, no one is completely sure."

Sabrina had already guessed about the Irish part, seeing his first name was Riordan. Mary slipped the cloak over her shoulders. "The young lady your father is presently courting is the second daughter of the Duke of Carlton. Talk is, she is rather plain of features and her father is eager to marry her off."

The poor young woman. Sabrina had half a mind to write her and warn her away from her father, but it would jeopardize her own plans. Or would it? Once her settlement money was safely tucked away, she could drop an anonymous note. "Mary, you are a treasure. Start gathering our possessions, pack the trunk. We may be departing sooner than we'd planned."

"Right away, my lady." Mary tossed her own cloak across her shoulders.

"I do not need a chaperone."

"So you keep telling me, but I'm coming anyway. Let's slip out the side door."

They quietly padded down the main staircase and entered the library. The oncoming dusk caused shadows to dance across the hardwood floor.

Opening the French door, they clasped hands and crossed the threshold, scurrying to the wooded area that acted as a border between the baron's land and the school.

"His cottage is about half a mile beyond the school."

Mary tsked. "Let's hope there are not any wild creatures about, my lady. I don't like the dark, let alone the woods."

The last thing Sabrina worried about was roaming or feral animals. What if Riordan Black told her no? Where could she turn?

"Speaking of wild creatures, who is that?" Mary whispered. She pointed to a large man with shoulder-length red hair unloading pieces of furniture from a flatbed wagon. "He is quite a specimen, built like a Viking of old," Mary murmured, admiration in her tone. "All that is missing is a sword and a fur cape."

"How do you know what a Viking looks like?" Sabrina whispered in return.

"I read romance adventures. You should give them a try, my lady. They are a pleasant escape from life's vile tasks."

About to answer, her breath caught in her throat when Riordan emerged from the cottage. He laughed at something the red-haired Viking said to him, and Sabrina found herself enchanted by Riordan's warm and friendly smile. With a confident stride, he moved to the wagon and lifted a small table onto his shoulder, then headed toward the cottage.

"Well, my lady. I don't believe I've seen you react like this to a man before, if you don't mind me saying."

Sabrina schooled her features to show complete indifference, but Mary had already seen her reaction. Her face flushed. Her breath caught. She tingled all over from the glorious sight of him. Why deny it? "What am I to do? I should walk away right this minute. I have no right to find him…him…"

"Handsome? Full of youth and vitality? Virile?" Mary interjected.

"Mary!" she admonished in a fierce whisper. But he was everything she'd described and more. Honorable, kind, capable.

"The young maids were right, my lady. He *is* lovely," Mary murmured, laying a hand on Sabrina's arm. "Better him than a mummified marquess. Who says this has to be temporary?"

"Mary!"

Her maid shrugged. "Are you going to talk to him?"

Not if there was a stranger with him. Who could the man be—a family member? "Not tonight. Not with the Viking there. I'm to see him tomorrow during the luncheon break at the school. I will speak to him then."

Linking arms, they turned and headed toward the woods and the baron's property. Sabrina sighed wistfully. *Who says it has to be temporary?* Mary had asked. But it *must* be. Keeping an icy wall about her heart had been the only way to protect herself from the constant hurt and disappointment she'd endured throughout her life.

No man, no matter how attractive or compelling, could be allowed to breech her frosty defenses; she had spent too many years constructing the barriers. Sabrina turned and took one last longing look as Riordan exited the cottage to unload additional items from the wagon. Oh, how he fulfilled all her youthful dreams of a heroic suitor. But those foolish imaginings had disappeared years ago and had no business rearing their heads at this stage.

She would remain resolute. Brave. No matter what he told her tomorrow she would continue to hold the reins and direct her own future. Yet a tiny part of her, a part she thought long dead, yearned for love. Ached for a man to hold her in his arms and whisper all will be well. Hungered for a man to take her to bed and show her all the ways a woman could be thoroughly satisfied and loved—for she knew nothing about it. Did not even know it existed. Except in the books Mary read.

No one would know of her secret longings. Especially a handsome, principled schoolmaster with a sensual mouth and sky-blue eyes.

Chapter 8

"I thought you did not need a chaperone, my lady?" Mary asked as they hurried through the woods.

"I do not, but if I am seen entering the school, it would be better served if someone were with me, to stem any gossip. Especially since it's the luncheon break and he is alone."

"What will we do if he says no?" Mary sounded worried, and for good reason. Sabrina also remained anxious. She'd hinged her entire future on the schoolmaster, but what choice did she have? Her options were limited.

"I shudder to think. Perhaps I can sell my jewels." But Sabrina knew that would be a short-term fix. The money would last them a year or two if they were frugal. At least it would give them time to formulate a different plan.

As they emerged through the cluster of junipers, the schoolhouse came into view. Sabrina's insides fluttered nervously, not only with the pleasant prospect of seeing Riordan again, but also with concern over his decision. Making an effort to arrange her features into complete indifference, she knocked, and, not waiting for a reply, entered the structure. Riordan sat at his desk, scratching away with his pen.

He lifted his head and smiled warmly. Her breath hitched again, and Mary squeezed her arm as if to agree. Or perhaps it was to give her courage. Riordan stood and inclined his head. "Good day, Sabrina." He moved out from around his desk and walked toward her.

Mary squeezed her arm tighter and murmured for her hearing only, "Good heavens."

Good heavens, indeed. He was dressed all in black, and it enhanced his porcelain skin, dark hair, and attractive blue eyes. "My lady's maid, Mary Tuttle. Mary, this is Mr. Riordan Black, schoolmaster."

Riordan took Mary's gloved hand and gave her a polite bow. "Pleased to meet you, Miss Tuttle."

Mary flushed. "Good heavens," she said breathlessly. "And pleased to meet you, sir."

Riordan let go of Mary's hand and stood upright. "Would you mind terribly if I spoke to your mistress in private? There's an alcove to the side with a comfortable bench, if you would not mind waiting there."

Mary looked to Sabrina questioningly. She nodded. As Riordan escorted Mary, Sabrina made her way to the front of the classroom and took a seat in the chair by his desk. Wringing her gloved hands, she waited nervously for his return. What *would* she do if he refused? With Sutherhorne arriving tomorrow, it was far too late to find another candidate. There was nothing else for it; both she and Mary would have to make a quick escape. Sabrina calculated the small amount of money she'd managed to tuck away before Pepperdon died: four pounds and ten shillings. Enough to hire a coach, to rent a small room—

"Sorry to keep you waiting." His deep, masculine voice caused her heart to squeeze with longing. It took great effort not to show her reaction outwardly. Lord, even if he did agree, how could she keep pretending his presence did not affect her?

"Do not leave me in suspense, Mr. Black. I must have your answer. What have you decided?"

Riordan sat. "I thought we agreed to use first names." He gave her another smile, making him even more attractive, drat him.

"It isn't proper. You should have never mentioned it," she muttered impatiently.

"Actually, *you* are the one who suggested it. Regardless, this entire situation is not proper, but here we are. There is no need to be haughty. I prefer the woman who came to my cottage after dark, sat in my parlor, and spoke from her heart." His beautiful blue eyes twinkled. "You do have one, you know."

Her mouth pulled into a taut line. "No, I do not. Your decision, if you please?"

His smile slowly slipped away, and she regretted her tone immediately as the warmth from his eyes also disappeared. "Very well, let us keep this about business. I did visit my solicitor friend, and, to be blunt, he tried to talk me out of it. Perhaps I should have listened. But in spite of his dire warning, I will assist you."

The overwhelming urge to cry with relief swamped her, but she bravely met his hardened gaze and murmured, "Thank you."

"William Chambers—he's the solicitor friend—suggested we use the registry near his office for the temporary marriage. He has agreed to keep your settlement under his safe auspices." Riordan's voice was cool, officious, and she further regretted her tone. But they must keep this about business or her heart would be in danger of harboring the fires of love and longing she imagined all hearts had potential for.

At that thought, she experienced a slight pang of melancholy, for her heart was cold, barren, and lonely. Forcing such thoughts from her mind, she asked, "What about Sutherhorne? For all I know he and my father have been corresponding. I am told nothing, except I'm to say yes to his proposal. And what grounds will we use for the annulment? And—"

Riordan raised his hand. Sabrina inwardly bristled, for she had had enough of men trying to silence her. "Concerning the annulment: William and I deemed it best you not be told the reason. Then you can genuinely and honestly claim you knew nothing about it."

Her mind quickly perused the various causes he had discussed with her earlier. *No. He wouldn't.* "I do not want for you to humiliate yourself over me. Truly, I sincerely appreciate that you have decided to help me, but I will not see you suffer publicly." For once, she did not hide her emotions; there was genuine concern in her tone.

A small smile formed about his sensual lips in response. "Ah, as I suspected. You *do* have a heart." His voice was husky, and the sound of it made her breath quicken.

"I assure you all evidence is to the contrary," she sniffed.

Riordan laughed, and jolts of heat cascaded down her spine. "As you say, my lady. The explanation we settled on is not one of those I mentioned last week. It is far less humiliating, I swear it."

"Well, we will set it aside for now. And Sutherhorne?"

"First, where will he be staying, with you and your father?" Riordan asked.

A chilling shudder replaced the warmth she'd felt at his sensual laugh. "Good Lord, I hope not. As I said, I'm told nothing. Seeing as my father despises visitors, I assume the marquess will be staying at the inn in town."

Riordan nodded. "Fine. I will pay the marquess a visit after he sees you tomorrow afternoon. I will convince him to withdraw his suit. Once he does, I will meet with your father."

"Withdraw? How? Let me guess: I am better off not knowing." Huffing in frustration, she pulled off her gloves and laid them on her lap. Oh, bother, it was unconscionably hot in here. It was either the woodstove or Riordan's compelling presence. Sabrina would lay bets on the latter.

"For the moment, you are better off," he replied. "I promise I will fill you in on the particulars later. I have a question for you: what will you do with your maid?"

Sabrina's brows furrowed and her heart dropped clear to her toes. "What do you mean?" she rasped.

Riordan arched an eyebrow. "You have seen the cottage. There is no room for a maid. I brought furniture from my visit home, so there is even less room. There is a chaise longue in the parlor I will sleep on."

"Well, Mary can stay in the main bedroom with me," she said firmly. Sabrina could not believe he was proposing this.

He chuckled softly. "There is only one bedroom and the bed is not large enough."

Her first instinct was to rail and cry, throw a tantrum only a baron's daughter and widow to an earl could possibly conjure up. She had been quite adept at them until her father beat the impulse out of her. "Mr. Black—Riordan—I cannot be parted from her. I rely on her." Her voice trembled on the last word. In a firmer, cooler voice, she said, "I will *not* be without my maid."

Riordan arched an eyebrow. "Of course. Silly of me. However will you survive?"

Was he mocking her? The corner of his mouth quirked slightly, but his expression was not cruel. She had no idea how to respond to this man, and it flummoxed her.

"She was with me throughout the entirety of my horrific marriage to Pepperdon. Mary was there for me, comforting me, especially when he… never mind." Blast it, she would not cry. "I know I'm not supposed to use her first name, but she is more than a lady's maid. She is my friend. Indeed, my only friend. Mary is…all I have." Now she'd revealed too much, and sounded pathetic to boot.

Riordan reached across the desk and gently clasped her hand, causing her to gasp in surprise. A slight touch as this should not be sending such strange sensations through her body. But it did. Could this be arousal? She had no idea. "Sabrina, I was teasing you, do not distress. I would not separate you from your friend."

Her life had become emotionally barren, and because of that she could not even recognize an innocent, teasing remark. His thumb brushed the top of her hand and a sigh escaped her lips even though she'd tried to stem it. The pad of his thumb was calloused, no doubt from gripping a pen for hours on end. The feel of it made her skin prickle with heated awareness.

"Call Mary into the room. We will find a solution." His smile was warm, encouraging.

As she called for her maid, he slowly released her hand, his fingers trailing hers. Oh, he was adept at that. Making an innocent touch into… more. Her senses had never been this heightened, nor had she been so aware of a man's masculinity.

"Ah, Miss Tuttle. Can I ask you what the baron has been paying you under his employ this past year?" Riordan asked.

Mary looked to Sabrina, biting her lower lip. "Well, sir, he paid me five pounds when we first arrived and said it was my wages for the year. If I dared complain or mention it to her ladyship, he claimed he would turn me out without a reference."

"What a miserable skinflint!" Sabrina cried. "Pepperdon may have been a lot of things, but at least he paid you a decent wage of twenty-five pounds per annum." Sabrina took a calming breath. "You should have told me."

Mary shook her head. "You had enough to deal with, my lady. I didn't want to be the cause of a row with the baron. Not with his vile temper."

"Here is the conundrum, Miss Tuttle: not only is the cottage I live in barely room enough for two, I cannot afford to pay you twenty-five pounds per annum. Not even for three months. I assume you know of what I speak? The arranged and temporary marriage?" Riordan asked.

Mary nodded. "I do, sir. May I say I find you extremely kind and generous for doing this for my lady?"

"Thank you. Now, with regards to your employment…" Sabrina began to sputter, trying to form words, but Riordan kept on speaking, not paying her any mind at all. "I may be able to arrange something. You may have to stay in town, but it is less than a mile walk from the cottage. You can manage it, I'm sure?"

Mary smiled. "I can, sir."

"Excellent. Now, Lady Pepperdon, I assume you will pay Miss Tuttle out of your settlement?"

Sabrina calmed, admiring the way Riordan took charge. He exuded such confidence, which she sadly lacked in her past but now worked toward regaining. "Yes, of course."

"Excellent. Miss Tuttle, how I envision this is you may work part of the time with her ladyship, and part of your day you may be required to help out at the inn to pay for the room. Do you have any objections?"

Mary shook her head. "Not at all, sir. After the first Lady Pepperdon passed away, I became a parlor maid. Cleaning and the like will be no hardship. I will earn my keep."

"Good. I will make the arrangements when school dismisses later this afternoon. I would suggest you both pack only the essentials, and do it immediately. This will all fall into place rather quickly, and a hasty departure may be imminent."

Mary gave a brisk nod. "Leave it with me, sir. We'll be ready."

Riordan nodded, then swung his gaze to Sabrina. "Once this plan goes into motion, we will make our way to London. Miss Tuttle will accompany us. We will have to go by mail coach, as the nearby train route is still under construction. William is making the arrangements; I only need give him a firm date."

Sabrina stood. "Thank you, again." She held out her hand. *With no glove.* Riordan stood and took it, then bowed briefly. He only touched her for mere seconds, but her body responded once again. Such fluttering over a mere brush of the fingers. She would have to learn to tame her response and ignore the emotions she had long buried—or so she kept telling herself.

"Until tomorrow. Good afternoon, Lady Pepperdon, Miss Tuttle."

As she exited the school, a weight lifted from her soul. Soon she would be free. Live her life on her own terms. Though Sabrina barely knew Riordan Black, a small part of her did trust him.

"My lady, if I may."

Mary's voice pulled her from her thoughts. "What is it?"

"May I make a suggestion?" Sabrina nodded. "In your future dealings with Mr. Black, you may wish to...soften your tone. He is doing you a great service and deserves your gracious consideration."

Sabrina halted. "Did I sound...harsh?" What a silly question—she knew she had.

"Yes, my lady. I know you don't mean to; how can you help it with what you've had to deal with? Mr. Black was teasing you, good-naturedly. I heard no mockery in his voice. I believe you've forgotten what affectionate teasing sounds like. Be open to his friendship. It will make the next three months all the more bearable and...enjoyable." Mary tsked. "I'm speaking out of turn."

Affectionate? Truly? "My dear Mary. You are well aware you may say whatever you're thinking. We are friends. I welcome your counsel." Sabrina sighed. "You're right. I cannot tell the difference between a teasing remark and a deliberate insult. I am not used to being treated with...with..."

"Respect? Compassion? Kindness?"

Sabrina smiled. "Yes. All of it." She looped her arm through Mary's and they continued toward the woods. "This is a fresh start in all ways. I will heed your suggestion and be more solicitous."

Sabrina glanced at her surroundings as they strolled toward home. Everything was enhanced and reflected vivid color and splendor, especially the autumn leaves with their shimmering red and gold tones. Birdsong filled her hearing, as did the crunching of the multihued leaves as they walked. Hours before her meeting with Riordan she'd taken little notice of such, and if she had it would have been a dismal cacophony of sound, and the leaves falling from the trees would have reminded her of death.

Today? All of it became a lush symphony of beauty and rebirth. Indeed, it was concerto of life itself. She looked up at the sun, closed her eyes, and inhaled deeply. For the first time in a long while, she was happy.

Mary squeezed her arm, returning her attention to the conversation. "You won't regret it, my lady. I knew right off he was a decent man when I looked into his handsome face. As my sailor father used to say, 'I like the cut of his jib.' He will do right by you. I know it."

"I am glad to hear it. Your opinion means a great deal to me. You know, I'm famished. Let's head to the kitchen when we return and see what cook can whip up for us. I foresee slices of chicken swimming in a creamy, decadent sauce. Something chocolate for afters."

Mary laughed as they stepped across the front entrance—but the laugh died in her throat as they were greeted by Sabrina's father, his face mottled and his expression angry.

In three long strides he stood before Sabrina and grabbed her arm. "Where have you been?" he hissed through clenched teeth. He squeezed and she cried out, pain shooting up to her shoulder.

"You are hurting me," she snapped, biting her lip to stem the acute throbbing from his cruel grip.

"I will do worse than this if you do not do as I say. Sutherhorne is here, and has been waiting for more than an hour."

Sabrina stopped struggling and her eyes widened in shock. "But…he was not supposed to be here until tomorrow," she gasped.

Finally, he released her arm. "Apparently he is anxious to see this marriage take place, and I am equally anxious to be rid of you."

And I you, Father. She nearly spoke the words aloud, but this was not the time to enter into an argument. "I'm not prepared to see or speak to him today," she said, her tone flat. Her insides roiled with apprehension.

"I do not care. Speak to him you will. And you will say one word: yes." He pushed her toward the sitting room.

"Wait. Let me give Mary my cloak."

She scurried away from her father, and as she handed Mary the wool cloak she whispered in her ear, "Run to the school. Inform Mr.

Black of the developments. Whatever he has planned must be put into motion immediately."

Mary gave her a quick nod and headed for the back stairs. Taking a deep breath and exhaling, she turned to face her father. How to handle this? She had not completely prepared herself for the conversation with the marquess. First, do not show fear. Not to her father or to Sutherhorne. Second, do not give a firm yes. *You can do this.*

"Come, we do not have all day." Her father held out his arm. Moving her shaking legs forward, she entered the sitting room. Standing, facing the fire, was a tall, thin man leaning on a cane. He turned to face her.

This man was not the marquess she had met at a ball, who smelled of horse and had missing teeth. That man was weak and harmless. This man was none of it. The Marquess of Sutherhorne was frosty and formidable.

This man was far worse than she had imagined.

Chapter 9

"Sutherhorne, my daughter, Lady Sabrina Pepperdon, widow of the late Earl of Pepperdon. Sabrina, this is Brendan Whiddon, the Marquess of Sutherhorne."

His cane hit the tiled floor as he moved toward her, echoing in her heart and sending a chill through her. This was not a wizened, weak shell of a man, but one whose cruel aura matched the baron's. This is what made him far worse: he reminded her of her wretched father.

Once, long ago, Sutherhorne was no doubt a fine looking man. But time had not been kind. He had a wraith-like appearance, from his pale, white skin to his full head of white hair and his icy gray eyes. Deep lines were etched into his face, reflecting years of harsh living. Did he have a weak heart, as her father had proclaimed? God, she had had her fill of old, cold men.

The marquess stared at her with shrewd, lecherous eyes. She scanned the long length of him. Far too slender, and the breeches and polished hessian boots he wore were two decades out of date. Although, on closer inspection, his long frock coat and double-breasted waistcoat were of a more recent fashion. What an odd ensemble.

He stood in front of her, and she caught the cloying scent of musky cologne—it made her nose twitch. Liver spots dotted his temples, and it was then she realized he sported a closely cropped goatee; it was as white as his skin and not completely visible at first glance. His cheekbones were prominent, no doubt an attractive feature in years past. Now they only enhanced his austere appearance.

"My dear Lady Pepperdon," he rasped, his voice as rough as sandpaper. He clutched her hand, which she had gloved on her way back from the school. She could feel the coldness of his touch through the fabric. It took all her inner resolve not to pull her hand from his in horror.

Mustering an indifferent but polite smile, she inclined her head. "My lord."

"I will leave you both to become better acquainted." Her father turned and marched from the room. Did Sabrina detect a spring to his step? *Miserable man.* He was genuinely happy to be rid of her. As hard as she tried to ignore it, the fact her own father did not love her still smarted.

"Were you offered refreshment? Perhaps I can order tea."

"No, thank you. I recently had a meal at the inn. Shall we sit?" he asked. A brief, brittle smile haunted his waxen features.

Sabrina immediately sat in the wingchair. She had no desire to sit next to him on the small settee. With a fling of the tail of his coat, he sat opposite, crossing his long legs.

"Allow me to give you a little information about myself. I am sixty-one years of age, in fine health, and in the possession of a modest fortune. I have been a widower for fifteen years, and I am of a mind to marry again. I do a fair bit of entertaining and need a hostess for these events." He leaned forward, his bony hands resting on the ornate knob of his silver cane. "But more than that, I am lonely. I want a companion, a friend."

Nothing he said caused her to be alarmed, but his narrowing gaze made her tremble involuntarily. *Fine health?* Her father had lied to her about the heart condition; she was not the least bit surprised. There was something not quite right about this man. He acted smug. As if he already owned her.

"Allow me to speak boldly, my lady," he continued. "I am of an amorous nature, and because of it, I wish for a willing bed partner—one old enough to appreciate experience and young enough to withstand my attentions." A slow, creeping smile spread across his face, like a malevolent feline spying a helpless mouse. "I already have an heir and a spare. I have no desire to have squalling brats running about my house. The fact you are barren appeals to me greatly."

The utter arrogance of men. They automatically believed the blame of not becoming pregnant lay solely on the woman. Pepperdon had made her see a physician, and the doctor had quietly relayed to her that all appeared to be in working order and perhaps the culpability, as it were, lay with Pepperdon. God forbid the doctor reveal such a fact to the earl. But neither did she. It would have only angered him further and no doubt subjected her to more humiliation.

Her father must have given Sutherhorne all the salacious details of her marriage to Pepperdon. *May all men rot in a fiery pit.* Well, except Riordan. Looking at the earl, she was glad she'd sought out the schoolmaster. Such a stark difference between them. Riordan was welcoming warmth, the marquess the complete opposite. A walking, talking icicle. He eyed her, waiting for her response.

Sabrina cleared her throat. "I appreciate your frankness. Allow me to do the same. My marriage to Pepperdon was loathsome, and he left me penniless. I have a few caveats before I will consider your suit." Her voice was strong, her tone confident. She was off to a good start.

He arched an eyebrow. "Indeed? Your father did not indicate such."

As I surmised. "I will be bringing my personal maid with me. Her yearly salary is forty pounds per annum, to be paid quarterly. By you." Sabrina decided to keep talking with the marquess, to allow both him and her father the illusion that she was even considering this marriage.

He gave her a slight shrug. "That is agreeable. The salary is a bit more than what is paid a lady's maid, but I will consent to it."

"I also will require a quarterly payment. Let us call it pin money. I want currency to call my own to spend as I please. I should not have to come begging if I wish to purchase new gloves or a book."

The marquess's steely gaze narrowed further. "Greedy little thing. Again, I do not object. Shall we say fifty…?"

"One hundred pounds per quarter."

He licked his thin, colorless lips. "I daresay you have more fire in you than your father led me to believe. What a pleasant revelation. It will bode well in the bedchamber."

The bedchamber again. The complete conceit of the man. Was she supposed to be charmed and excited by this? Instead it made her stomach churn. Sabrina decided to ignore his statement. "I require you to stipulate in your will that upon your death, I will be granted a yearly stipend of three thousand pounds until my death, and a place of residence of my choosing. All I require is a comfortable, modest place by the sea. Before I agree to any marriage, I must see all these provisions in writing, in a legal and binding document." There. The requests should delay things long enough for her to make her escape.

"Well. Marriage to Pepperdon taught you much. What you are requesting is not unreasonable. Any man of honor would make sure his widow was provided for. Pepperdon was a lout. Rest assured I will meet your demands." He stood, and Sabrina did the same. Apparently the meeting was concluded. What a relief. "I will go at once to the solicitor in town." He patted his coat pocket. "I already have a special license, signed by the archbishop himself. I will pay a visit to the town vicar and make arrangements. We will be married before the week is out."

"Perhaps you are getting ahead of yourself, my lord?"

He stalked toward her, and without thinking she backed up several steps until she found herself against the fireplace mantel. He leaned in; his heavy, pungent scent nearly made her retch. "I have waited eleven years for this, Sabrina, and I have run out of patience. You see, your father chose Pepperdon over me. There was more than one suitor for your hand. Quite the…contest." A cruel smile spread across his face. "All I know is I wanted you then, and I want you now. More than ever." He whorled the shell of her ear with his tongue, causing her to cry out. "I will have you, make no mistake," he whispered before he stepped away. "I shall return tomorrow with the appropriate agreements, and I will expect your answer. Good afternoon, Sabrina." With his hand on the door handle, he paused, turned, and stared at her with a neutral expression that developed into a slow, wide grin. With a slight cackle and nod, he opened the door and left.

As if out of a Gothic novel, cracks of thunder sounded as he exited the room. Heavy rain thrashed against the windows in concert with her beating heart.

Sabrina whirled about and grasped the mantel to keep from collapsing into a heap. Never had she been so frightened. She covered her mouth to keep a scream from clawing its way up her throat. What did he mean by a contest? Sabrina did not like the sinister way he'd conveyed the sentence. As if it had an underlying and ominous meaning.

Regardless, the path was clear. She could not stay here no matter the circumstances. Nor could she allow herself to be trapped in another loveless marriage with an old peer.

For a brief moment, when Sutherhorne had agreed to her demands, she'd considered going through with the marriage. It would ensure her future… and Mary's. But in the end, she could not do it. Not for all the money and comforts in the world.

Her future now lay in the hands of a schoolmaster. She had to place her complete trust in Riordan Black and pray he managed to wring a settlement out of her father and turn Sutherhorne away. How could it be accomplished? There were too many variables. It could all go wrong in many ways. The more she thought about it, the more she realized the mad scheme had no chance of success.

Sabrina had no choice. There was only one thing to do.

Run.

* * * *

A rumble of thunder sounded overhead, causing the students to gasp and gaze worriedly at the heavy rain lashing against the windows. Howling winds rattled the panes and tore leaves from nearby trees. Riordan had not witnessed such an intense thunderstorm in October before. "Settle down, students. We're safe. No cause for alarm. The roof will hold and not spring any leaks, I am sure of it. Now, where were we?"

Charlie raised his hand. "You were showing us the globe."

Riordan's personal curriculum did not follow the standard one in use for smaller, rural schools, where emphasis lay on physical labors instead of intellectual ones. Why would a farmer care where the Russian Empire is located on a map? was the general thinking. Riordan did not subscribe to teaching knitting for girls and shoemaking for the boys, for example. Developing the mind was a far more useful skill.

It had taken some doing to convince the board, and there were a few in the town who objected to his "radical" teachings. Like the vicar. He wanted a curriculum that leaned heavily on religion, infusing bible study as part of the daily routine. Riordan had managed to convince the vicar—and the board—that religion was best left to an expanded Sunday school period.

Riordan reached for the large globe and held it up in front of him. "There is a huge world out there beyond Great Britain." He spun the globe. "Earth moves about in space just like this, but perhaps not quite this fast." The children giggled. "As we discussed yesterday, this is how we have day and night, the sun setting in the west and rising in the east. This is where science and geography intersect."

A couple of the younger students looked at him with puzzlement. Sometimes, he forgot he was teaching children ranging from age seven to seventeen, the majority between the ages of ten and thirteen. "Intersect means to overlap, or to divide by passing through or across. For example, Weldon Road intersects with the town. Understand?" Everyone nodded. "Remember, if you do not understand the meaning of a word, raise your hand and I will gladly explain—"

A booming crash of thunder drowned out the rest of his sentence. His youngest student, a sweet girl named Annabelle, screamed and vaulted from her desk, then ran toward him. She flung herself at him, clutching his legs as if looking for protection. God, the poor wee thing was trembling.

His protective instincts went into full alert and he scooped the frightened child into his arms. She immediately hugged him about his neck, holding on for dear life. "There, child," he whispered soothingly. "No need to be afraid. Thunder and lightning can be loud and overpowering, but they are merely a facet of weather, just warm air and cool air slamming against each other. It will be over soon, I promise." He walked about the front of the class, humming quietly until Annabelle settled.

The young girl did not have a father; the man had disappeared when she was a baby. Annabelle ran to Riordan for protection because she had no other male influence in her life except him. A sad state of affairs, but Riordan soon learned many of his students looked to him as a father figure, and it was humbling indeed. He carried Annabelle to her desk and made sure she was calm and comfortable. Another crash sounded. *Wait.* It wasn't thunder. Someone was pounding on the door.

"Students, study the drawing of the map of the world in front of you. When I return, we will discuss the continents. Clara, watch over the class." The older girl nodded and moved to his desk. Clara had expressed a desire to be a teacher, and he often used her as a de facto assistant.

With the class under control, Riordan strode toward the alcove and the front entrance beyond. He flung open the door and a soaking wet Miss Tuttle stood before him, gasping and out of breath. "Mr.…Black …" she wheezed.

He clasped her arm and assisted her across the threshold. "Good God. What is it?"

She took several deep breaths and exhaled. "I…I ran all the way. One moment." Regaining a more regulated breathing, she gazed up at him, her worried expression certainly cause for concern. "When we arrived, the earl was there. Sutherhorne."

Damn. "He wasn't supposed to be there until tomorrow."

Miss Tuttle nodded. "Yes. Not expected. Lady Pepperdon was shoved into a room with him. She bade me to come to you, and to say whatever you've planned will have to be put into action immediately."

"Come sit by the woodstove and dry off. Unfortunately, I can do nothing until class dismisses in two hours. Hopefully by then it will have stopped raining. In the meantime, stay as my guest, Miss Tuttle."

"Thank you. Please, call me Mary as Lady Pepperdon does."

"Very well, Mary." Still clasping her arm, he escorted her to the woodstove and saw her settled. "Class, this is Miss Tuttle. She is taking refuge from the storm and will be our guest for the rest of the afternoon."

"Good afternoon, Miss Tuttle," the class said in singsong unison.

Riordan's mind raced. What he'd planned would have to be put into action right away. A good thing Garrett had not departed for home yet—he would need him. But first…he turned toward his eager students. "The continents…"

* * * *

The rain had let up by dismissal. After assuring Mary he would act immediately, he made for his cottage. Upon entry, he found Garrett sitting in the overstuffed armchair with one long leg dangling over the side. He had a book in one hand and a whiskey in the other. A roaring fire crackled in the hearth. Riordan stood in front of it and warmed his hands.

Garrett looked up from his book. "Dismissal already? Where did the afternoon go?"

"Don't you look comfortable."

Garrett slammed the book shut. "I am. I do not often take a respite like this. I must do it more often. Your housekeeper brought a kettle of beef stew by, along with a fresh loaf of bread. I'm famished. Let's tuck in."

Riordan turned to face his uncle. "The meal will have to wait. I have a favor to ask of you. All you need to do is stand next to me and look menacing."

Garrett cocked an eyebrow. "Does the wretch deserve to be menaced?"

"Yes. He does."

Garrett stood. "What are we waiting for?"

"First, I must ask you not to repeat to grandfather and father anything that happens or anything you hear. Rest assured I will attend the first of November's family meeting and reveal all. I have already asked the board and was granted a personal day."

"Jesus, what in hell are you doing?"

"I'm assisting someone in dire need. It is what we do as a family, is it not?" Riordan gave Garrett a brief smile. "The wretch in question is a marquess. There is a baron involved. And his daughter, the widow of an earl."

Garrett closed his eyes. "Aw, hell."

Riordan wrapped his wool muffler about his neck. "It could become messy. But I gave my word to the lady in question."

Garrett's eyes snapped open. "The widow? Again I ask: what the bloody hell are you doing?"

Riordan marched toward the door. "Rescuing a damsel in distress. It is too bad the horse isn't white, but I will ride up on a noble steed nonetheless."

Garrett grabbed his cloak and followed Riordan outside. The heavy rain had turned into a light mist, but the road into town was muddy and full of ruts. A nondescript brick building, the Carrbury Inn, came into sight. After handing off their horses to a young lad, Riordan pulled Garrett aside. "Go inside and ask for the Marquess of Sutherhorne. Tell him the Earl of Carnstone awaits him. I better not go inside, as the innkeeper sits on the education board. Having the schoolmaster threaten a peer would definitely be cause for dismissal."

Garrett arched an eyebrow. "You think? I bloody well hope you know what you're doing, Nephew." With a grunt of disbelief, his uncle headed into the inn.

Actually, he had no idea what he was doing. He did not make a habit of threatening anyone, but could rise to the occasion if needed. No one stood in his way once his mind was made up. An unfortunate family trait, but it came in handy for their progressive causes. And this was a significant cause. Women should never be treated as property or chattel with no rights of their own.

Garrett stepped outside, bending slightly to allow the doorframe to accommodate his height. "Well, the message has been delivered. Now to see if he comes on his own. He does have a couple of men with him, no doubt his valet and a coach driver. I suppose you will do the talking and I will threaten bodily harm."

"Yes. Thanks for this, Garrett. I will explain a little more when we return to the cottage."

"Carnstone? Where are you, man? And what is the meaning of dragging me away from my warm fire—"

Garrett growled, clasped the marquess's arm, and pulled him into the shadows of the alley next to the inn.

The older man stammered in protest. He had come out alone, a lucky occurrence. "Sorry, no Carnstone. You are to leave this vicinity immediately. There will be no marriage between you and Lady Pepperdon." Riordan barked, though he kept his tone as quiet as possible in order to not be overheard.

"You insolent blackguard. Who are you to make demands?" Garrett growled once again, grabbed a fistful of the old man's coat, and lifted him bodily from the ground. It looked to be no hardship, as the man probably weighed nothing more than a leafless twig. Sutherhorne cried out, struggling to free himself from Garrett's tight grip to no avail.

"No one of significance, but know that my friend here will break you in half over his knee like a rotten piece of kindling if you do not agree to depart. Tonight." Riordan paused. "But not before you write a note to the baron withdrawing your suit. How much is he paying you for a settlement?"

The marquess stopped struggling and glared at him. Riordan stayed in shadow and hoped his face was obscured from any possible identification. "Paying me? I am paying *him*!" Sutherhorne snapped.

Riordan's insides twisted at the news. "There is no money?"

"No, there isn't. Durning makes a habit of selling his daughter. He held a secret auction the first time around, I was there…and lost. Not again. I ensured I'm the only one in the running, as I offered him eighteen thousand pounds, which is to be paid before the marriage takes place. The baron and I have a deal, in writing, you cannot…"

Secret auction? Riordan could not believe his ears. Though Sabrina had said she was sold to the highest bidder, he'd thought it was merely a turn of phrase. Yet she'd spoken of a dowry paid to Pepperdon. Where did the truth lie? God, what a mess. "I can and I will. Since you have not paid for her yet, you can easily withdraw from the transaction. I have powerful friends, and I will let it be known that you were involved in illegal doings."

Sutherhorne squeaked as Garrett lifted him higher. "Call off your damned beast! I will write the letter and leave tonight. But know this: I will find out who you are, and you will pay for interfering. Both of you. This I promise." The last sentence dripped with menace. They had made an enemy here tonight.

"Take him inside to write the note."

Garrett gruffly lowered the marquess, then commenced dragging him toward the inn. His uncle was certainly playing his role with a good deal of relish. Riordan ducked farther into the darkened alley and waited.

One statement was startling: if Sutherhorne was paying to marry Sabrina, there would be no dowry or settlement. How in hell could he break the news to her? Things had already been set into motion; there was no going back on the plan now. "Habit of selling his daughter…secret auction." Which meant Pepperdon had paid for her as well. Disgusting, arrogant men, bartering for a young lady. Again, no dowry or settlement. It explained why Pepperdon had left her penniless. The late earl had obviously decided she did not deserve it, since he'd laid out a good deal of capital in order to marry her. *Damn it all.* He believed Sabrina was truly ignorant of these facts.

If the earl wasn't already moldering in a grave, he would have ensured he be put there without hesitation. Both the marquess and the baron deserved the same fate. The potency of his growing anger alarmed him. Never had he come this close to committing murder.

Moments later, the inn became a beehive of activity. The marquess's carriage was brought around, trunks hurriedly loaded on, and Garrett emerged from the inn with Sutherhorne in tow. He loaded the cursing marquess into the carriage and slammed the door. With a crack of the whip, the horses whinnied and trotted off out of town.

Garrett handed Riordan the sealed letter. "There is nothing to stop the bastard from sending a message to the baron anywhere along the road."

"Yes, I thought of that. I'd better head to the baron immediately and inform Sabrina of what has transpired."

"Sabrina, is it?"

"Garrett, if you could please procure the room Sutherhorne just exited, I would be grateful. Lady Sabrina and her maid will be staying here tonight. Probably the rest of the week. I'll meet you at the cottage."

Garrett was about to speak, then changed his mind. He clapped Riordan on the shoulder and gave him a look of what could be admiration.

Now to make his way to Baron Durning.

And to Sabrina.

Chapter 10

Once Riordan announced that he carried a note from the Marquess of Sutherhorne, who had ordered it be delivered personally into the baron's hands, he was quickly bustled into the library. While waiting for the baron to arrive, he glanced about the room. Not well-stocked as libraries go, and the draperies were worn and frayed along the edges. The baron must be in financial straits. What other motive could he have to sell his daughter? It would take every ounce of his restraint not to pummel the oaf as soon as he made an appearance.

The door banged against the wall and Baron Durning strode in, his look arrogant and imperious. Early fifties, Riordan guessed, and in fine fettle. Close to six feet in height and broad of shoulder—could he take him in a fight? He was taller and younger than the baron, it could be accomplished.

But this wouldn't come to an altercation. They were hardly drunk laborers arguing in a pub. They were gentlemen. However, that did not stop Riordan from using his brawny uncle to threaten the marquess. Desperate times call for...well, perhaps he could have handled this entire situation in a more civilized manner. But he was on this path, might as well see it through. His anger certainly fueled his actions. "I'm to wait for a reply, my lord."

Durning snatched the note, tore it open, and scanned it, his face turning purple the more he read. "What is the meaning of this?"

"The marquess has departed the vicinity and returned to his home. There will be no wedding. However, I offer myself in his stead. I am Riordan Black, schoolmaster."

"School...schoolmaster? Is this a joke?" Durning thundered.

Riordan took a step closer. "I am removing your daughter and her maid from these premises at once. You will not be able to sell her any longer, nor use her for your nefarious and selfish means."

The baron's eyes narrowed. "I can do with her as I please. However, you want the bitch? Take her. She comes without a farthing."

"I am aware. The Marquess of Sutherhorne was most forthcoming with the information regarding your transaction, including your previous secret auction," Riordan snapped. "I aim to offer my protection to Sabrina and because of it, you will never tell her there is no settlement or that you tried to sell her. In fact, you're to have no further contact with her. Do I make myself clear?"

"Or you will do what, exactly? One word from me and you will be dismissed from your post and run out of this county." A malicious smile spread across the baron's face.

"No, you will not. I'm guessing you want to be rid of your daughter more than you wish to take revenge on a lowly schoolmaster. Besides, I have powerful allies: a viscount and an earl. Do not force my hand."

"You. Lie." The baron spat the words, and a spray of spittle hit Riordan's cheek, stoking his fury to untested levels.

"Care to call my bluff? I will also ensure the authorities are made aware of the underhanded and illicit scheme to sell your daughter. There have been prosecutions in court for what you are doing. I'm guessing your finances are in a precarious position. May I suggest you find another way to procure income?" Riordan whispered dangerously. "Sell yourself in marriage instead."

The baron snorted, his look turning from anger to pure abhorrence. "You have cost me more than money, and it's not something I will soon forget."

Riordan stepped away. "I seem to be collecting enemies today. Let me return the threat in kind: if you dare reveal any of this to your daughter, dare to speak of her or to her again, I will see you ruined. Arrested. Humiliated before Society." Riordan leaned in close and whispered menacingly, "I will see you suffer in every way imaginable."

"You arrogant puppy," Durning cried.

Riordan collected himself. This heated situation was getting out of hand. But he was utterly furious at the way Sabrina had been treated. It made his hasty decision to assist her more urgent and equitable. But even more surprising was the desire to do anything to protect her. "Send for your daughter."

* * * *

"Quickly, Mary. We must make a hasty escape." Sabrina tore about her room like a whirling dervish, tossing various garments into her trunk.

Mary gently laid her hand on Sabrina's arm. "My lady, remember Mr. Black instructed us to only bring what we cannot do without. We must travel light. Do you truly care for these clothes?"

Sabrina glanced at the pile of silk and velvet. No, she didn't. All it did was remind her of her life with Pepperdon. Though her life with him was abhorrent, she had wanted for nothing. "I thought we could eventually sell them, but no, I don't care for them. I will leave the trunk. Only what we are able to carry." She marched to her dressing table and snatched up the sterling silver comb and brush set. "And what we are able to sell. The sun is setting; we will leave as soon as it grows dark."

"Shouldn't we wait until Mr. Black arrives?"

Sabrina shook her head sadly. "I doubt Mr. Black will be able to assist us. What was I thinking? A schoolmaster against a baron and a marquess?" She stuffed the vanity set in her large carpet bag. "The plan is doomed."

"Well, I spent a couple of hours in his classroom today, and he had a commanding presence with complete control of his students. I don't think he is a man who will be easily pushed around, not even by peers." Mary smiled. "He had me mesmerized. I thought my education was solid and thorough, but even I learned a few things about the continents. I wonder what else he could teach a woman?"

"Mary!" Sabrina froze.

"Well, not me. I'm old enough to be his mother. But you, my lady? You're attracted to him, you're blushing even now. You will be alone with him in a small cottage and—"

Sabrina held up her hand. "No. I cannot. I have no heart left. I have nothing to give any man."

Mary moved to her side. "How will you know unless you allow it? Be open to new experiences and emotions, my lady. I promise you will not regret it." Mary shook her head. "I'm not suggesting that you seduce Mr. Black, good heavens. But as I said earlier, be open to friendship. And if it should lead to more…" She sighed, her expression wistful. "My lady, you have no idea how wonderful an intimate relationship with a man can be. It can enrich your life. I'm not merely speaking of physical intimacy, though that can be extraordinary. I mean friendship, sharing secrets, trusting that person with your life. Sharing a quiet evening when you are both in the room, each lost in their own pursuits but content in the companionable silence."

"My heavens, Mary. How do you know of such things? Do not tell me it is from your romantic books."

Her maid did something Sabrina had never seen before: she blushed. "No, not only from the books."

A knock at the door made them both start. "Oh, no. We should have left an hour since," Sabrina whispered.

"Who is it?" Mary called out.

"It's George, my lady. Your presence is requested in the library."

Mary marched to the door and flung it open. "Who is in the library with the baron?" she demanded.

The young footman jutted his chin in the air and did not answer.

"Oh, stop being contrary, George. It doesn't suit you," Mary snapped. "Who is it?"

"I recognize him, it's the schoolmaster," he muttered.

Sabrina let out the breath she'd held. Not the marquess. Thank God. Smoothing her skirt, she walked toward the door. "Continue packing, Mary." She followed George downstairs, her legs shaking the entire way. Crossing the threshold of the library, the tension hanging in the air was palatable. Her father faced the window, his fists at his sides. By his stance, she could tell he was angry. Sabrina slid her gaze to Riordan. He also looked furious.

"We are leaving immediately. Mary as well. The bags should be brought down, I have a wagon outside," Riordan said, his voice tight.

George looked toward the baron, who kept his back to everyone. "My lord?"

"Do it," the baron barked.

George scurried away, looking relieved to be departing.

"Then we shall take our leave," Riordan said in a clipped tone.

"Good luck with her," the baron stated coldly. "The late earl said she is a contrary, frigid hag who couldn't even manage to give him an heir. She is spoiled, taciturn, and thoroughly unpleasant. I'm glad to be rid of her."

Sabrina gasped and covered her mouth in shock at her father's hateful words.

Riordan's expression turned dangerous, and with three large strides he spun her father around until he stood toe-to-toe with the baron. "You are not to speak of your daughter in such a way ever again." Riordan grabbed a fistful of the baron's cravat. "Remember what I said. I will follow through, have no doubt."

The quick burst of violence from Riordan made her blood run cold with fear. Good heavens, he was no better than every other man in her life.

As if sensing her distress, Riordan released the baron and moved to her side, gently clasping her elbow. "Come, Sabrina. We are departing." He leaned in and whispered, "Don't look back. Do not *ever* look back."

Biting her lip, she nodded. Strangely, tears clustered on her eyelashes. This part of her life was over. Her father would not even look at her or say goodbye. Fine, neither would she. With shoulders straight, she left the room, allowing Riordan to steer her toward the front door.

The sky had cleared and the sun all but set. Pink clouds hovered across the horizon, showing proof tomorrow would be a glorious, sunny one. *A new beginning.* Though many questions formed in her mind, she knew if she put voice to them, she would begin to weep. Liberation. Freedom. She was on the path to achieve it, and it made her heart soar.

He helped her up onto the bench seat, and she stiffened at his touch. "I will be escorting you and Mary to the inn, where you will stay until we can depart for London. The marquess has left town."

Riordan did it. Everything he'd promised. How could she ever repay him? Perhaps she should raise his share of the settlement to twenty-five percent. He deserved it. But now was not the time to broach the subject. His expression was thunderous, and peppering him with questions could annoy him further or lead him to believe she did not trust him. How surprising to find she did. Yet fear lingered.

Shortly after Mary and George emerged, Riordan helped load the few pieces of luggage and assisted Mary into the rear of the wagon. With a quick, fluid movement, Riordan sat next to Sabrina on the bench. He snapped the reins and they were off. "I am sorry you witnessed my temper. You must never think I would turn it on you. I will never harm you. Believe it."

Oh, she wanted to believe him. "It is not easy for me to trust any man, but I will endeavor to do so with you," she said.

He gave her a quick glance and nodded. "Before I came here, I met with one of the board members and they granted me Friday afternoon. We will leave for London then," Riordan said.

"You must keep an account of the costs you've been incurring, postage, the inn, the loss of salary. I will reimburse you immediately, from the settlement."

Riordan did not reply. His expression was stony and hard to read.

"There is a settlement?" she asked worriedly.

He patted his pocket. "I have it all in hand."

He'd said that earlier. Did he have the signed contract in his pocket? Was that the reason he patted his coat? "Thank you, Riordan." Her voice quivered with emotion.

He clasped her gloved hand and kissed it. “It was my distinct honor.”

Her insides fluttered. *Be open to new emotions*, Mary had said. Dare she allow it? *No.* She could not open her heart to this attractive, principled man. It was far safer to feel nothing at all. No chance of getting hurt. As she pulled her hand from his she took a deep breath. Exhaling, she marveled at the fact of how easy it was to breathe. She gazed at the road ahead. Her future lay open for this first time in her life. Sabrina couldn’t wait.

* * * *

Riordan made it to his cottage close to eight o’clock. Garrett immediately jumped from his chair and crossed his arms. “Right. You had better tell me all, Nephew.”

Riordan removed his hat and wool muffler and hung them on the hook by the door. “May I eat first?”

Garrett pointed to the table. “Sit. I’ll serve you, I’ve already eaten.”

With a weary sigh, Riordan sank into the wooden chair. God. He had pulled it off. Reaching in his side coat pocket, he pulled out the form he’d made the baron sign before Sabrina came downstairs. It was an utterly useless endeavor and could not be enforced, for there was no payment at all. But if Sabrina asked for proof, he could show her the fake paper. Lying made his insides roll with nausea. But she had been through enough, why add to her misery?

After settling Sabrina and Mary at the inn, he decided on his way home he would instruct William to use ten thousand pounds of his inheritance and pass it off as the dowry settlement. In reality, he should come clean, tell her the truth, and give her the money outright with no marriage needed, temporary or not. But he knew enough about her to surmise she would not accept the money as a gift, or even a loan. She was as stubborn as he.

He wanted to protect her and give her the chance to start a new life. Most of all, he wanted to erase the look of fear that haunted her beautiful eyes—his rare flash of temper had not helped matters. Cursing inwardly, he admonished himself for allowing the baron to bait him.

Deep down he knew that he cared about her, about what would happen to her. The transitory marriage would give him time to convince her to accept the money. Or perhaps he wanted to know her better, see if the sparks of attraction crackling between them could lead to something more...permanent. Yes, he was seriously considering this option.

It would be challenging. Sabrina Durning Lakeside had tucked her heart away years ago in order to protect it. He may not be able to find her heart and breathe new life into it. Every touch of her skin inflamed his passion to greater heights. How deluded he had been to think progressive causes alone would stir him. Never did he realize an emotionally closed off widow would make him feel more alive than…anything.

Garrett set the bowl of stew in front of him, along with a small plate of bread, then sat opposite. "Well? Do I have to drag it out of you, Nephew?"

Slipping the folded paper into his coat pocket, he gave his uncle a sly smile. "I agreed to assist Sabrina in extricating herself from an unwanted marriage to an abhorrent marquess, and at the same time rescue her from the clutches of her greedy, detestable father." He shrugged as he sprinkled pepper on the beef stew. "Mission accomplished."

Garrett reclined in his chair, regarding him. "There is no money. The marquess was to pay the baron for his daughter. Completely repugnant and illegal, I agree. But what is the widow to use for money? How will she live? I assume she is penniless. How do you factor into this, besides being her knight?"

Riordan didn't want to lie, as he would be doing enough of it in the next three months. "I am going to marry her." He shoved a spoonful of stew into his mouth.

Garrett jumped to his feet. "Have you gone mad?" he cried. His uncle started to pace.

"Temporary only. We will seek an annulment in three months. She will receive the money when the marriage is dissolved."

Garrett stopped pacing. "What money?"

"The money I'm going to give her." He explained the situation as his uncle slowly slumped into his chair, his expression incredulous. By the time Riordan finished the stew, he'd concluded his narrative.

To his surprise, Garrett laughed, but soon sobered. "You're deluding yourself if you believe you can stay detached from a young, nubile widow in this tiny cottage. I assume she's attractive?" Riordan nodded. "Have you heard nothing I have told you the past several years? Women are poison. They infect your heart and soul, then leave you all alone. The curse is real."

Riordan scoffed. "Jesus, Garrett. Not the curse again. I cannot believe you take that fairy tale seriously." Though he had to admit: he half believed in it himself.

His uncle's expression turned dark. "Have you been to the graveyard? My mother, Julian's mother, my half sister, and all the women who came before. The old earl, my grandfather and your great-grandfather, buried two wives. And his father before him buried three. Shall I continue? I can recite all the way to the beginning of the seventeenth century if you require proof. It *is* real." Garrett exhaled and ran his hands through his long hair. "Never mind the legal ramifications of what you're doing. It smacks of fraud, and it's not worthy of you no matter how earnest your intentions. You must have feelings for her already or you would not be barging ahead." Riordan looked away. "Damn it, Nephew, I thought you smarter than this."

Reluctantly, Riordan met his uncle's worried gaze. His annoyance grew; the last thing he wanted was to argue with Garrett. "This has nothing to do with love. Not that you know anything about it."

Garrett crossed his arms. "And what makes you think I know nothing about it?" he replied, his voice soft. "I know more than I ever wished to. You may think you're in charge of the situation, but it will spin out of control, mark my words."

This was a surprising development, for what did his uncle mean about love and knowing about it? When had he ever been involved with a woman? One of the summers he'd visited his Scottish relatives?

Garrett shook his head. "I can hear the gears turning in your head. Do not even ask. This is about you, not me. What about your father and grandfather?"

"I will reveal all when I come for the meeting."

Garrett scoffed. "By then it will be too late, the deed done. I should tell them of your insane plan. Have them talk sense into you."

"Uncle, give me credit for having a functioning brain. I'm not a stupid schoolboy, but a grown man out earning my keep. I've discussed this in-depth with William Chambers, my friend and solicitor, and this is all aboveboard. I had no idea the baron was selling his daughter, or had in the past. I was led to believe he would pay a generous settlement to be rid of her."

Garrett banged his fist on the table. "Exactly what makes you think this widow is not playing you for a fool? Eliciting your sympathies, trifling with your compassion for humankind? Your desire for progressive causes? All to gain money from you?"

Riordan bristled. "All she knows is that I am a penniless schoolmaster. She has no clue of my family connections. My God, you are cynical."

"Bah." Garrett shook his head. "There is no arguing with you."

"Please, allow me to break the news to father and grandfather. Will you?"

"It's against my better judgment, but fine. You'd better attend the meeting in two weeks time or I *will* tell them what's going on." Garrett raised an eyebrow. "For argument sake, let's say the widow is innocent. How do you think she will react when she finds out the money did not come from her father, but from you? And the fact you lied to her.... Think on it, Nephew." He spoke the last couple of sentences with slow, emphatic deliberation.

A throbbing ache formed in Riordan's left temple. He didn't want to think about it. At least, not tonight. All he was concerned with was getting her away from her father and the marquess. To protect her, see her safe, and ensure she would not be used and abused anymore. To keep Sabrina from harm he would prevaricate, cheat, even kill. The depth of his turbulent emotions had him worried about how he was going to survive the next three months.

Chapter 11

Two days had passed since Riordan brought Sabrina and Mary to the inn. Sabrina had seen him only once, last night, to inform her he'd heard from William Chambers and they would be leaving by mail coach noon Friday. Reservations were made for two rooms at an inn near the law office and the registrar's office. The brief civil ceremony would be held Saturday at noon, with Mary and Mr. Chambers acting as witnesses. There would be no music, no rings, and no solemn pronouncements before God. They would immediately return to Carrbury.

Just as well, since she'd already had a fancy wedding in a large church and it had led to nothing but misery. Also during this period, arrangements were made for Mary's own room and employment. It would be an adjustment not to have Mary around day and night. She would come to Sabrina in the mornings, prepare her for the day, see to her lunch, and then return to the inn for her afternoon duties. In the evening she would come to Sabrina to prepare her for bed.

Sabrina took Mary's words to heart: it wouldn't hurt to be friendly and solicitous. Try and banish old fears. Could she do it when every instinct screamed for her to remain aloof? Especially after his show of temper with her father, though he deserved to be threatened. Her obligations to Riordan were accumulating at a swift rate.

Taking the silk bag from her valise, she spread her jewelry across the small table. There was a jeweler here in Carrbury; would he buy select items from her? Then she could pay Riordan instead of waiting for the settlement to be processed. Her fingers trailed across the pearl hair comb. As far as she knew, these were real pearls. A wedding gift from Pepperdon. It meant nothing to her, then or now. Surely it could fetch twenty pounds or more. Sabrina pushed it aside. Her wedding ring, a plain gold band. Again, it meant nothing. Not a fancy piece, but enough to garner a few more pounds, at least. Nodding, she laid it next to the comb. There could be enough to not only pay Riordan, but buy herself a simple wool dress or two. She would save the more expensive pieces of jewelry for later bargaining if required.

Sabrina had stayed in her room the past two days because she believed her father or the marquess would seek her out. Snatch her away. Paranoid, to be sure, but as much as she decided to move forward, old doubts still lingered. However, she would not allow dread to rule her life any longer with regards to any man. After scribbling a note for Mary informing her of her whereabouts, she readied herself for her departure.

It was another pleasant autumn afternoon; a cool breeze ruffled the remaining leaves on the trees lining the main thoroughfare. If she remembered correctly, the jeweler was located at the corner of the thoroughfare and Weldon Road next to the bakery. A few men touched the brim of their hats as she passed and she nodded in reply.

The pleasant odors of the bakery filled her senses. Baked apple and cinnamon, fresh bread. Perhaps she would stop in on her return to the inn and purchase a treat for herself and Mary. Pushing the door open to Davis and Sons Jewelers, a bell dinged overhead to signal her arrival. An older man stood behind the counter and gave her a polite smile. "Good afternoon, my lady."

"You know who I am?"

"Yes, indeed. You are the widow of the Earl of Pepperdon. It is common knowledge that you have returned to the area. How pleasing to see you out and about. May I assist you, my lady?"

"Do you buy jewelry, Mr. Davis?"

He scratched his whiskery chin. "Well, my lady, I do. For select customers. I should reveal you would fetch a far better price if you sold the pieces in London. Alas, I can only offer a fraction of the going rate."

Sabrina pulled the small silk bag from her reticule. "I assumed as much, Mr. Davis. I would still like to sell these."

Taking out his handheld jeweler's loupe from his pocket, he snatched up the pearl comb and inspected the piece closely. "Good quality pearls. Not the best, mind you." He laid the comb on the counter and picked up the wedding band. "Hmm. I can give you ten pounds for the lot."

"Let us agree on thirteen pounds, Mr. Davis. You will be making a significant profit here when you resell them. I'm desperate enough to absorb a loss, but not to accept an insulting offer." She gave him a polite smile.

"Ah. Shrewdly bargained, Lady Pepperdon. Thirteen pounds it is. Will notes suffice?"

"Absolutely."

The jeweler bowed and turned to open his cash box. Sabrina looked absently about the store, when the corner of her eye caught her father walking by the large shop window. She froze, and old fears surfaced once again. Through sheer inner strength she collected herself and hurried to the window to watch as he strode down the street. He entered the solicitor's office. Blast, the one time she decided to leave her room she encountered her miserable father. Several minutes passed. Then she recognized her father's carriage as it pulled up to the office.

"My lady?" Mr. Davis questioned.

She waved her arm. "A moment please, Mr. Davis." Sabrina continued to observe, and minutes later her father emerged from the office, a large brown envelope tucked under his arm. Once he climbed into the coach, it was off, spraying mud and water in its wake as it turned the corner. Exhaling a sigh of relief, she rejoined the jeweler, taking the pound notes he held out to her.

Tucking them into her bag, she nodded at the older man. "Thank you, Mr. Davis."

He bowed elegantly. "A pleasure doing business with you, Lady Pepperdon." He escorted her to the door and held it open.

Clutching her reticule, Sabrina hurried along the walkway, pleased she'd spoken out regarding the price. In the past, she would have accepted the offer without uttering a peep. As she rounded the corner, a familiar and unwelcome voice brought her up short.

"Hello, Daughter."

Sabrina gasped and froze in her tracks. Her father. But she had watched him depart!

"I saw you standing at the window at the jewelers. I had my driver circle the block. Out and about town? Selling choice pieces?" He stepped closer, a cruel smile curved about his mouth. "You think you have escaped your fate. But you haven't."

She glanced about, wondering if she should cry out for help. Cursing under her breath, she admonished herself for allowing fright to grip her. Her hands trembled and she clutched her reticule tighter. The baron took another step closer, and Sabrina took one in reverse as she tried to remain outwardly indifferent.

"Allow me to inform you of a salient fact about Sutherhorne," her father said in a cool but steady voice. "The marquess is a determined and dangerous man to cross, and you and your self-important schoolmaster have stoked his anger. There will be consequences, mark my words. He does not forget—nor forgive. He exacts revenge."

Blast her father for still having a firm hold of her emotions! "You don't frighten me. Not anymore. I won't let you. I am free from you at last. And that miserable marquess."

He laughed. "You always were a foolish girl. As foolish and stupid and useless as your mother. Like most useless women, you need a man to support you, to keep you in the custom to which you have become used to. Well, the schoolmaster will not be able to dress and feed you as you wish. You will be living in a shack."

Not for long. She would gain control of her own life, and she was tempted to tell her father of her plan. Instead, she sniffed dismissively. "I'd rather live in a shack with an honorable man than live in a manor house with you or Sutherhorne."

"We will see," he whispered ominously. When a couple passed them, her father touched the brim of his hat and gave a false smile, while he said for her hearing only, "This isn't over."

He continued along the sidewalk, not giving her a second look, leaving her shaking with both anger and cold fear. What did he mean about the marquess? The bit of anticipation she'd experienced for this small excursion scattered into nothingness and she continued on her way. She stopped in front of the dress shop—her lavender silk gown trimmed with white lace was on display in the window.

The garment had been one of many she'd left behind when she departed. Good heavens, her father had sold them? It is not as if he needed the money, considering he'd paid out her settlement. Then why? Besides being a penny-pinching miser and a complete bully, apparently he wished to erase every last trace of her from the premises. Again, her heart stung. Now hurt mixed with the anger and the lingering fright.

Dejectedly, she ambled past the dress shop and bakery and continued toward the inn. She didn't care that her skirt dragged through the muck when she stepped into the muddy street.

"Lady Pepperdon."

There was no mistaking the deep, masculine voice. Glancing up, Riordan hurried toward her. Lord, he was breathtaking, and the sight of him made her aching heart throb for a different reason. Today he wore a calf-length black wool coat and a top hat. The fashionable coat was a snug fit, accentuating his broad shoulders. It was tucked in at the waist, as was the fashion.

How could a schoolmaster afford such well-made garments? Perhaps he was not as poor as she was led to believe. Occasionally, she had the distinct feeling he was keeping secrets from her. Well, she would keep her own secrets—like meeting the baron on the street, for she did not want to rile Riordan. Or facilitate another confrontation between him and her father. A smile broke out on his flawless face, and try as she might to return it, she couldn't.

Standing before her, he touched the wide brim of his hat. "Mary informed me you were walking about town. Is there somewhere I may escort you?"

Polite, kind, a gentleman in the truest sense of the word, at least outwardly. But she had witnessed the burst of violence from him. Could he be, deep down, the same sort of man as her father and the marquess? No. Riordan did not deserve her suspicion, as he was doing her a great service. He'd apologized for his burst of temper, and it was best she put it behind her. "I'm heading to the inn."

Crooking his arm, he said, "Let us make our way."

Take his arm? It would be an insult if she didn't. Yet the thought of touching him for an extended period caused her insides to tumble with yearning. Steeling herself, she slipped her hand through, resting it as lightly as she could on his sleeve. Even through the coat, muscle flexed under her fingers. *Say something.* "School is out already?"

"Dismissal will be at half past three instead of five for the rest of this week, as a number of students are needed on family farms. It is why the board agreed to dismiss school at noon Friday—it will please the parents. Apparently it is time to make final provisions for the harvest, and there are other chores to prepare for the oncoming winter."

A fair number of passersby gaped at them as they strode along. It would be all over town that she was arm-in-arm with the schoolmaster. In years past, she used to care about such talk, but since they were marrying on Saturday, it was hardly worth giving any mind.

"No luck with your shopping trip?" he asked.

Well, he wasn't put off by her sullen mood, she would give him credit. "I lost all interest when I spotted one of my gowns on display in the dress shop window."

He cast a quick glance. "How did that come about?"

"I left behind a trunk full of expensive gowns when I departed. I assume my father sold them. It cannot be for the money. It leads me to conclude he wished to erase every last trace of my existence from his home."

"I meant what I said, Sabrina: don't ever look back. No regrets. He is not worth your consideration in any way." He patted her gloved hand with his own and the gesture made her want to cry. "I did bring the wagon; we could have brought the trunk with us."

"No, they meant nothing. Remnants of my life with Pepperdon. I wish to start fresh, and that includes my wardrobe. Besides, many of the gowns are inappropriate for the sedate life I plan to live going forward." In all her eleven years with Pepperdon they did not speak this freely—they hardly spoke at all. Sabrina decided to keep the conversation going. "I sold two of the pieces of jewelry I'd been gifted from Pepperdon. I wish to pay you with some of the proceeds. For the inn, the mail coach, any upcoming expenses."

With a quick turn, Riordan led her into a darkened alley. Swinging her around, her back touched the wood clapboards of the building. He stood close, staring down at her. "Do not feel beholden to me. I'm happy to help. I do not expect payment." Riordan's voice was tender, but firm.

"I know, but paying you for these expenses means a great deal to me. It is the first act of my newfound independence. My new life. I'm already under obligation to you. This small recompense will lessen it, and ease my conscience."

He arched an eyebrow. "It's important to you?"

"Yes. I wish to do my share, pay my way. Will five pounds suffice?" He nodded. "Excellent. I'm relieved. You ask for so little, I'm glad to give a bit in return for once. In the future, if you wish anything of me, you merely have to give voice to it."

"There is something I wish from you." His voice was husky, sensual in its cadence. "I long to see you laugh. Throw back your head, laughing for the pure joy of it." His gloved finger traced her bottom lip. "Even a smile, a genuine one, reflecting happiness and contentment."

"I cannot remember the last time I did," she whispered.

"It will give me a goal these next months," he murmured. "Meanwhile, I will settle for a kiss."

Sabrina blinked, not believing what she'd heard. Surely, he cannot be serious.

"A sweet, brief kiss, a gentle meshing of our lips. Nothing predatory or untoward, I promise." He continued to caress her lower lip, causing her legs to turn to jelly.

"Why do you wish to kiss me?" Her voice shook, her tone incredulous, for she truly could not understand why he would ask for such intimacy.

"I have wanted to kiss you from the beginning, even though you annoyed me with your supercilious ways." She sputtered in protest, but he ignored her and continued on. "Besides, you have eminently kissable lips. You appeal to me, Sabrina. You should know it now, in case you have second thoughts on our temporary arrangement." He pulled his hand away. "I am going to touch your cheek, will you allow it?"

Her response dried up in her throat. How to explain that she'd never received a proper kiss from a man? Pepperdon had never bothered. The few she'd received from the old earl during the beginning of their marriage consisted of polite busses on the cheek. There was no affection in them, and when he came to her bedroom, there was no preamble before he roughly rutted her. Sabrina cleared her throat. "We are out in public."

"The sun is setting; no one can observe us here in the alley. May I…touch you?"

Against her better judgment, she gave him a brisk nod. He removed his glove with his teeth, letting it drop to the ground. The warmth from his hand caused her eyelids to blink rapidly. "Soft, as I imagined. Like the finest silk. Your skin is glorious to the touch." Riordan caressed her cheek with the pad of his thumb. Slowly, he leaned in, angling his head for the kiss. As soon as his lips brushed hers, she could not keep the gasp from escaping her throat, for the contact was electric.

Riordan hesitated. Then he kissed her again, the barest touch. She had no idea what to do. How to react. This was the last thing she expected to occur between them. Perhaps she should follow his lead and return in kind. She moved her mouth across his, and now he was the one who gasped, though it sounded more like a moan. His lips were surprisingly supple. His scent was subtle, masculine, a mixture of lime and bergamot, no doubt from his shaving soap.

In slow increments, Riordan ended the kiss. Exhaling, he smiled. "Better than I imagined. Thank you."

Her heart banged furiously against her ribcage. One innocent kiss had upended her world. Made it spin out of control. Blast, she should have never allowed it! Feigning indifference, she pushed away from the wall. "Shall we continue on our journey?" Her tone was aloof, the exact feeling she wished to convey.

Riordan's mouth twisted into a half smile as he bent to retrieve his glove. "As you wish."

They did not speak the rest of the way, and on the stoop of the inn, she opened her reticule and passed him five one-pound notes. "Thank you again…Riordan."

He touched the brim of his hat as he stuffed the notes into his coat pocket. "Until Friday at noon. We will drop most of your luggage at the cottage before we depart. Pack only what you need for overnight. Relay the same to Mary." She must have been frowning, for he added, "It was only a kiss, Sabrina. Tell me now: did it disturb or disgust you to such a degree that you wish for it to never happen again?"

Here lay the opportunity to dismiss this mutual attraction in no uncertain terms. To inform him in as cool a tone as she could muster that he was *not* to touch her ever again. Explain they were better off ignoring what sparked between them, and in three months they could depart and live their own lives, stay polite strangers and never think of each other at all.

She could not do it.

However, there must be parameters set between them. "No, it did not disturb me in the way you think. But you must see that this cannot happen again. There must be boundaries we cannot cross if this agreement is to work."

Clasping her gloved hand, he brought it to his lips. With lids half hooded, he glanced up at her. "I will respect certain boundaries. But, in all honesty, I cannot promise it will not happen again." He paused, his eyes alive with blue fire. "For there is nothing I wish to do more at this moment than to pull you into my arms and kiss you again. Deeply. Thoroughly." He let go of her hand. "Good evening."

He turned and walked away, leaving her trembling by the front entrance. Oh, she was hopeless. For there was nothing she wanted more than for him to pull her into his arms and kiss her. And there lay certain trouble. Or paradise.

Or both.

Chapter 12

The trip to London passed by in a complete blur. Sabrina and Mary sat on one side of the crowded carriage, while Riordan sat opposite. They were all crammed in like sardines in a tin, which made private conversation difficult. The older woman next to her continually sneezed the entire trip, and she smelled of olive oil, which supported the sardine analogy.

When they arrived in the city they took a hansom cab from the carriage stop to the inn. Thankfully it was not far, as the conveyance barely had room for the three of them. Sabrina became engulfed in heat—Riordan's body pressed against hers from shoulder to calf. Since the kiss, she reacted to his nearness more than ever before.

Settled in their room, Sabrina expressed her desire to take a nap, but Riordan had acquired a small private dining area for supper. Mary informed him that she would take a tray in the room, effectively leaving Sabrina alone with Riordan. "I insist you come with me," Sabrina pouted when they were alone.

Mary pulled a book from her carpetbag. "I would rather curl up here by the fire, read, and eat at my leisure."

"So would I," Sabrina replied.

"My lady, you should join Mr. Black. He's gone to a good deal of trouble to arrange all of this for you. Besides, you had best become used to being alone with him. He is not the old earl. Mr. Black will wish for you to engage in conversation, act interested in him and what he's doing or saying. I know it will be an adjustment after the lonely life you spent with that horrid man." Mary paused, giving her an encouraging smile. "Come out of the shadows and look at the sun full on, my lady. Revel in the comforting heat and glory of the dazzling light. And I must say, Mr. Black is all warmth and brightness."

Mary was correct, as usual. "Yes," Sabrina replied. "He is." Should she mention the kiss? Not tonight. No doubt it had been an aberration, nothing more. "Yet I cannot allow myself to grow attached to him. He is younger and beneath me socially, at least Society says it matters. I do not want or need a man for the long term." She crossed her arms defiantly.

Mary shook her head. "None of it will matter if love is involved. Remember to be open to new experiences, wherever they may lead, my lady."

"I will try, but I must protect…protect…"

"Your guarded heart? Your sensitive soul? Your hurt feelings?"

"Oh, Mary, you do have a way of getting directly to the core of the matter. Yes. Everything you mentioned. But also my damaged trust and deep-seated fears. My wounded pride. My lost innocence." Sabina tossed her shawl about her shoulders. "I do not *want* to like him…but I do. I do not *want* to be attracted to him…but I am. It can go no further."

Mary nodded, though her expression was dubious. "As you wish, my lady. Enjoy the meal and the conversation."

Giving the slightest hint of a smile, Sabrina grabbed the doorknob. "And bask in his brilliance?"

Mary laughed. "Yes. Revel in it, in fact."

Sabrina opened the door to find Riordan standing there. What had he overheard? Thank goodness he gave no indication that he'd heard any of the conversation. He wore his frock coat, with a white cravat tied simply at his throat. She stepped into the hall, closing the door behind her. Acting the gentleman, he placed his hand at her back, barely making contact, but enough for her to be aware of his touch. He guided her toward the small dining area in the rear of the inn.

"We are in luck; a private room was available. No peers staying here tonight. Well, besides you. I do hope you like roast turkey. I'm told it is the main course."

They entered the room, and Sabrina was struck by how cozy and welcoming it appeared. A fire blazed in the stone hearth, and nearby stood an oak dining table set, complete with linen tablecloth and lit candles. Riordan pulled out her chair and she took a seat. "The journey has made me hungry," she said as she arranged her skirts.

"Me as well. You don't mind that we will return to Carrbury as soon as the ceremony concludes? Well, two hours after." He sat opposite her. "There are a couple of shops in the vicinity you may wish to browse before we catch the mail coach. There is a bookshop, a dress shop—"

"Oh, yes. Especially the book dealer. I'm a voracious reader, as is Mary. How thoughtful of you."

Riordan smiled broadly. "Your eyes are twinkling. First time they've done so since we've become acquainted." He leaned in and murmured, "The green shade in your hazel eyes is pronounced, and it glitters like emeralds."

Heat infused her cheeks. Oh, he was a shameless flirt, but the words were not insincerely spoken. It pleased her, for she was not used to such attention from a man, mainly because she was never given the opportunity to enjoy a season, or the company of any gentlemen close to her own age. Pepperdon could not be bothered with compliments and words of affection. He preferred insults, or hurling licentious phrases at her when he bothered to speak at all.

No. She would not think of that disgusting man. Not while she basked in the glow of Riordan's company. Oh, Mary had the right of it. *Warmth and brightness.* No more cold darkness. "Thank you. I believe you're the first man to compliment my eyes."

"Am I? I'm honored. I confess I'm not a skilled flirt, so any praise is sincerely meant. I shall endeavor to do it more often." He took a sip of water. "It is settled. A shopping excursion before we depart."

A woman bustled into the room carrying a large tray laden with food. She was followed by a man, no doubt the innkeeper. The woman laid full platters in front of them as the man poured white wine into the crystal goblets. "If you need anything else at all, Mr. Black, let us know," the woman said.

"Fresh bread perhaps?"

"Oh, blimey! I knew I forgot summat." She scurried away.

"Mr. Beacon, this is my fiancée, Lady Pepperdon. My dear, this is Mr. Beacon, owner of this fine establishment."

My dear? Fiancée? The words arrowed straight to her heart, causing it to swell with delight. She gave the innkeeper a polite incline of her head. Good heavens, she was a fiancée.

"A lady?" The innkeeper bowed, clearly flustered from the revelation that she was of the peerage. "Welcome, my lady. Anything we can do for you, the wife and I are at your service."

Mrs. Beacon returned with bread and butter, then the couple left the room, whispering between them.

"Looks appetizing," Riordan stated. "Perhaps not as fancy as you are used to."

"The late earl did not care for grand meals. It does look appetizing." She laid her napkin across her lap.

Riordan raised his wineglass. “To new beginnings. To banishing the past. To…independence.”

She raised hers and gave him a brief smile. “Hear, hear.”

“A small smile as well. My cup overfloweth.” He winked teasingly.

Sabrina was beginning to understand the difference between lighthearted banter and mocking, at least as far as Riordan was concerned. She cut into the tender poultry and took a bite. “Oh, lovely. It has been ages since I have partaken of turkey.”

Riordan popped a piece into his mouth and swallowed. “It is good.”

“Now that we are alone, can you disclose the amount my father settled on me? I will sleep better knowing the details.”

He didn’t answer right away, and a spark of anxiety took root inside her. “It’s ten thousand pounds. William is handling the details. As I mentioned before, we will visit his office and sign the papers before the ceremony.”

She let go of the breath she’d been holding. “Oh, thank heavens. I’m not sure how you managed it, but I am eternally grateful.” Relieved, she ate a few forkfuls of the meal. “I meant to ask: who was the large man with the red hair at your place?”

Riordan chuckled. “When did you happen to see him?”

Sabrina buttered her bread. “I confess; Mary and I went for a walk at dusk a few days past. I was curious if you had returned from your journey. Where exactly is home, by the way?”

“To answer your first question, the red-haired beast is my uncle, Garrett. He is only six years older, so he’s more of an older brother, really. To answer your second question, my home is near Sevenoaks, in Kent. My uncle has already journeyed home.”

“Do you mind if I ask questions?”

Riordan cut his potatoes into bite-sized pieces. “Not at all. Shall I give you a brief biography? I come from a household of men. My father is involved in factory work, my Irish mother died of a heart ailment when I was three. I never knew her.”

Oh. She was genuinely sad to hear he’d lost his mother. Feeling empathy for others—another sign she was reclaiming her life. “I also lost my mother at a young age; I was twelve when she passed. I never did find out from what. She had been ill three years before, never leaving her bed.” It still hurt to mention her. Because her mother had been absorbed by her infirmity and her deep unhappiness, she’d had little time for an emotionally needy daughter.

“She died at the age when you needed her most,” Riordan stated.

"Yes. When it happened, I became angry, feeling abandoned. How could my mother leave me alone with my cold, unyielding father? It took many years for me to realize that she did not die on purpose." After swallowing a forkful of buttered carrots, she said, "A household of men. Sounds like the Wollstonecraft family. They live in Kent, I believe. Do you know of them? The patriarch is an earl…I forget his title."

Riordan started coughing. Oh no, was he choking? His face turned red, and he snatched the napkin from the table and covered his mouth. He immediately drank a half glass of water until the coughing ceased.

"Are you all right? Shall I ring for more water?" Truly, she was worried for him.

He shook his head. "No. I'm fine. Thank you. A piece of potato became lodged in my throat. All is well."

"What were we discussing? Oh, yes, I asked if you knew of the Wollstonecrafts."

"Do you?" Riordan asked.

"No, not personally. But I have heard of them. There is silly talk of a curse with regards to them finding love or some such. I also read that the young heir had been involved with one scandal or another. They're champions for the poor, always tied to one cause or another. My father finds them detestable—not that he knows them personally either, but he would scoff and sneer whenever they appeared in the newspaper." She sipped her wine. "I believe he called them 'smug, do-gooder attention mongers.'"

"Indeed? I know *of* the family, but not well. We do not exactly move in the same circles," Riordan murmured.

"You're of the middle class? Oh, I am prying, but you're well educated, your clothes are of a fine quality. Mary heard your father owns a factory. That explains it." Satisfied with the answers to her nagging questions, she enthusiastically continued her meal. Riordan grew quiet, but the silence was not awkward.

When the dishes were cleared and tea and a plate of raspberry tarts had been served, they were alone once again—this was the last time they would be before the marriage. She should say her piece and be done with it. "Riordan, may I be honest with you?"

"Of course. You must always speak your mind with me."

"When I first proposed this—let us call it what it is, a mad proposal, I originally thought I could enter into a temporary marriage, and after the ceremony take a room at the inn until an annulment could be acquired. I'd have no contact with the man in question, I'd simply wait it out then move on with my life." She paused, and caught Riordan gazing at her with an intensity that took her breath away. "You see, I wanted to use a man for my own gain for once, instead of the other way around. I did not expect to *like* you, Riordan. Not at all. I believe we are becoming…friends."

"Yes," he said kindly. "I believe we are."

"This is not easy for me, conversing, being pleasant. If at any time in the next three months I withdraw, either physically or emotionally, please know it is *not* you." Blast! A lump formed in her throat; confessing such a defect in her character had exposed her. As much as her vulnerability often rose to the surface, she'd learned to keep it deeply hidden. Why was she telling this man her secrets? A man she'd only known barely three weeks? Because he deserved to know. Riordan Black was sacrificing his life by assisting her in her plan. This marriage could damage his budding career. The selfless act humbled her. "You see, the only way I could avoid being hurt was to hide, in whatever way I could. It's a habit I'm finding difficult to break. Mary claims I live in shadow, and she's been encouraging me to step into the light. I will endeavor to try."

"Mary means a great deal to you."

"Yes. As I said before, she is more than a lady's maid. She has been a friend, sister, aunt, and even a mother all rolled into one." Sabrina glanced at her tightly clasped hands resting on her lap. "I would not have made it this far without her support."

"If you wish to discuss your past, I am a good listener. It does take a weight off to talk about it; it makes the journey forward easier to bear." His voice was comforting, making it tempting to confess.

Slowly, she raised her head and met his eyes; they were soft with sympathy. "I'm not sure I can ever discuss it, but thank you for the offer."

Once they concluded the meal, Riordan escorted her to her door. Grasping her chin, he caught her gaze and held it. "Until tomorrow." He kissed her forehead, much like a brother would do. It was what she wanted, wasn't it? Friends and nothing more?

As he turned and walked toward his room, Sabrina experienced a sense of loss at his absence, for secretly she yearned for him to kiss her goodnight as a fiancé might—how had he described it? *Deeply. Thoroughly.*

Tonight she would dream of him. For that was where Riordan belonged and where he should stay: in her nocturnal fantasies. It would take all of her resolve not to allow her true feelings to become reality in the clear light of day.

Chapter 13

Lack of sleep affected Riordan from the moment he woke. At breakfast, he drank three cups of strong coffee—not his preferred hot beverage—hoping it would shake the cobwebs from his mind—and dissipate lingering images of Sabrina writhing with passion in his bed.

The kiss. God, the kiss. He had indulged in a few dalliances, kissed his fair share of young ladies. But the brief one he shared with Sabrina in the darkened alley made every woman fade into the mists of his past. Her hesitance showed she'd not been kissed much. Not with genuine affection. But she'd soon returned it, pressing her lips to his. He wanted to devour her, taste every inch of her hot mouth, but he instinctively understood he would have to be patient.

For he had no intention of keeping his distance. Boundaries be damned. He'd never felt this way before. Never would he have believed that he could find an emotionally damaged widow appealing—by her own admission, Sabrina was all that and more. Behind her protective wall, he truly believed that a passionate woman waited for someone to show her affection and attention. How he yearned to be the man to scale the barrier and hold her in his arms. Show her what true intimacy consisted of.

After all, he had overheard part of her conversation with Mary before supper. He hadn't meant to; he was about to knock when their voices carried into the hall. *Blasted thin walls.* She spoke of damaged trust and deep-seated fears, wounded pride and lost innocence. It tore at his heart, yet explained much: the aloofness, the pulling away from his touch, and the fright he'd observed in her shuttered expression at various intervals. Her marriage must have been worse than he originally imagined.

But now a spark of hope flickered in his soul. "I do not *want* to like him…but I do. I do not *want* to be attracted to him…but I am. It can go no further." His heart had soared at her words, proof that he more than liked her. Hell, he could even be falling for her.

He had less than three months to show her that the attraction and liking *could* go further. It would be a challenge, and one he should not rush. The fact they were becoming friends was an excellent start. Slow and careful would win the day. Yet telling lies was not a solid foundation on which to build a relationship. Last night at dinner he'd been nauseous repeating the factory story. Technically, thousand pounds came from her father, but he doubted that she would parse his words that finely when his deception came to light.

When Sabrina mentioned the Wollstonecraft name he had choked. Kent was not far away; could he manage to keep his identity secret? What a tangled web. Damn her loutish father for calling his family "smug, do-gooder attention mongers." This from a man who could not even be bothered to sit on the local board of education. The baron probably spent most days in his study, drinking brandy, content to allow others to attend to societal tribulations.

He must be in dire straits if he sold his daughter's wardrobe to the local dress shop. Sabrina did not suspect. Riordan would do all in his power to protect her from the truth. She would be devastated to learn that her father sold her not once, but twice. How could a man treat his only child with such contempt and utter disregard?

As he escorted the ladies into William's office, he banished such disturbing thoughts. After introductions, they all took their seats, he and Sabrina in front of William's desk, Mary in a chair along the wall, close enough to participate in the conversation.

"I have two agreements for you to sign, my lady," William explained as he opened the folder.

"Sorry to interrupt," Sabrina said, "but I would like to make a slight amendment to the settlement. Instead of twenty percent, I wish for Riordan to have twenty-five percent."

Damn. He was touched by her generosity. He was about to speak, but William beat him to it.

"Lady Pepperdon, Riordan has indicated to me that he does not want *any* part of the settlement. The full ten thousand is to go to you on the day the annulment is finalized. This agreement reflects his request."

She turned to look at him; her beautiful eyes glistened with unshed tears. "Oh, Riordan. You're kindness itself. But you are making a huge sacrifice and should be compensated accordingly. You deserve it." Yes, underneath was a woman of immense emotion, and when it managed to bubble to the surface, it made her all the more alluring. Though her vulnerability was appealing, so too her determined desire to move on with her life on her own terms. God, he admired her for it.

Taking her hand, he brushed a kiss across it. "You will need every last farthing for your new life. Allow it to be my gift to you."

Sabrina did something he didn't expect: she leaned in and cupped his cheek with her free hand. He closed his eyes, drinking in the warmth from her touch. Time stood still, as if there was no one else in the room with them. *But there is.* He snapped open his eyes and found William staring at them incredulously, with one eyebrow arched.

Riordan cleared his throat. "The agreements?" Sabrina pulled her hand away and faced William.

"Of course." William dipped the pen into the ink and handed it to Sabrina. "Read them over. The first agreement states that the money is yours on the day the annulment is granted. The second agreement is signed by your father, claiming the money will be deposited here after the marriage takes place. All the arrangements have been made with the baron's bank." William slid the papers across the desk for her to reach.

"What if…what if the ecclesiastical court does not grant the annulment?" she asked. "It could happen."

A small part of Riordan hoped it would be the case. Marriage appealed to him. He was not his brother. Empty affairs soon lost all his interest. It had not taken long to come to the conclusion that he would much prefer an intimate, long-lasting relationship. A partnership. Lovers and friends. But this was about Sabrina and her fervent wish for independence.

"It could, but the chance is remote. However, if it happens, there is a clause in this agreement stating that the money is yours, and no one else can lay claim to it, not even your husband." William paused, inclining his head toward Riordan. "On the slim possibility the annulment is refused, Riordan will not stand in your way if you wish to continue on with your plans regardless. Your independence—on your terms. You will live separately, though legally married."

The ramifications of this significant point hit home with Riordan. If she decided to move ahead with her plan to live by the sea, he would be left in marital limbo. There would be no remarriage. No children. No future with any woman, unless he took a mistress. Rather bleak, when he thought about it. His father and grandfather had certainly had one or two short-term mistresses throughout the years, and they were content enough with their lives. But they had been married previously, and were widowers with children. In his haste to assist her, he had not fully comprehended all the variables.

Sabrina must have been having similar thoughts, for she turned toward him. "You're giving up far more than I realized. How utterly selfish of me."

"Sign the agreements, Sabrina," he encouraged. "I will have a full and satisfying life, you need not worry. This will ensure that you will as well."

Taking the sheets of paper, she reclined in the chair and read the forms. As she did, William turned his attention to Mary. "Miss Tuttle, Riordan would like to give you a portion of the pay that was owed to you by the baron. Unfortunately, the man refused to see to the obligations of your employment. Riordan will be reimbursed when the money comes through. Would five pounds suffice, with the balance of fifteen pounds and what you are owed for three months to be paid on the date of the annulment? Again, if not granted, I'm sure Lady Pepperdon will see that you are compensated."

"Thank you, Mr. Chambers, it will be more than sufficient," Mary replied.

Riordan glanced at Sabrina. Her brows were furrowed as she continued to read the documents. The room was quiet as they waited for her to sign. "I need to speak to Riordan. Privately. Do you mind, Mr. Chambers?"

William stood. "Not at all. Miss Tuttle and I will wait in the outer office. Though I must remind you of our appointment at the registrar's office at noon."

"Yes. Thank you."

William and Mary departed, closing the door behind them.

"What is it, Sabrina?" Riordan asked.

She set the papers on the desk. "For once in my life, I'm not going to think of myself. I cannot allow this to go forward. I must admit that in my haste to escape my father and his abject plans for me I did not take in all considerations. For either one of us. This could go wrong in many ways." She turned to face him. "You are a young man. What if you meet a woman and fall in love? You could never marry her if we were still bound together—if the annulment is not granted. What of children?" She shook her head. "We must call this off."

Damn. After all he went through to get them to this point. "And how will you live?" he asked quietly.

"I have more jewelry to sell…and other items."

"It will not be enough to live on for any extended period. You've broken with your father. There is no going back, only forward." He paused, wondering what to say next. He did not want to force her into this temporary marriage. "Perhaps I can raise enough money…."

"No. Absolutely not. I cannot be beholden to anyone. The debt would hang over my head, and I have no way to reimburse the amount. I could never accept a loan, from you or anyone else." Her tone was firm and adamant.

Wonderful. He rubbed the bridge of his nose. How could he ever reveal it was his money and not the baron's? *Tell her now,* his inner voice whispered. *Before it's too late.* He decided to take another tack. "Have you considered the possibility that we could make this marriage work?"

She blinked at him, her mouth slightly agape, no doubt from shock—he'd shocked himself. Yes, he'd briefly considered it, but sitting here with her, his emotions in turmoil, the idea held merit. "Hear me out: We get along. As you said, we're already friends. It is more than some people have. Perhaps more than most." He took her hand; it trembled in his. "I would never make demands of you, dominate you, or humiliate you. As far as the physical aspect, I'm a patient man, and I would wait until you are comfortable with us—"

Sabrina pulled her hand from his. Her expression held a degree of horror. "You're no better than the marquess or my father, after all. You're trying to…trap me."

Damn it, was he? "No. Never."

"I don't want a real marriage. If we do this, it is a temporary arrangement. I must have your word on this, or I cannot go through with it."

Well, he'd bungled this thoroughly. A wave of disappointment rolled through him. It appeared he was young and foolish after all. He'd splayed open his heart, literally handed it to her, and she'd tossed it back at him. "My apologies for suggesting it. You have my word. If you wish this to be temporary, then it shall." He took her hand again, holding it firm. "Allow me to explain about myself. I don't like being told what to do or being pushed about any more than you do. Nor shall I be told how and what to feel. I will not act as a stranger toward you. I can only be who I am. You must accept this, or *I* cannot go through with it." He threaded his fingers through hers. They had removed their gloves when they first stepped into the office, making the touch of skin against skin stimulating—even more heated than when she'd touched his cheek earlier. "Make a decision, Sabrina. Stand up for what you want. For I shall. Every time." *And to my complete astonishment, I want you.*

* * * *

The way he looked at her. The intensity of his gaze. Sabrina's mind was in a whirl. Make the marriage work? He'd no idea what she'd endured. Perhaps she should have told him, at least enough to make him understand the reason why she did not want such an arrangement again. This false, transitory marriage she could endure, knowing at the end she could walk away and start her new life.

Could she take him at his word? He did state this would be temporary... but what if the decision was not theirs to make? Sabrina glanced down at their clasped hands. Her skin burned where he touched her. Her insides were aflame. *This must be desire.* What else could it be, unless she was suffering from a stomach ailment? *I can only be who I am.* Why did the statement simultaneously thrill and alarm her? The way he spoke, with such firm conviction, confidence, and emotion...she was not used to it at all.

Make a decision.

Her desire for freedom took on fresh significance. This was her plan, and she wanted to be in complete control of it. But whatever power she held over the situation slipped away in Riordan's presence. Every time he touched her. If she wanted the money and her future, she had to move forward. *Make a decision.*

Slipping her hand from Riordan's, she snatched the pen from the desk, dipped it in ink, and signed the forms. It was done. Sabrina pushed her chair from the desk and stood. "We had best recall Mr. Chambers and Mary and depart."

Riordan stood and clasped her shoulders, turning her to face him. "You won't regret this, Sabrina. It will all work out the way you wish."

She walked away from him and opened the door. "You may come in. The forms are signed." Mr. Chambers and Mary entered the room.

"Are you well, my lady? You look pale," Mary whispered.

Sabrina glanced at Riordan, who stood close to Mr. Chambers. They were deep in conversation and examining the papers. Riordan picked up the pen as Sabrina turned to face Mary. "I'll be fine. Last minute doubts. Let us get this over with."

Within minutes they were strolling down the street to the registrar's office. Riordan escorted Sabrina; Mr. Chambers walked beside Mary. Once they entered the office and introductions were done, the registrar wasted no time. The words were brief, spoken officiously. They exchanged vows they had no intention of keeping. "Solemnly declare...no lawful impediment... take as your wedded husband..."

It passed in a blur. Before she knew it, Riordan had taken her hand. "I promise to care for you above all others, to give you my love and friendship, support and comfort, and to respect and cherish you throughout our lives together." The words brought her up sharp, startling her out of the haze she'd been in. Were these words part of the civil ceremony? Why did they make her heart ache with longing?

She blinked, more than once, not knowing what to do or say. Everyone looked at her, waiting for a response. "I…promise to care for you above…" Her voice died. She couldn't remember the rest. Her mind drew a complete blank.

"All others," Riordan gently encouraged.

Sabrina made the mistake of gazing into his striking face. *Oh.* No man had ever looked at her with such affection before. It was as if he meant the words—no, he acted the part of the eager groom, nothing else. "All others…to give you my…my…"

"Love and friendship," he replied, his voice soft and husky.

This was far more intense than she'd imagined it would be. The air was thick with emotion. With a determined effort, she quickly recited the rest of the words without hesitating. The registrar declared them married.

Then Riordan cupped her face, his thumbs caressed her cheeks. My heavens, was he going to kiss her? He leaned in close. "I thought a kiss was not part of the civil ceremony?" she whispered.

He angled his head, a small smile curved about his mouth. "It's part of this one." He captured her lips with a bracing, wild kiss she did not expect. Not possessive, but bold and confident, passionate, and she gasped from the pleasurable shock of it. As she gasped, Riordan deftly slipped his tongue into her mouth and swept it about, tasting her, causing her legs to tremble.

It was over. The registrar offered his congratulations. "My best wishes, Mr. Black. My lady." The voices grew fainter as the room began to spin. No, she would not swoon. She reached out, looking to grab something to steady herself. Riordan slipped his arm about her waist and pulled her close. His enticing scent of lime and bergamot allowed her to focus.

"I've got you," he murmured close to her ear. His warm breath fanned her neck, causing the hairs at her nape to stand upright.

That's what worried her. Had she stupidly placed herself in the possession of yet another man? A lump formed in her throat. Only this could be the one man she did *not* want to escape, and the prospect frightened as much as it excited her.

She was married. To a handsome man who stood as the ideal hero of her youthful dreams. How on earth would she be able to protect her heart?

Chapter 14

It had been a long day, with the ceremony, the shopping, and the return trip by mail coach. Luckily, Riordan had arranged for Farmer Walsh, his student Charlie's father and the farmer who'd boarded his gelding, Grayson, to meet them at the coach stop and escort them home. During the journey the decision was made to escort Mary to the inn first, which meant Sabrina would see to her own preparations for the evening.

Once they arrived at the cottage and the luggage and shopping purchases were unloaded from the wagon, Riordan thanked Farmer Walsh profusely, then informed the man he'd just been married. Seeing that Walsh had raised his heavy brows at the prospect of Sabrina staying at his cottage, he'd had no choice *but* to explain. Though he'd asked for the farmer's discretion, he had no doubt it would be all over the district before tomorrow afternoon.

Riordan watched the wagon disappear into the darkness, then turned and entered the cottage. Sabrina was nowhere to be found. Seeing the place was small and cramped, there weren't many places she could hide. He poked his head in the bedroom and found her sitting on the edge of the bed, her hands tightly clasped and resting in her lap.

"Tired?" he asked, giving her a smile.

"Yes…and no. I am rather wound up."

He understood completely. "I'm about to make tea. Would you care for a cup? I see Mrs. Ingersoll delivered beefsteak sandwiches earlier today. Come and join me, Sabrina."

"I thought to take a tray here, in this…room."

And, in point of fact, hide. Riordan wasn't going to have it. "First, I don't own a tray. Second, Mary is not here to bring it in to you even if I did. I will not act the footman. Wouldn't know how to go about it, at any rate." He chuckled. "But I can make tea, and will do so…if you come and sit at the table with me."

A sigh escaped her as she laid her hand flat on the quilt. "The bed is quite comfortable." He would miss his feather mattress, only had it three weeks. "Perhaps I should sleep in the parlor."

"Nonsense. What kind of gentleman would I be if I allowed you to sleep on the chaise longue? This bedroom is yours…while you're here. Make yourself at home."

She gave him a brief but tremulous smile. "You are kind."

Opening the door wider, he held out his hand. "Let us have a bite to eat. Together."

Nodding, she stood and walked toward him, even slipped her hand in his. He was pleased that she'd done it without hesitating; he reveled in the warmth of her touch. He escorted her to the small wooden table and pulled out a chair for her to sit. Then he moved to the kitchen and busily prepared a light meal. After bringing the teacups and saucers to the table, along with the bowl of sugar, he laid the sandwiches on a small platter with pieces of cheese and pickle. Lastly, he brought out the teapot and a pitcher of milk. "Will you pour?" he asked.

Sabrina nodded, giving him one of her brief smiles. He sat opposite. "How wonderful that you can make tea."

"It has been an exercise in failure and triumph. I've also learned to fry eggs and ham. Not much else, I'm afraid. It is why Mrs. Ingersoll has been employed by the board—to ensure I do not starve. Now she will cook for two. Mostly meat pies and stews, I hope you don't mind."

She nibbled on a wedge of sandwich. "Not at all. I know nothing of the kitchen."

"I do not expect you to learn," he teased. "I will show you how to use the pump so you can at least fetch water should you need it. Also, there is an outdoor privy, and a chamber pot under the bed. As far as bathing, there is a large copper tub. It's stored outside in the lean-to. Simply tell me what day you wish to use it, and I will bring it inside before I depart for school."

Sabrina sipped her tea. "Good heavens, such a personal conversation."

Riordan laid two wedges, cheese, and pickle on his small plate. "Best to get it out of the way, as it is all part and parcel of sharing a living area."

She peered at him over the rim of her cup. "And when will you be taking a bath?"

The air between them snapped with sensual energy. "Well, I would imagine it would be in the evenings. You will have to stay in your room.

Unless…" He gave her as sultry a smile as he could muster. "You wish to assist me, scrub my back and the like."

He waited for the look of horror. A rebuke for his bold forwardness. Sabrina placed her cup on the saucer. "I'm sure Mary would be thrilled to help you scrub all your bits, including your back."

Riordan laughed. "Well done, my lady. Very amusing." He placed a piece of cheese in his mouth and swallowed. "You recognized the teasing and replied in kind. A good sign."

She nodded. "It is a good sign."

"Tomorrow is Sunday. I must ask; do you attend church services?" Riordan asked.

"Not as a rule. The earl did, at Christmas and Easter, and I accompanied him."

"Ah. I'm not a steady churchgoer myself; however, I did make a compact with the vicar when I accepted the position of schoolmaster."

"Oh? What kind?" She looked at him with genuine interest. How wonderful to have someone to converse with in his lonely cottage. It lessened the homesickness. Someone to tease. A lovely woman to gaze at and admire. *And desire.*

"The school's curriculum caused a good deal of discussion in many quarters. As you can imagine, the vicar pushed for one based in religious studies. I proposed we extend Sunday school instead. The vicar—who, I found, is a shrewd negotiator—agreed, so long as I attend services twice a month, to show a good example for my students. Another of his demands was that school on Sunday must be three and one half hours in duration."

Sabrina snickered. "How shrewd."

"I must attend tomorrow, and I believe it best you accompany me."

Her slight smile disappeared. "I think not. It's best I stay cloistered away until we are able to obtain the annulment."

Unbelievable. "Sabrina, I already told Farmer Walsh you're my bride."

Her eyes widened. "Why would you do such a thing?" Annoyance hovered at the surface of her voice.

"The farmer witnessed you carrying your luggage into my cabin. Imagine the scandal. Besides, this is a small town; you will be seen. You cannot hide in this place for three months, it is not feasible."

Her full, lower lip thrust out in an attractive pout. "Well, I had hoped to attempt it, at least."

Riordan took a sip of tea. "Best to appear together and show a brave front. Granted, the town will be abuzz, but they will settle down soon enough. We will be forgotten, and then we will quietly obtain the annulment."

Taking a bite of the sandwich, he chewed and swallowed. "I have to visit Grayson tomorrow. He needs a long run."

"Who is Grayson?"

"My gelding. There is no proper place to keep him here at my cottage, so he boards with Farmer Walsh. When I can spare a moment, I take him out. Exercise for the both of us. Usually on Saturday and Sunday."

"Do you have many horses at your family home?" Sabrina asked.

It annoyed him to have to hesitate and try to figure out how to answer her questions without blatantly lying or exposing his identity. "A few. Growing up there was always a dog and cat underfoot as well. Did you have any pets?" Best to steer the conversation toward her.

A look of sadness covered her pretty features. "I was never allowed to have a pet of any kind. My father was adamant. The earl would not allow it either." She paused. "Once I asked for a kitten. One of my friends offered one, as her cat had given birth. My father replied that if I brought the mangy feline home, he would wring its neck and toss it outside for the wild animals to feast on." She looked away. "I was ten years old."

Anger tore through Riordan. "Have I told you how much I despise your miserable father?"

"He does not inspire warmth, to be sure," she answered, her voice quiet.

Damn the man. Riordan now wished he had planted a facer directly on the baron. His grandfather often used the phrase, and it fit here. The baron deserved to be punched—and more. Sabrina's childhood must have been as cold and lonely as her marriage—which made him all the more determined to draw her out of her protective shell. "Do you ride?"

"I have, but not since I returned to my father's. He only has the two horses for his carriage and he refused to allow me to ride them."

Yes, the man deserved a pummeling. Riordan reached across the table and took Sabrina's hand. Again a jolt of sizzling heat tore through him. "Attend church with me, and after we'll head to the farm. Farmer Walsh has a fine mare. We can go riding. Say you will." He could see her hesitation, and gently squeezed her hand. "No hiding, Sabrina. Never again. Time to live your life. Starting now."

Another brief, tremulous smile curved about her sensual lips. "You're right. I will attend church with you, and go riding."

"That's my darling girl." He smiled broadly as he slowly and incrementally released her hand, trailing his fingers along hers as he'd done before. She seemed to like it, and the blush staining her cheeks proved he was correct. The color was a welcome change from the stark paleness she'd exhibited most of the day. Pleased at her reaction, he snatched another piece of sandwich. "What do you plan to do in the afternoons when you're alone?"

Giving a slight movement of her shoulder, she reached for a piece of cheese. "I imagine I'll do the same thing I have done for the past several years: read. Thank you for assisting me in my selection at the bookshop. I'm looking forward to *Wuthering Heights*."

"Why don't we read it together, in the evenings? We can take turns reading passages."

She nodded, giving him another of her brief smiles. "I would enjoy that."

"The books you donated, were they yours?"

"I must confess, they were from my father's library. He'll never miss them."

Riordan laughed. "Again, well done. Do you partake in any other ladylike pursuits?"

It dawned on him that he wanted to know all about her, but was he rehashing the unpleasantness of her past? The last thing he wanted was to churn up terrible memories.

"When my mother died, I was shipped off to the Blackwell School for Young Ladies. My education before that was sporadic at best; father's choices for governesses left a lot to be desired. I learned more from reading than I ever did from those dour women." Sabrina placed another wedge of beefsteak sandwich on her plate. "At the boarding school? They sprinkled a little academia throughout the endless, boring classes of needlework, French, and the pianoforte. I'm afraid I do not excel at any of it."

"I admire you for wishing to expand your mind. It is a fallacy girls cannot be educated the same as boys. Yet those in power believe females should only learn enough to prepare for their roles as wives and mothers. I do not hold with the view. My curriculum is for all children, regardless of gender."

"Your students are indeed fortunate that you're forward-thinking. I admire it. I admire…you."

Riordan sipped his tea; the compliment pleased him.

After a few moments, Sabrina stood. "I believe I will retire. All of a sudden, I'm fatigued."

Riordan rose from his chair. "Allow me to escort you to your room."

"It is barely a few steps away."

"Nevertheless." He took her arm and escorted her to the door. Turning her to face him, he cradled her face, gently stroking her cheeks with his thumbs. "Good night. Sleep well." He kissed her forehead, then laid gentle kisses on each of her cheeks. Her eyelids lowered, and he placed kisses on them as well. The temptation proved hard to ignore. Taking a chance, he leaned in and tenderly kissed her on the lips. Brief, but scorching.

Stepping away from her, and about to turn and head to the parlor, Sabrina moved toward him, encircling her arms about his waist. Her ample breasts smashed against his chest, causing blood to rush to his shaft, hardening it. It was the same fierce embrace she'd given him the afternoon they shared a picnic lunch in his schoolroom. "I'm sorry," she whispered, "that I said you were trapping me like the earl and my father. Nothing could be further from the truth."

Sabrina laid her head against his chest and hugged him tighter. Her enticing citrus scent filled his senses as she softened all around him. God, she felt glorious. A perfect fit. He was completely aroused. "You're not like those poor excuses for men. No comparison at all. You're the best man I have ever known." He stroked her hair as her generous words made his heart swell.

As quickly as she hugged him, she let go and hurried into the room, closing the door behind her. Already he was bereft by her absence. Her scent lingered in the air, and the only sound was the ticking of the mantel clock. Or perhaps it was his heart, beating at a fast pace.

Damn. His entire body throbbed with need. He rested his forehead against the door and took a shuddering breath. How in hell would he be able to stay emotionally detached? The truth was he couldn't, and he would not even try. This was moving beyond a surface attraction into a deeper bond. The challenge lay in making Sabrina admit that there was far more going on between them than friendship.

A challenge he gladly accepted.

* * * *

Sabrina had been awake since shortly after dawn. She lay in bed, not knowing what to do. Should she rise, or wait for Mary to arrive? The small cottage was silent, indicating Riordan must still be asleep, and she did not want to disturb him. Thankfully, she'd slept through the night, the stress of the day tiring her far more than she'd thought. Pulling the covers up to her chin, she glanced at the sun pouring in through the sheer draperies. It would be a fine autumn day for a ride.

I am married. Despite her second thoughts and last-minute apprehensions, Sabrina had come to the conclusion that she'd made the right choice. Besides condemning her and Mary to a life of poverty, there was no other option. Many revelations filled the day. The first, Riordan insisting that she keep the entire amount of the settlement. That she had not expected.

The gesture, generous at its core, spoke of the honorable man she'd come to know—and wanted to know better.

But one of the biggest surprises? His suggestion that they make the marriage work. It had shocked her. Complete fright overtook her, hence the reason she lashed out and compared him to Pepperdon and her father. The earl, during the first months of their marriage, had tried to make an effort. But when it was clear that she abhorred his attentions, he turned cruel. Rough. The vindictiveness spilled over into their daily lives. As did the coldness.

During her first day married to Riordan, she experienced none of this, thank heavens. Sabrina closed her eyes, reliving his passionate kiss after the registrar declared them married. Then his tender kisses last night. After the ceremony, he was solicitous, engaged in every aspect of their shopping trip, assisting her in selecting books and giving his opinion when asked about the couple of dresses she'd purchased. He'd made her tea. Acted interested in what she had to say.

Sabrina was not used to any of this. Though overwhelming, she found she took great delight in not only his company, but his attention. All her talk of boundaries and still he kissed her. Regardless of the limitations she tried to place, she did not stop it, for she quite liked it. Her fingers brushed her lips, the memory of him still upon them. Gathering the sheets and blankets, she held them up to her nose and inhaled. His lime and bergamot scent. Masculine. Enticing.

The sound of Riordan moving about caught her attention. Was he dressing? Her cheeks flushed as she imagined it. There was no mistaking: he was a fine figure of a man. The strange sensations when they touched, when they kissed. She wanted more. As quietly as possible, she rose from the bed and crept to the door. *Voices.* Mary had arrived. Cracking open the door, she listened.

"I will attend church services with you both, Mr. Black. Then I will return here and ensure her ladyship is settled in. Regarding lunches, sir."

"Yes?"

"I'm not much of a cook, but I can manage certain meals, as well as make scones and biscuits. I'll handle Lady Sabrina's lunch. Will you be coming here for your break, or staying at the school?"

Sabrina waited for his response with bated breath. See him every day for luncheon? Her heart swelled with anticipation. How odd. She never expected to have these feelings toward any man. What feelings, exactly, remained a mystery.

"Most days I will stay at the school. I manage to accomplish much during the break, planning, correcting, and the like, but there are days I will come here for the meal. I will give you plenty of notice," Riordan answered.

"Very good, sir."

"Make a list of what needs to be purchased. There is not much here, seeing as my meals have been supplied by Mrs. Ingersoll. I usually take what remains from supper for lunch the next day."

"Leave it with me, sir. I'll speak with Mrs. Ingersoll and we'll work out the meals between us. I should see to her ladyship. She doesn't rise much before nine."

Sabrina scurried to the bed, climbing under the covers. Mary entered the room, closing the door behind her. "Good morning, my lady."

"Good morning, Mary."

"We best get you ready for church. You should have a bite before we depart, though there's not much here. Sandwiches from yesterday will have to do." Mary tossed aside the covers. "Sleep well?"

"I did."

Mary leaned in and whispered, "I think I woke Mr. Black. He answered the door looking disheveled and appealing."

"Mary!"

Her maid winked, then commenced bustling about the room, opening Sabrina's luggage, laying out the newly purchased dark blue wool dress with pearl buttons. "This will do nicely. Understated, but elegant." Mary lifted a cloth bag onto the bed. She removed a book and handed it to Sabrina. "Not what you're used to reading, but I recommend it."

"*The Bold Seduction of Miss Featherstone*?"

"Yes, my lady. It is erotic. More sensuous than salacious." Mary tapped the cover of the book. "Time you knew what passion consists of, though by your expression when Mr. Black kissed you yesterday, I believe you're beginning to understand what pleasure can be had with a man."

"This is entirely improper...."

"Oh, bosh, my lady. Read it. It involves a rake, the son of a viscount and an ex-soldier." Mary sighed. "What a delicious hero. Reminds me of Mr. Black, with the dark hair, blue eyes, and broad shoulders." Mary cleared her throat. "Well, best to get the day underway. I suppose you heard my conversation with Mr. Black."

Sabrina chuckled. "You know me well."

"We'll get it all sorted, my lady, don't you worry. The meals and the cleaning and whatnot. Three months will fly by."

Sabrina trailed the tips of her fingers across the gold-embossed title of the book. Seduction? Passion? Mary was correct, as usual: she absolutely knew nothing about it. Did she wish to learn? Perhaps she was incapable of base emotions.

She had close to three months to discover if such were the case. But if her reaction to his kisses was any indication, and the fact that she'd impulsively embraced him twice already, Sabrina suspected she may have found the one man who held the key to her locked away and hidden emotions. What to do about it was another question entirely.

Chapter 15

"May I present Mr. and Mrs. Black?" Reverend Thackeray declared. Sabrina stood at the front of the small chapel, her hand lightly resting on Riordan's arm. The entire congregation stared at them, some with mouths agape. Shocked murmurs rose from the pews. "Isn't she the baron's daughter?" One young lady even cried out, "No!" Sabrina scanned the small crowd and found the woman. The look of distress on her face showed she harbored a tendre for Riordan. No doubt more than one young lady had found herself infatuated with the handsome schoolmaster.

When services concluded, the vicar insisted upon announcing the marriage. Sabrina made a point of asking that he not call her Lady Pepperdon. She could've kept the courtesy title while married to a commoner, but in truth she was glad to be shunt of the earl's name. Next would be to banish him from her memory entirely.

Initially, the vicar had acted affronted that they'd traveled to London to see the deed done, and then aghast when Riordan told him they'd married at a registrar's office. The man had the audacity to ask to see the certificate. Riordan must have guessed that he would, because he had it tucked in his coat pocket. Once Reverend Thackeray established they were indeed married, he stated that the announcement must be made.

Good heavens, she didn't like being on display like this. Riordan must have sensed her stiffen next to him, for he laid his hand on top of hers and squeezed it gently. Eventually a small number of people came forward and offered congratulations, but the rest followed the vicar toward the main entrance to make their exit.

"Let's slip out the side door," Riordan whispered.

"Oh, could we?"

Riordan nodded toward Mary, who returned a smile as she headed down the aisle. Stepping out into the sunshine, Sabrina exhaled.

"It's over with. After a bit of tittle-tattle over tea in various parlors and kitchens, everyone will move on with their lives and forget us," Riordan said, his tone reassuring.

Sabrina had grown up in this area; it had been always a focus of gossip. Thankfully, her father had not attended Sunday services today. His attendance over the years had been sporadic and unpredictable. *Move forward. No looking back.*

"The farm is not far. A good stretch of the legs."

"I could do with a pleasant constitutional," Sabrina stated, remembering when she'd last ventured on a walk: the day she had discovered Riordan and his mesmerizing, melodic schoolmaster voice. A small smile curved about her mouth.

After arriving at the Walsh farm and exchanging introductions, the mare was fixed with a sidesaddle and Riordan helped Sabrina mount. His large hands grasped her on either side of her waist, and his touch seared. The sensation was growing in intensity with each contact. As she collected the reins, she patted the butterscotch-colored mare's strong neck.

Riordan climbed onto his magnificent horse with relative ease. Pulling on the reins, he brought the gelding about to stand next to her. "The mare's name is Goldie."

"I can see why yours is named Grayson. He's beautiful. The black mane offsets his dapple gray color."

As if he had heard the compliment, the horse kicked the dirt with his front hoof and nickered, giving his head a shake. A giggle escaped her.

"And he is a bit of a show-off. Shall we head out? Start with a trot and work up to a canter?"

As they travelled along the path leading from the Walsh farm, Sabrina tilted her head toward the sun. Though the air was slightly cool, the sun held comforting warmth. Birdsong sounded from the surrounding oak and juniper trees. The colorful autumn leaves shimmered with vibrancy. Everything was enhanced, bringing all her senses alive as never before. *Because of Riordan.*

"A beautiful day, is it not?" he asked.

"Completely glorious," she replied dreamily.

"See the brook ahead? I'll race you."

"Hardly fair; I'm riding sidesaddle. Now, if I were astride, it would be a true race. In fact, I could beat you."

He laughed, and the deep resonance of it made her heart skip a beat. "Then I will give you a head start."

Leaning over Goldie, Sabrina shortened the reins and gave the mare a gentle kick with her heels. The horse needed no further encouragement; she vaulted forward, leaving Riordan and Grayson behind. It didn't take long for pounding hooves to fill her hearing. Riordan caught up to her, and with a jaunty salute passed her. She dared not go any faster.

When she reached the brook, Riordan had already dismounted. She pulled up on the reins, slowing Goldie until the mare came to a full stop. "Being a gentleman, I should have let you win. But Grayson would not have it. He is from racing stock, and blood will win out." He reached up to help her dismount. Heavens, he would be touching her again. Steeling herself from any reaction, she placed her hands on his shoulders.

Riordan lifted her from the saddle as if she weighed nothing at all. He held her aloft, his gaze searing and smoldering. Then he lowered her, close enough that his body made contact with her own. Her breasts brushed by his chest, her legs tangled with his. The friction was like flint to tinder. Still he held her gaze, and she could not look away. Blue fire crackled with life and danced in his eyes.

At last, her boots hit the ground. His hands remained about her waist. Gazing up at him, she marveled once again at his nearly flawless face. Already she could see dark bristles forming along his firm jawline. How she ached to run her fingers along it. "We should allow the horses to drink," he said.

"Yes, of course."

He stepped away and grabbed the reins, urging Grayson to the edge of the brook. She did the same with Goldie. "We should have brought a picnic lunch. It is still warm enough to enjoy one." He pointed to the cluster of trees. "Right under there, it's perfect."

She glanced to where he pointed. It *was* perfect. Flat ground tucked under a shelter of trees. Sun shone through the gaps in the branches, creating a magical effect. "Perhaps next week, if the weather holds," she offered.

"Ah." He inclined his head toward the horses still drinking. "They will be fine." He took her gloved hand, threading her fingers through his. He did it naturally, as if they always held hands. "Next Sunday I'll be heading to my family home. Nothing serious. I will return Monday night. The board has granted me a personal day. I'm sure it will be the last one for a while."

"Oh."

"You will not be alone. I'll ask Mary to stay with you for the night I'm away."

"Thank you."

"You look lovely today."

A hot flush spread across her cheeks at his compliment. She wore merely a plain wool dress and her cloak, with a gray linen bonnet with a silk flower on the brim. This morning, Mary had wound her plait into a bun pinned at the nape of her neck. "Thank you."

"Not used to compliments?"

"Oh, dear, does it show? I'm not. But I do appreciate it."

"The fresh air and ride have done you a world of good. You are flush with health and color. It's entirely appealing. Enhances your natural beauty. And I'm not spouting false praise to win your favor; I mean what I say. Always."

As if he had to win her favor. She innately understood his sincerity was genuine. His words warmed her more than the autumn sun high in the sky. "Allow me to compliment *you.* I'm in awe of how you have handled this entire situation, from my bizarre request to managing my father and the earl, and the plans for the actual marriage. The agreements and the living arrangements…all has gone smoothly. Your career as an organized schoolmaster does you credit."

He lifted her gloved hand to his lips and laid a quick kiss on it. "Why, thank you, my lady. Let us hope all remains smooth."

"What are your plans for the future, regarding your career? What do you want from life?" she asked.

They stopped under the cluster of trees. The horses stayed by the edge of the brook, alternating between drinking the water and grazing on the grass growing nearby. "All I can think about is what I want right now."

"Oh? And what is that?"

He caught her gaze and held it. Again his expression smoldered. "To lean you against the trunk of this oak tree and run my hands over your lovely curves. Across your waist to your glorious breasts, where I would cup and caress them until you gave a sensual moan in reply." He stepped closer. The husky tone of his voice caused her to tremble with yearning. He should not be speaking to her this way. Not at all. But she could not tear her eyes away from him, nor muster the words to tell him to stop.

"I would continue on my journey, pull the pins from your hair. See it hang long about your shoulders. Run my fingers through the silken strands while I inhale your citrus scent. Nuzzle your delicate neck, pull you close into my embrace."

Both of them were breathing hard. *Aroused.* Yes, she was aroused from his heated, sensual words. *Dear heavens. How to respond?*

Riordan took another step. They were inches apart. "Do you feel it? What is between us?" Sabrina could only nod. "Despite what I want, what I…desire," he continued, "I will settle for a kiss."

Finally, she cleared her throat. "Should we keep doing this? Kissing, I mean."

"Yes. In the same way we should keep breathing." He did not give her a chance to respond, just swept her up into a bracing kiss. He clasped the nape of her neck, sending her bonnet slightly askew. "Kiss me in return, Sabrina," he rasped.

His gently spoken but urgent demand gave her courage. She threw her arms around his neck and followed his movements, brushing her lips across his until a husky moan escaped his throat. When it did, she thrust her tongue into his mouth as he had with her yesterday. Sinful. Completely wonderful.

"Oh, God," he murmured. In response, he wrapped his tongue about hers, caressing it, sending the flames of desire to a full roil. Sabrina was caught in a maelstrom of sensations. She wanted and needed more. Riordan clasped her cheeks, gasping, then leaned his forehead against hers. "Listen to me. Any chance I am able, I will be kissing you. I can't *not* kiss you. Do you understand?"

She nodded, gulping deeply, trying to regulate her breathing as she did.

"Do you want me to kiss you? If not, tell me. Here. Now. We will coexist as friendly acquaintances and nothing else."

How would she survive the next three months? The Sabrina of the past would have coldly rebuffed his passionate plea, even acted pitiless in the face of his raw and honest emotions. But in the span of mere weeks, she'd changed. It was all due to Riordan. She longed for his kiss. *Yearned.* At this moment? It was all she wanted. "Yes. Kiss me. Always."

He pulled her into his arms and she melted. "Brilliant. I don't know what I would have done if you had said no."

They stood together for several minutes. Sabrina did not even care that his arousal was pressed against her. She did not pull away in horror, but instead soaked in his warmth. The hardness of him. For the first time in years she felt…safe. Protected.

Grayson nickered loudly and they parted. Riordan chuckled. "I believe the horses are anxious to be on their way."

"Could we walk along the brook first? The day is lovely, and the winter season will soon be upon us. I want to savor it." *And savor you.* Yes, she shamelessly wished to be as close to him as possible. Take his arm, lean against his tall, muscular body. How astounding that she did not find any of this abhorrent. Perhaps the six years in which Pepperdon had left her alone before he died had allowed her to heal somewhat. But how much? Enough to allow more than kisses? Not possible. Pepperdon had ruined her from ever wanting a deep intimacy with any man.

Or had he?

* * * *

Once they arrived at the farm, they headed to the stable to leave the horses. Sabrina stumbled and Riordan rushed to her side.

"You're tired. I will take you to the cottage on Grayson."

"No, I will be able to walk."

Riordan leaned in and whispered in her ear, "Whether or not you are able to walk, indulge me. I want you in my arms."

Another roll of heat moved through her. Riding together on his horse? "Will he manage both of us?"

Riordan handed Goldie's reins to Farmer Walsh. "Absolutely." He lifted her up onto the saddle and gracefully mounted behind her. "Farmer Walsh, I will return shortly."

The farmer touched his forelock. "Grayson will enjoy the extra exercise, sir."

"That he will." Riordan urged the gelding forward at a slow trot. In a low voice that only she could hear, he said, "And give me an opportunity to be close to you."

Pleased at his words, she leaned against his chest and sighed contentedly. Riordan kissed the exposed area of her neck between her bonnet and the collar of her cloak. This continued for several moments, until a small girl's voice broke through her dreamy thoughts.

"Mr. Black, Mr. Black!"

Sabrina sat upright, her gaze sliding toward the sound. A girl, probably no more than six or seven, stood on the path. She wore a shabby pinafore over a plaid dress, her golden blond hair pinned haphazardly, with several tendrils hanging loose, framing her pretty face. She clutched several pieces of paper. Her face lit up at the sight of Riordan. Goodness, he even charmed small children.

"My youngest student. One moment." He slid off Grayson and strode toward the small girl, who immediately broke into a sprint, throwing herself at him. Riordan hunched down and held out his arms. The girl laughed with pure joy as Riordan gathered her into a warm hug and lifted her upward. The sight of Riordan with a small child tugged at her heart, making it ache with longing. Someday, once he was free from this situation, he would make a fine father.

"Momma told me you got married. I drew you pictures," the girl cried.

"Did you? Does your momma know you're here?"

The girl shook her head. "She's asleep."

"Annabelle, this is my wife, Mrs. Black. Say hello."

"Good afternoon, Mrs. Black," the girl answered in a singsong voice.

"Good afternoon, Annabelle."

Riordan lowered the child. Annabelle held out the papers toward him, and he took them and studied them closely. "Well done. Is that me standing outside a church?"

Annabelle nodded vigorously as she chewed on the side of her finger. "Uh huh. And your wife. She's holding flowers."

"Pretty bluebells, or are they daisies? I will hang these pictures in my cottage, I promise. But we must get you home, Annabelle, before your mother starts to worry. Are you cold?"

"A little." The child was wandering about in the late autumn air without a cloak. Riordan slipped out of his frock coat and gathered it around Annabelle, causing Sabrina's heart to squeeze once again at his thoughtfulness.

Riordan helped Sabrina down from the saddle, then handed her the papers. "I'll drop Annabelle off at her home before returning Grayson. She is a handful, slipping out while her mother naps. She has no siblings, and the father left years ago." It explained much. The girl looked to Riordan as a father figure.

"Of course. I will ensure Mary has tea ready for your return."

Riordan smiled as he trailed the back of his fingers down her cheek. "Thank you, Mrs. Black. The cottage is straight ahead over the small rise. You can't miss it."

Oh. She flushed at his touch, the warmth slowly spreading through her.

Riordan gathered the child and placed her on the saddle, then mounted. "Wave goodbye, Annabelle."

The girl giggled and gave Sabrina an enthusiastic wave. Sabrina returned it and watched as they rode away. She opened the papers and inspected the first pencil drawing. The picture was crudely drawn, as only a young child could accomplish. Annabelle had drawn Riordan as a tall stick figure with a broad smile and a head of wavy hair, hand-in-hand with a female figure in a long gown who held flowers. A large sun shone over them, and the girl had drawn what looked to be a rainbow arching over their heads and beds of flowers at their feet.

Tears gathered in Sabrina's eyes. The picture moved her, for it captured her mood since marrying Riordan. Sunshine, warmth, smiles, and happiness. It hit her hard. She wanted this. With Riordan. For the rest of her days. But it was a fairy tale, and no more real than a drawing with stick figures. A dream. Tears spilled down her cheeks as she hugged the picture against her chest and watched Riordan and Annabelle disappear through the trees.

She was falling for the schoolmaster and had no idea what to do about it.

Chapter 16

Heading toward Wollstonecraft Hall for the first-Monday-of-the-month family meeting, Riordan was apprehensive. Garrett must have kept his word and said nothing, because his father and grandfather did not descend on him in Carrbury, demanding an explanation for his actions. And they would have, if they'd known about his hasty marriage.

There was no meeting last month, as his father and grandfather had been busy with parliament. It struck him he hadn't heard from Aidan since moving to Carrbury two months past. For all his brother's excesses, they usually stayed in touch. He'd specifically asked his twin to correspond with him, but he'd received no word at all. Well, he would be at the meeting. Aidan wouldn't dare ignore a summons from the earl.

As for his marriage…his thoughts drifted to the previous Sunday and the magical afternoon he and Sabrina had spent together. *Any chance I am able, I will be kissing you. I can't* not *kiss you. Do you understand?* But since his passionate confession he'd only kissed her twice. Riordan thought it best to slow things down, more for Sabrina's sake than his own. At least for this week—even though she'd responded to his desperate plea with, *Yes. Kiss me. Always.* As soon as he returned, he would fulfill her request with enthusiasm.

At his core, he was a sensible man, raised to take responsibility for his emotions and actions no matter how riotous. He'd married Sabrina in order to assist her with her plight, but that was only part of his motive. He'd been attracted to her from the moment she showed up at his door hidden under the hood of her cloak. Kissing her had been a revelation. Apparently he knew nothing about desire, because everything he'd experienced before did not even come close to what he felt when Sabrina was in his arms.

If he wanted to try and convince her there could be more between them than this temporary legal arrangement, his original assessment of taking things slow had been the correct one. The way she'd melted in his arms showed passion existed in her. He need only allow her the time to acknowledge her hidden sensuality.

His trepidation grew as the tree-lined drive leading to Wollstonecraft Hall came into view. The property consisted of magnificent grounds, ideal for hunting, though none of the Wollstonecraft men did it for sport, as they found it barbaric, particularly fox hunting. The original house, done in the Tudor style and constructed in the sixteenth century, had all but been demolished, except for the timber-framed entrance and front hall.

The additional wings were Gothic Revival and Georgian, light beige brick with Palladian windows. The small Gothic wing sported black brick with lancet windows. As the sprawling building came into view, Riordan smiled. In spite of its strange, eccentric look, this was home. His arrival had been anticipated, for Martin stood by the door while a young lad from the stable hovered nearby to take charge of Grayson.

"Good to see you, sir," Martin said. His deep voice resonated but had a gentle, firm tone. The no-nonsense butler had been around as long as Riordan could remember. He'd been hired as a young footman about four decades ago. Around the age of Riordan's grandfather, Martin commanded respect from the other servants and ran the hall in an efficient manner. Tall, lean, and gray-haired, he stood ramrod straight, motioning to a young footman who'd appeared in the doorway to take Riordan's valise.

"Good to be home, Martin. Am I the last to arrive?" He slid off Grayson, giving the horse an affectionate pat on the neck before handing the reins to the stable boy.

"No, sir. Master Aidan has yet to make an appearance. You will find the earl, the viscount, and Master Garrett in the library. Dinner will be at eight." Riordan had departed at the crack of dawn in order to have most of the afternoon to visit.

"I'll go the library first and greet the family, but will wish a bath before dinner. Who will attend me?"

By their own choice, both he and Aidan did not have their own valets, nor did Garrett. Usually one of the footmen stepped in when needed, such as preparing for formal occasions or seeing that baths were prepared. Otherwise, the twins looked after themselves, shaving, dressing, and the like.

Handing his hat, gloves, and cloak to Martin, Riordan strode through the hall, steeling his spine for the confrontation ahead. Should he tell them now? At dinner? Tomorrow morning at the meeting? Spilling the information over brunch before he departed was the coward's way. Not his style at all.

Stepping into the library, he found his grandfather, father, and uncle sipping whiskey and sitting in the half circle of leather chairs before the large stone medieval fireplace. A roaring fire crackled in the hearth, the logs snapping noisily on the grate.

"Riordan, my lad," his grandfather called out, a warm smile on his face. Martin had followed Riordan into the library and was already pouring a tumbler of scotch. When Riordan sat, Martin handed him the drink. "Thank you, Martin. That will be all." The butler bowed toward the earl and left the room.

"You look well, Riordan," his father stated. The viscount, though self-contained and not as outwardly affectionate as the earl, felt things profoundly. Riordan never doubted that his father loved him. One only had to look at his astounding record in parliament, fighting and speaking passionately for progressive causes, to see the proof. But it was not only in his work—he'd spent as much time as he could with him and Aidan as they grew.

"As do you, Father." Once settled in with his drink, he savored the comforting warmth, not only from the fire, but also from being with his family. Which reminded him. "Where is Aidan? Sleeping?"

His father frowned. "We have not heard from Aidan. At all. Not once in the past two months."

Riordan looked to Garrett, who said, "It's true. We sent runners out to his usual haunts and...nothing. He's gone to ground."

Riordan did not like the sound of this. "How odd, he's never done that before. He has always stayed in contact, no matter how deeply immersed in his vices. But I haven't heard from him either." He ran his hand through his hair in frustration. "Damn, I've been caught up in my own... Is anything being done to locate him?"

His father nodded. "Of course. We have people in Bath and London and points beyond. He will be found. And dealt with." His father's expression turned stony. Aidan was in deep trouble. He'd been sinking for months, but this was the final straw.

"Tell us about Carrbury and your teaching. Garrett was sparse on details," his grandfather said, no doubt glad to change the subject.

Garrett laughed. "Da, I wasn't in the schoolroom with him. I was only there for a couple of nights."

Riordan stared into the depths of his whiskey. Why put off the inevitable? Might as well reveal it. "I was married. Last week."

The silence was deafening. The only sounds came from the fire crackling in the hearth and the pendulum clock on the mantel ticking away the awkward minutes.

"What did you say?" His father's tone was incredulous.

"It's a temporary marriage of convenience only. I'm assisting a widow left penniless by her earl husband. She was about to be literally sold off by her miserable baron father to an old marquess."

Garrett blew out a breath, then took a long swig of whiskey. His father turned his thunderous look toward his brother. "Were you aware of this?"

"I knew a little of his plans," Garrett murmured.

"And you thought not to tell us?" the earl cried.

"He asked me not to. Riordan is of age, and able to make his own decisions. He's here now to tell you of it. Listen to what he has to say," Garrett replied.

"What do you mean by 'assist' and 'temporary'? Explain yourself," his father barked.

Riordan took a fortifying drink, savoring the burn. Once he swallowed, he commenced giving his family as thorough an explanation as he could. The earl looked shocked, but his father's expression darkened.

"The money. Where did it come from?" his father whispered, his tone clearly expressing his growing irritation and anger.

"It is mine."

Julian stood and threw his glass of whiskey into the fire. The alcohol exploded in the flames. "I gave you the money, a mere taste of your inheritance, when you turned twenty-five because you had shown through word and deed that you were responsible, sober, and sensible. Apparently, I was wrong. I should have held the money in a trust as I did with Aidan's." His father began to pace. "I never had to worry about you, not one moment from the cradle onward. I trusted you. Believed in your judgment." He stopped pacing and faced Riordan. "What a crushing disappointment to find that you are as vapid and stupid as your brother."

"Julian, wait a moment—" the earl began.

"No, Father. This is between me and my son. Years ago, I agreed to stay here under the condition you never interfere with my dealings with my sons. Do not start now." The earl's mouth pulled into a taut line, but he said nothing. "Riordan, tell me why you've done this. What possessed you?" Julian cried.

He had never seen his father as livid and distressed as this. Throwing the glass into the fire was a rare show of emotion. Riordan placed his tumbler on the nearby table. "She had nowhere to turn. As you're aware, women have no rights whatsoever. I wished to assist her. It is a good cause. You know all about it, Father."

"And what if you are trapped with this woman for life? A woman older than you. What then?"

"It will not be a hardship," Riordan murmured.

"God, he's infatuated," Garrett stated incredulously.

"Is this true?" Julian demanded.

"Yes. I hope to convince Sabrina to make the marriage permanent."

"You should have informed me of this before acting. We discuss everything in this family, especially anything to do with our causes. You *will* be getting an annulment. I will brook no argument on this matter." Julian kicked the nearby stool and charged from the room.

Riordan's insides twisted and he clenched his jaw. His father had never spoken to him that way before. *Vapid. Stupid. Crushing disappointment.* The words were seared into his heart. He grabbed his nearby glass and tossed the rest of his whiskey down his throat, the burn no longer comforting.

* * * *

Julian strode angrily from the library, only stopping long enough to gather his greatcoat before heading outside. He would try and walk off the dangerous fury roiling inside him. The strong breeze whipped his long coat about his legs as the gravel crunched under his heavy tread. Damn it all. Riordan was the last one he expected to act as foolhardy as to marry a stranger, and gift her with a substantial sum besides.

Perhaps he'd drilled his passion for progressive causes into the boys a little too fervently. Not that any of it got through to Aidan. Julian huffed out an exasperated breath at the thought of his oldest son. A complete reprobate. A notorious rake. Thoughtless, selfish, and depraved. Reports about Aidan had recently come to his attention: tales of drunken orgies, itinerant and reckless gambling, and, even more worrying, visits to low class East End brothels to partake in opium.

It made it all the more urgent to find Aidan and bring him home. Opium could be his motivation for dropping out of sight. Julian shook his head. Blast both of his sons! Riordan should have spoken to him about his plan. He smiled grimly. Well, at least the lad did what he believed was the right thing. The noble thing. Though such notions always paved the road to perdition.

He shook his head a second time. Was his uncharacteristic outburst truly about Riordan, or was it more about Aidan? Yes, he had taken his temper out on the wrong son. Perhaps it was a mercy Fiona could not witness what a thorough and botched job he had done raising their twins.

A sharp pain squeezed his heart at the thought of his late wife. She had been dead more than twenty years, and still the loss and heartache lingered. As much as he tried to bury his emotions, he was a passionate man. No one else had touched his heart since Fiona. Perhaps no one ever would. He was better off. His father agreed and lived his life the same way.

A parade of women, enough to satisfy certain carnal urges, and sufficient reforms to be worked and completed would keep him well occupied until the grave. Yet a part of him was…empty.

Julian rounded the corner at the rear of the hall. Not far from the servants' entrance was a kitchen herb garden, along with a patch of brown mushrooms—Julian's favorite. He'd brought them from France on one of his many trips, carefully and lovingly tended them, and instructed the cook that they be fried in red wine and served with his beefsteak. But there in the middle of the cluster of mushrooms sat a hedgehog, happily munching away on Julian's prized fungi. "Blasted pest," Julian growled. The hedgehog must have heard his dangerous tone, for it immediately curled into a ball to protect itself from retribution.

"Don't you hurt my Daisy!"

Julian turned and faced the source of the loud cry. A giant of a young man lumbered toward him. Hell, the man was nearly as tall as Garrett. He wore muddy trousers and his shirt hung loose on his left side. What struck Julian was the angelic, beautiful face. Perfect symmetrical features any human, man or woman, would desire to possess. Or perhaps just simply desire.

The young man plundered through the mushrooms and scooped up the hedgehog, cradling it close to his chest. "There, Daisy. I found you. No one will hurt you," he murmured gently to the trembling creature.

"Do you mind? You are trampling my mushrooms," Julian snapped.

The young man looked up at him and blinked, as if not comprehending what had been said to him. *Ah.* Julian realized the man was simple of mind. To look like Adonis yet possess the mind of a child…what a tragedy. But he supposed it was all a matter of perception. Banking his temper, he said in a friendly tone, "Could you please not step on the plants?"

The man looked down at his booted feet. "Oh. All right." He turned to leave.

"Wait. What is your name? Do you live nearby?"

The Adonis continued to cuddle the hedgehog as close as one could with a prickly animal. "Jonas. I live over there." He pointed across the vast expanse of the estate, toward where Sir Walter Keenan had resided. The new owner must have taken possession. What had Garrett said? A widowed niece of Sir Walter. Who was this fellow?

Julian stepped forward and held out his hand. "I am Julian Wollstonecraft." Jonas glanced at the hand, then looked away. "Take it, lad, and shake. I won't hurt you…or Daisy. You have my word."

Jonas met his gaze and briefly shook his hand. "Hello, Julie."

Julian fought back a laugh. "Perhaps you had better call me by my title, Tensbridge."

The lad smiled broadly. "Tens!"

This time Julian did laugh. "Whatever you like."

"I have to go. Bert will worry."

Who the deuce is Bert? Curious, Julian asked, "Do you mind if I walk with you?"

Jonas shrugged and set off toward the Keenan residence. Julian fell in step next to the young man. He continued to cuddle the hedgehog, which had come out of its protective shell-like position and licked Jonas's hand. "Is this hedgehog your pet?"

"I have lots of pets," Jonas answered. He listed a litany of names as they continued on their journey. They reached the boundary of the property; the fences were in various stages of repair and decline, and the hedgerows were overgrown. Julian then recalled Garrett stating he was assisting the widow with certain renovations.

"Bert, I found Daisy," Jonas called out. In the middle of a thatch of weeds a wizened old man dug into the dirt with a small spade. He was small, hunched over the weeds wearing heavy cotton trousers and a baggy plaid coat with a wide brim straw hat. The man stood and turned, wiping dirt from his face.

It was not a wizened old man, but a woman. At least, the face showed feminine features, though it was hard to ascertain the exact gender because of the loose-fitting clothes. If female, she possessed no shape whatsoever. She lifted her head and caught his gaze. This "Bert" had the most incredible amber eyes he had ever seen. They shimmered gold in the setting sun. "I see you have become acquainted with Jonas." She pulled off her glove and held out her slender hand. "I am Alberta Eaton, new owner of this menagerie."

Bert. Alberta. Of course. Her voice was smoky and entirely sensual, and the touch of her cool hand caused his insides to tumble. *Hell.* It had been quite a while since he experienced such a swift reaction to a woman. "Julian Wollstonecraft, Viscount Tensbridge, at your service."

"Of course." She pulled her hand away and held it above her eyes to shield them from the late afternoon sun. "Garrett's older brother. I remember you, my lord."

"Have we met?"

She laughed, and it caused a ripple of lust to travel through him. Why he found this elfin lady attractive was beyond him. "Not formally, but I used to visit my uncle Walter on occasion while growing up. The last time I visited was fourteen years ago. He grew increasingly hermit-like in his final years." She smiled. "I attended a formal dinner at Wollstonecraft Hall with my friend, Abigail Wharton."

"I do recall, now that you mention it." Julian pointed to Jonas, who stood inside a pen. "Your son?"

The widow crossed her arms and squinted at him. "Dear me. I look old enough to be his mother? No, my lord, he is my brother-in-law. My late husband refused to have Jonas institutionalized, as those asylums are barbaric. I made a promise on his deathbed to always care for him. Their parents have passed and there is no one else. Jonas is sweet, but has the mind of a twelve-year-old, when in fact he is twenty-four."

She sighed wistfully. "I love him as if he were my son. I hope he did not disturb you, my lord. I warned him to stay on our property."

Julian clasped his hands behind him. "Daisy the wayward hedgehog was making a meal out of my rare mushrooms."

The widow Eaton smiled. "I'm sorry, my lord. She is one of an array of hedgehogs that Jonas looks after. He also has a llama called Poppy. She resides in a pen behind the house, a pen your brother generously built for us. He has been a godsend, for my uncle let the place go to ruin, as you see."

Once Daisy was settled in her pen, Jonas ran over to where they stood. "Tens, come see Poppy." The lad acted with such infectious enthusiasm, Julian could not find it in his heart to say no.

"I see Jonas likes to give nicknames," Julian ventured.

"He does. I hope you are not offended, my lord. I can correct him and encourage him to call you by your title."

"It's not necessary. I am not offended in the least. You may call me Tensbridge, if you like. I would rather it than 'my lord.'"

They trudged behind the house, and Julian observed crumbling brick and peeling paint along with overgrown, shabby shrubs. The place would need a great deal of work and attention.

"See Poppy? Isn't she pretty?" Jonas cried.

Julian had seen a llama at the zoo in London, but he never imagined anyone having such an animal as a pet. As he stepped closer, the wretched beast glared at him imperiously, then hocked deep in his throat and spit at Julian. The spittle landed on the front of his greatcoat, angering him afresh.

"Oh. My heavens." Mrs. Eaton rushed forward and wiped at his coat with her garden glove. "She's never done that before. I do apologize, Tensbridge."

"Sorry, Tens," Jonas murmured. "Poppy, don't spit at Tens. He's our friend."

In response, the animal nuzzled Jonas and made a noise similar to a sigh.

"It's fine. Do not worry." Julian's irritation dissipated at the look of the contrite Jonas and the obvious affection the llama showed the lad.

Mrs. Eaton stood incredibly close. She gazed up at him, for she was petite in height. He could drown in those golden eyes of hers. "Come in for tea; let me make it up to you."

By God, he was tempted. "Another time. My son is visiting, and only here until tomorrow afternoon. I must return home. But I will, next I return from London, I promise."

She gave him a warm smile. "Please do."

After saying goodbye, Julian headed toward Wollstonecraft Hall. By the time he entered the library, much of his temper had faded. Only Garrett was in the room, slumped in his chair, his long legs stretched out in front of him, another glass of whiskey in his hand. "Where is everyone?" Julian asked.

"Father has retired to his study. I imagine Riordan is upstairs bathing, removing the dust of his journey."

Julian tore off his coat and tossed it on the settee as he headed toward the whiskey decanter. He poured a generous amount. "I cannot believe you didn't tell me. You are *my* brother, not Riordan and Aidan's. Your loyalty should be to *me*."

Garrett scoffed. "Don't pout. It doesn't become you. We may have a greater concern than Riordan's hasty marriage."

Julian sat next to Garrett and took a sip. "Such as?"

"What do you know of the Marquess of Sutherhorne and Baron Durning?"

"The baron? Next to nothing. Sutherhorne? I believe Father is more acquainted with him; they're a similar age. We've conversed once or twice. To be honest, I did not care for the man. A cold, disagreeable sort."

Garrett rubbed his glass between his large hands. "Well, we'd better find out what there is to know, for the marquess has made a definite threat toward both Riordan and me. He is not aware of our family ties...yet. It will not take him long, for Riordan used father's name to induce Sutherhorne to come downstairs."

Julian uttered a foul oath under his breath.

"I believe we've made enemies, ones who will seek retribution. We'd best be prepared and investigate what kind to expect," Garrett said. "It may please you to know that Riordan handled himself well. Complete control of the situation." He went on to relay the exchange outside the Carrbury Inn.

Brilliant. On top of everything else, now they must deal with vengeful peers. Julian had to agree: he did not like the tone of the threat, and Garrett would not exaggerate. They had best inform Father of the incident. Now to try and make Riordan understand the seriousness of his consequences.

And to make certain the damned annulment goes through as soon as possible.

Chapter 17

They all made an effort to dress for dinner. The menu was impeccable, as cook was no doubt glad to be able to prepare a large meal for once. Riordan was famished after the journey, and thankful that his father did not broach the subject of his marriage while they ate. Perhaps he'd walked off the bulk of his anger, or at least decided to set it aside for the rest of the evening. Riordan could only hope. He did not like being on the outs with his father.

The meal started with crayfish soup, a Dover baked sole, medallions of foie gras (not Riordan's favorite), along with a saddle of mutton, potatoes, brussels sprouts, and French beans. Dessert consisted of peach pie, raspberry tarts, and vanilla cream.

The conversation stayed civil, the topics varying from the estate to recent news events and doings at parliament. Afterwards, while everyone sat around the table with brandy and cigars, though Riordan had never developed the tobacco habit, the discussion turned to him.

"Riordan, you must see this marriage cannot stand. You married the woman under false pretenses regarding your name. I understand it's why you chose the annulment, and it is a logical choice." Julian paused, swirling his brandy in his snifter. "Allow me to contact Miller Kenworth. Perhaps we can start the wheels turning and dissolve this marriage immediately. Negotiate a parting settlement with Lady Pepperdon for a few thousand pounds."

Kenworth. Head of the law firm, and his friend William Chambers's employer. It would be simple to become annoyed, start another argument. But Riordan tried to avoid conflict when possible. "Father, I gave my word to Sabrina, and it states in legal documents we both signed that she will be entitled to the entire ten thousand pounds on the day the annulment is finalized." He sniffed the brandy, then took a sip, allowing the spicy taste to linger in his mouth before swallowing. "Beyond that, I have feelings for her. They are deepening with each passing day. I'm in no hurry to dissolve the marriage."

Julian bristled, but his grandfather laid a hand on his son's arm as if to calm him. "Why this woman?" the earl asked, his voice soft.

All eyes were on Riordan. "To begin with, she is attractive, with light brown hair and golden highlights seemingly added with a painter's brush."

"Jesus," Garrett muttered. "He's more than infatuated."

Riordan shrugged. "Perhaps I am. You must understand, Sabrina has had a loveless, cold life. From her miserable father selling her to the old earl, to the horrific marriage she endured. I am not aware of specifics, but judging from her aloof nature and abhorrence for anything physical, it may be worse than I could ever imagine. I want to protect her from more hurt. I want to give her what she longs for the most: her independence. Her freedom. And I will do anything in my power to give her what she most desires."

"Admirable grounds," his grandfather acknowledged. "Then give her the freedom now."

"Exactly," Julian interjected. "If you promised Lady Pepperdon the money, I suppose we have no choice but to follow through. But you cannot be handing out money to everyone with a sad story."

"I'm well aware of that fact, Father," Riordan said. Tamping down his annoyance was becoming difficult as the conversation continued. "But it is my money, and it is my decision how I choose to spend it. It is a stain on this country that women cannot vote, are considered property, and cannot hold any property of their own. Nor can they escape a detestable marriage. Women are mistreated, abused, and when their husbands die, they can be left with nothing. If their only living male relative refuses to assist them, where can they turn?" Riordan continued to swirl his brandy. "I cannot rescue every woman in dire straits, but I *will* rescue this one. And if during the three months I'm able to convince her to open her heart and allow love and light to enter it, there may be no need for the settlement at all. Yes. It is more than an infatuation, more than merely physical. More than a cause. I want to explore the attraction already sparking between us." He smiled. "There is a passionate woman beneath the outer layer of frost—I'm determined to find her."

Garrett rolled his eyes. "I tried to warn him. Emotional attachments to women will only lead to trouble. And what of the curse?"

Riordan stared at his uncle. The man lived and breathed the damned curse. "I suppose I'll lay the particulars of the curse before her and allow her to decide whether it is worth it. For my part? I have doubts. Why put a woman you care deeply for at risk? But then, why deny love on the premises of a medieval tale of woe?"

Garrett bristled, but Julian held up his hand to stay his brother's response. "You speak passionately," Julian said, "But you could be heading for heartache, and I'm not speaking merely of the curse, which is tangible no matter what you think. Even though you say there's an attraction, there is no guarantee the lady will wish anything permanent with you."

Riordan frowned. He didn't like being reminded of such an outcome. "I will deal with that if it should happen. I'll not stand in her way if she wishes to leave—for whatever reason. As I said, I will give her what she most desires."

"And if you are able to convince her to stay, what of children?" the earl asked.

Riordan turned slightly to glare at his grandfather. "What of it? I'm not the heir. It is not my responsibility to procreate and carry on the Wollstonecraft legacy."

"Who is to say?" Julian replied. "Your brother is not showing an inclination to take his responsibilities seriously."

"Besides," the earl interjected, "she was married to Sutherhorne for years and there was no issue from the union. Granted, the fault may not be hers."

Riordan took another sip. "Here is my last word on the subject. I've listened to all your concerns and I will take them under advisement. Ultimately, however, it is my life and my decision. If it is a mistake, I'll live with the consequences. Heartache or no. Meanwhile, no interference from any of you. Trust me to make my own choices."

The table was silent. Perhaps too silent.

"Father?"

"I will not contact Kenworth. At least, not for now. I still stand by my belief that you should end this marriage, sooner rather than later." His father blew out an exasperated breath. "Best we change the subject. I met our new neighbors this afternoon."

Garrett grinned as he took a puff on his cigar. "Mrs. Alberta Eaton and her brother-in-law, Jonas Eaton."

"What can you tell me about them?" Julian asked.

Riordan glanced at his father; he was interested in what Garrett had to say. All of a sudden, so was Riordan.

"Mrs. Eaton is thirty-nine. She was married to Mr. Reese Eaton, barrister, for ten years before he died of heart failure. I believe she said her husband was close to twenty years older. And Jonas? A late birth for

Mr. Eaton's mother, one she did not survive." Garrett sipped his brandy. "Alberta said the cord was wrapped around his neck at birth. They thought him stillborn until the doctor brought him around by massaging his chest. Was he deprived of air for too long? Or is this the way he was meant to be? No one knows the answer."

Julian stubbed out the remains of his cigar. "Unfortunate. How is it you are privy to this information?"

"Many a cup of tea in the parlor over the past several weeks. Do I detect a spark of interest in the widow, Brother?" Garrett's eyes twinkled with amusement.

Julian scoffed. "Hardly."

The men gave him dubious looks, including Riordan. His father had not shown any curiosity toward a woman in recent memory. Oh, he was aware that his father had a few affairs through the years, but he never mentioned any of them. Interesting development.

"Riordan, over brunch tomorrow we wish to hear a detailed account of your schoolroom adventures, and the results of your progressive curriculum," the earl stated.

"Of course, Grandfather."

He would depart immediately after and head home. To Sabrina. This visit had made Riordan all the more determined to pursue a permanent bond between them. He'd spoken the truth: he was more than infatuated. Taking a chance with his heart? Perhaps. But she was worth the risk.

In all ways.

* * * *

He stood, resplendent in his soldier red, the breeze ruffling his thick, black hair. Tall and broad-shouldered, he looked every inch the hero. Handsome beyond measure, with eyes that rivaled the summer sky above, he gave me a sly smile and a slight bow. My insides somersaulted as a heated yearning tore through me, culminating in my body reacting in the naughtiest of ways. I wanted to possess him; I wanted him to possess me. It was then I knew I would sacrifice everything I was raised to believe in order to have him in my bed for one night

Sabrina closed the book and heaved a sigh. Last night she'd started to read *The Bold Seduction of Miss Featherstone* and found herself swept up in this young woman's tale of sensual awakening. The entertaining read was a combination of the heroine's journal entries interspersed with third-person narration.

Much of what was described in this story, Sabrina was slowly becoming aware of: the tumbling of her insides, the reactions of her body, whether naughty or not. There was no doubt about it. Finally, when in a man's presence, she experienced arousal. *In Riordan's presence.* This never happened with her husband. Not once.

She'd enjoyed their first night of reading *Wuthering Heights*. It certainly highlighted how all-consuming passion could be—and how tragic. The thought of Heathcliff standing before the open window, beseeching a ghostly Cathy, his heart's desire, to come to him made her eyes fill up. But it was not only the story itself—it was Riordan's mesmerizing voice, and the emotion he injected into every word.

Mary bustled into the bedroom. "Luncheon is ready, my lady. Come to the table… Oh! You're reading the book."

Sabrina slipped it under her pillow. "Yes, and I have questions."

"Come, before it grows cold. I made us poached eggs on toast. Ask me what you will while we eat."

Sabrina smiled as she stood and followed Mary into the parlor area. "Not as fancy as we are used to." Since coming to the small cottage, she and Mary had shared meals, the line between lady and servant further blurred, and Sabrina did not mind in the least.

As Mary poured their tea, Sabrina cut her egg and toast into small pieces. Her maid cut generous slices of Cheshire cheese. "Mrs. Ingersoll and I have made a workable plan between us. Since the foodstuff order has been delivered, I will be able to prepare a few extras outside her domain." Mary laid pieces of cheese on Sabrina's plate. "We will follow Mr. Black's meal pattern. Breakfast, luncheon, and supper. A bit different from the breakfast, afternoon tea, and late dinner of your class."

"I will adapt, Mary, never fear."

"Mrs. Ingersoll will arrive at four o'clock each afternoon, do a little light cleaning, and leave supper behind for you both. I will be done with my own duties and supper by seven, and will come to you directly after eight to prepare you for bed. If that is satisfactory, my lady."

"Sounds as if you have it all planned out. You do not mind the work at the inn?"

Mary shook her head. "Not at all. Tidying rooms, making beds, assisting at the front desk…it's no problem, my lady. I would have made the sausages, but I thought we would save those for a luncheon when Mr. Black can join you."

Popping a piece of egg and toast in her mouth, Sabrina chewed and swallowed. "Speaking of Mr. Black."

Now seated and cutting into her egg, Mary lifted her head and caught her gaze. "Yes?"

"As you witnessed, Mr. Black—Riordan—kissed me with a good deal of enthusiasm at the registrar's office. But he kissed me before, and after too."

Mary smiled. "You allowed it?"

"I did. And I…enjoyed it." Sabrina sipped her tea.

Mary laid her utensils across her plate, and her smile slipped away. "I was with you through those long eleven years of your marriage to that wretched man. Many a night the other servants had to restrain me from marching into the bedroom and tearing you away from his deviant clutches." Mary's eyes welled with tears. "I wish now I'd mustered the courage."

"Oh, Mary." Sabrina patted her hand. "It only would have fueled his anger, and he would have taken it out on you." She paused, wondering whether to reveal anything of what had gone on behind closed doors. She'd never told anyone in any detail. "Do you remember a winter's night in the fifth year, you knocked at the door asking if I was all right? I know there was more than one occasion." Mary looked up at her, dabbing the corners of her eyes with a napkin, and nodded. "The earl had me tied to the bed. Facedown. Committing an act I now know is sodomy." Mary gasped. "When you knocked, he bade me to say all was fine, or he would pull you into the room and do the same to you, and make me watch."

Mary cried out. "Oh, my lady."

"You know he would have done it. When at last he became bored of me and realized I would not become…pregnant, he left me alone. He also left me dead inside. Completely numb. But not all physical relations between a man and a woman are what I endured, are they?"

Mary shook her head as she picked up her utensils and speared a piece of egg with her fork. "No. Not at all." Her maid sighed. "I'm not a virgin, my lady. I have known contentment in a man's arms…and in his bed. We were to be married, you see, but he was a sailor like my father." Her expression softened. "Oh, he was a considerate lover. You'd think he would be rough and uncouth, considering his occupation, but my Billy knew how to love a woman good and proper. Unfortunately, he was on the same ship as my father and was lost at sea."

Now Sabrina's eyes welled with tears. "Oh, my dear. How tragic."

Mary continued eating. In between bites she said, "I had no time to mourn. It was left to me to provide for my mother and me. But I stray from the point. Going by the look in Mr. Black's eyes when he gazes at you…I saw the same in Billy's. Respectful and loving. Mr. Black would be a caring and thorough lover, I'm sure of it. Maybe even a little wild. You can tell about a man from his kiss. Was Mr. Black aggressive? Forceful?" Sabrina shook her head. "Good. For I will reveal that when complete trust exists, a little wildness in the bedchamber can be exciting." A flush of embarrassment colored Sabrina's cheeks at Mary's blunt words. "But if he starts off gentle like, understanding of your reaction, and then kisses more deeply, allowing the desire to flame between you…there is nothing better. Am I describing Mr. Black?" Mary asked.

Sabrina quickly shoved a small bite of egg in her mouth and nodded.

"It is not always easy to forget the past, but you must not allow it to rule your life. Perhaps, my lady, you could try."

"I would like to," Sabrina whispered. "I miss Riordan. I'm longing to see him again. Mary, what is happening to me?"

"You're falling for him," Mary replied matter-of-factly.

"But I cannot. We have plans. We must follow them through…."

Mary shrugged. "Life rarely follows the earnest plans we make. Do not close this door, my lady, see what develops." Mary continued with her meal.

See what develops. Dare she? Oh, she was confused, her emotions in a jumble. It would be quite a step from being a baron's daughter and an earl's wife to be with a mere schoolmaster. In the past, such an obstacle would not have even been considered. She had been brought up to believe that one stays in one's own class. She didn't think as such anymore. What had her class given her? Nothing but misery.

Turning her attention to her meal, Sabrina began to eat in earnest. Yes. Why not see what develops? A few passionate kisses did not have to lead anywhere; she could continue on with her original plan of her and Mary finding a small place to live out their days. Yes, this would be the more prudent path to take. And if she could manage to learn more about the schoolmaster, all the better.

But Sabrina could not deny that she'd never felt more alive than when she was with Riordan.

Gaining independence meant she was at last in charge of her own life. Truth be told, she wanted—*ached*—to bask in Riordan's warmth and attention.

Chapter 18

The autumn sun was setting as Riordan arrived at the Walsh farm. It was November third; the air held a decided chill and most of the leaves had fallen. He was exhausted, not only from the journey, but from the drama and emotions his marriage announcement had stirred up. Over brunch before he left, he expounded in great detail everything he'd implemented within the schoolroom and the successes he had garnered.

His grandfather had instructed Martin to take copious notes as Riordan spoke, and by the time he'd concluded it was well past the hour for departure. His farewell with his father was cool but civil. Julian's harsh words were a heavy weight on Riordan's mind. But he was determined to follow his own path, and hopefully his father would come around to his way of thinking. The men all agreed, finding Aidan was a top priority, and Garrett volunteered to begin the search in earnest by hiring an ex-copper friend of his.

A shiver traveled down Riordan's spine. From the rain shower he'd been caught in? Perhaps. He had sought temporary shelter at an inn, but his clothes were still damp. No, the shiver had more to do with Aidan. They shared a bond, but it wasn't as if they shared emotions and pains, like the fictional characters in *The Corsican Brothers* by Alexandre Dumas. Yet Riordan could not deny that there were instances when he sensed something was not right with Aidan. He sensed it now.

Truthfully, he should be assisting Garrett in finding his brother. But other responsibilities pulled him in a conflicting direction. With the colder weather growing ever closer, he doubted he would be given any further personal time for trips to Wollstonecraft Hall and beyond. He had implored Garrett to keep him apprised of any developments.

Farmer Walsh raised a hand to greet him. Riordan pulled up on the reins, then slid off his horse. Patting the gelding's neck, he said, "Grayson has had quite a workout. I hastened his pace part of the way. He's lathered, weary, and, I imagine, hungry."

Farmer Walsh took the reins. "I will see him well looked after, sir. A rubdown, your special mix of oats, and plenty of water. Will you stay for a mug of tea?"

Riordan released the strap that held his small valise on Grayson. "It is tempting, but I should head for home and—"

The sharp, piercing cry of an animal came from the nearby barn. A desperate howling. "What is that?"

"Oh, Charlie chose a kitten from the barn cat's litter weeks ago. Brought it in the house and trained it, but the wife has taken to sneezing and the like, so the animal has been banished to the barn." Farmer Walsh scratched his whiskery chin. "Got to find a new home for it; it's useless as a barn cat. Won't survive."

Kitten. The lonely mewing cut straight to his heart as he recalled Sabrina sadly relaying the fact that she'd not been allowed to have a pet. Should he? It was an impulsive thing to do. "How much for the kitten? I believe my bride would welcome a pet."

"Nay, sir. No charge at all. You pay me far above what is expected for boarding a horse, and Charlie thinks the world of you. Never seen him so keen to go to school. Unlike most of my neighbors, I believe an education is important. Wish I had one." The farmer chuckled. "Though I don't see how this type of learning benefits a farmer."

"There is a saying in Latin, '*ars gratia artis*,' which means 'art for art's sake.' Learning for learning's sake. Are you interested in having your son become something beyond a farmer, as wonderful as that is? Perhaps a doctor or a solicitor?"

"Aye. I want my son to have more opportunities."

"Only with learning and knowledge can this happen. Instilling a sense of wonder and awe." Riordan smiled.

"Aye. Awe. I'm learning too, as Charlie tells us all you've taught him every night at supper."

Riordan was humbled by the words. To be given proof that his way of teaching was having an impact on his students' lives—and their parents'—was more than he could ask for. "Thank you, Farmer Walsh. Then it's all worthwhile, isn't it?"

"That it is, sir. Come into the barn with me while I see to Grayson. You can meet the kitten. Charlie called her Mittens, but I imagine your missus can call it whatever she wants."

Riordan placed his luggage on the ground and followed Farmer Walsh in. The warmth from the barn drove off the chill from his bones, and the familiar odors of hay, horse, and leather reminded him of home. "Are you sure Charlie will not mind parting with his pet?"

"He said he'd prefer she has a good home, and he'll be thrilled you took the kitten in rather than anyone else." He pointed to the far corner. "She's there. Once I put Grayson in his stall, I'll see if the wife has a closed hamper you can borrow. In fact, I'll see you home on the wagon, sir. You'll need the basket the kitten slept in, the container she does her business in, the sand…."

Riordan laughed. "I will accept the ride gladly."

He walked to the small pen. Huddling and shivering in a pile of hay was a white kitten with patches of orange across its small body. She looked up at him, her green eyes full of misery. Leaning down, he gathered the frightened kitten in his arms, expecting a hiss and a scratch for his efforts. Instead, Mittens burrowed close to his chest and mewed softly. Already he was taken with the small feline; he hoped Sabrina would be as well.

By the time they left the Walsh farm darkness had blanketed the sky, the moon and stars their only guide. Mrs. Walsh gifted Riordan with a fresh loaf of bread and a raisin pie. The kitten had mercifully stopped yowling. As they pulled up to the cottage, the door swung open and Sabrina stood on the threshold. Farmer Walsh elbowed him. "Your young bride is happy to see you, sir." The farmer gave him a wink.

Was she? As usual, her expression was shuttered, though the light from the parlor illuminated her enough that he was able to see a small smile curved about her lovely lips. *God.* His heart leapt at the sight of her. He was tempted to jump down from the wagon and run to her, pull her into his arms, kiss her with every scorching sensation tearing through him. Tamping down his arousal, he slid from the bench seat and assisted Farmer Walsh in unloading the wagon. Holding out the pie as an offering, he approached Sabrina and kissed her on the cheek. "From Mrs. Walsh."

"How kind," she murmured. More loudly she said, "Farmer Walsh, do thank your wife. Kind of both of you."

The farmer touched his forelock and carried the items into the cottage. After saying their goodbyes, Sabrina and Riordan were left alone in the parlor. Riordan reached for the covered basket and held it out toward her. "For you. I thought you would like a little company during the afternoons."

Her brows furrowed as she took the hamper and lifted the lid. A loud meow emitted from it. She gasped, then dropped the lid. Thrusting it in his hands, she turned and fled.

Damn it all. What had happened? Then it struck him. She was overwhelmed. He placed the basket on the floor. "Stay. We will be returning." Pulling off his coat and muffler, he tossed them onto the chaise longue and headed to the bedroom. The door was closed—he tried the handle—but not locked. Turning it, he entered the room and found Sabrina with her back to him, staring at the flames dancing in the small fireplace.

He walked up behind her and gently placed his hands on her shoulders. "It's all right to feel, Sabrina. To show emotion." He nuzzled her neck, and to his genuine pleasure, she did not shrink away from him.

"No one has ever given me such a thoughtful gift before," she whispered. "Not ever."

Riordan turned her to face him and lifted her chin with the tips of his fingers in order for their gazes to meet. Tears streamed down her cheeks and his heart clenched in response. Cupping her face, he soothingly brushed away her tears with the pads of his thumbs. "I can convey, based on personal experience, that there is nothing lovelier than reading by the fire with a pet cuddled up next to you. I believe you and Mittens will become fast friends."

"Mittens?"

"You may name her whatever you wish. Farmer Walsh tells me she is about four months old. Completely trained to use a box of sand for her doings, a house cat in all ways. His wife suffered a form of hay fever and the poor thing was banished to the barn—the kitten, not Mrs. Walsh."

A small giggle escaped Sabrina.

"Ah. There. The beginnings of a laugh." He kissed her, but kept it brief. Before he ended it, she actually kissed him in return. A soft pressing, a searching, and he was sorely tempted to take it deeper. *Patience.* The kiss ended on her sigh, and he pulled her close to his rapidly beating heart.

Sabrina slipped her arms about his waist and embraced him in return. They stood together for interminable minutes, until finally he said, "Shall we introduce Mittens to her new home? She may become distressed if we leave her in the basket for much longer."

"Thank you again. Only I know next to nothing about having a pet," she whispered.

He kissed the top of her head, and her enchanting citrus scent surrounded him. He was fully aroused—there was no hiding it, and he didn't even bother to try. Daringly, he rolled his hips, and his erection pressed closer against her thigh. Sabrina gazed up at him, her expression questioning. "You do this to me every time you're near, whenever I kiss you or hold you. I cannot control it, nor do I wish to," he revealed.

"You want me?" Her tone was incredulous.

"Yes. Desperately. But I will abide by your boundaries." To show that he meant what he said, he released her and took a couple of steps in reverse. It was one of the hardest things he'd ever done.

Her gaze rolled over him, lingering on his obvious hard shaft pressing against the fall of his trousers. Then, as her cheeks flushed a deeper crimson, she met his eyes. "In the past," she began, her voice barely above a whisper, "a man in such a state filled me with abhorrence. With you? I feel…none of it."

A spark of hope took root deep inside him. "Do you wish to discuss it?"

"Not tonight, but…soon. Perhaps later in the week."

Riordan would not push her. Instead, he held out his hand. "Let us see your cat settled and find us a bite of supper."

Another brief, slight smile. And perhaps an expression of relief. Sabrina took his hand and they headed for the parlor. Riordan picked up the basket. Opening it, Sabrina peered in. "She's beautiful."

"Take a seat and I'll pass her to you." Sabrina did as instructed. Taking great care not to spook the feline, Riordan lifted Mittens from her wicker imprisonment and held her close, speaking in soothing tones to calm the trembling animal. "She's nervous, no doubt glad to be out of the barn, but not sure where she is and why. Don't be alarmed if Mittens struggles or lashes out. Don't take it personally."

Riordan passed the kitten to Sabrina. The animal stared up at her with its large green eyes as if asking for her love and acceptance. "Go ahead and pet her, scratch under her chin," he instructed. Sabrina did and was rewarded with loud purring. A brief giggle left her throat and the sound was glorious. "Where shall we set up her bed, here or in your room?"

Still petting the kitten, she gazed up at him. "Oh, my room. Next to the fireplace. What is the other container and the sand for?"

"As I stated earlier, Mittens is a house cat. She cannot be allowed outside on her own. She will be doing her business in the sandbox, and it will have to be cleaned daily. There is a lot of responsibility to having a pet. Are you willing to take it on? If not, I can find another home for Mittens."

Sabrina hugged the kitten tighter. "No. I will take on the duty of caring for her."

With a broad smile, Riordan motioned toward the kitten. "Allow her to explore and become acquainted with her new home."

Sabrina seemed reluctant to let the kitten go, but when she did Mittens immediately moved about the parlor, taking in her surroundings.

"We should have supper."

Jumping up from the chair, Sabrina clasped her hands together. "Allow me. You've had a long journey. Take a seat at the table."

"Are you sure?"

She nodded and hurried toward the kitchen. To be honest, he was fatigued—but not enough to dissipate his arousal. Blast, how could he function in this condition for the next two months? Eventually they would have to talk about it. Her past. Their feelings. And their future. By God, he wanted one with her.

Sabrina hurried toward the table with a plate and utensils and set them before him. "Mrs. Ingersoll brought cold ham slices and salad, easy enough to prepare." She was pleased with herself. No doubt the first time she had ever waited on someone. "I'll slice the bread—Mary showed me this afternoon, along with how to cut and serve a pie. Would you care for a glass of cold water from the pump?" She gave him another small smile. "I've learned how to use it as well."

"Thank you, I would." This from the spoiled woman of the peerage. What strides she had made toward her independence! After a couple of trips to the kitchen area, Sabrina sat opposite. "You probably would have preferred a hot meal."

Riordan cut into the thick slice of ham. "Not at all. I ate a hearty brunch before departing. This is perfect. Especially served by you."

"Do you mind if I ask a question?'

"Of course not."

"Does your father own a factory? Did you attend university? I know next to nothing about you. I would like to learn more."

Damn. He laid his utensils across his plate. Thus far, he'd managed to deflect her queries with vague truths. How to answer?

"He doesn't own it, but has an important position. And yes, I did attend university, thanks to the generosity of a peer." Not a lie; his grandfather had paid for his education at Cambridge. "Frankly, I don't see why you wish to know more when we will be parting in about two months. I'm not one for talking about myself."

She gave him a puzzled look. "Well, I only wished to start a conversation. If you would rather not talk about it, then we will not."

"Not tonight, at any rate."

Mittens began meowing loudly at their feet. Riordan was grateful for the distraction.

"I should feed her. What does one give a growing kitten?" Sabrina asked.

"Cats need meat, even more than dogs. We must inform Mrs. Ingersoll to add Mittens to the daily meal plans. We used to feed our indoor cats twice a day, meat mashed up with potato and water or milk. Or fish. There are cat meat sellers in the larger cities. They sell horse meat and other scraps especially for cats."

"Horse meat?" Sabrina cried, clearly horrified.

"Well, yes. Horses that die of injury or old age are often sent to the abattoir, their meat put to good use for other animals."

Sabrina gave Mittens a strange look.

"She's a carnivore. If she was an outdoor cat, she would be hunting for her supper. Still want to keep the little beast?" He gave Sabrina a teasing wink.

Her look softened. "Yes. I want to keep her. She's darling. As are you, for gifting her to me."

Damn. His heart melted. If he were able, he'd cut open his chest and hand it over to her. For she owned it. Completely. He was in love. Absolutely smitten. It tore him in two that he was keeping secrets, but he was doing it to protect her. Because he loved her. He would not see her hurt for the world. How to convince her that she deserved to be loved more than anyone he'd ever known?

Chapter 19

Sabrina's soul was decidedly lighter when she awoke the next morning. Though she didn't wake of her own accord; Mittens's meowing did the trick, but Sabrina was not the least bit annoyed. Somehow, the last pieces of the protective wall she'd built around her heart were crumbling away.

Though vulnerable, it was also exhilarating. Her emotions, often confused of late, demonstrated clarity of purpose. Her self-confidence, battered most of her life, had been repairing itself the past few years, and since meeting Riordan repairs had accelerated and now she was fully healed. All was right with the world.

Mary was certainly shocked to find a kitten making itself at home, curled up on the small scatter rug before the fireplace in the parlor. "Mr. Black bought her for you? Oh, my," Mary murmured. *Oh, my indeed.* She gathered the kitten into her arms and nuzzled its silky fur. Already she loved this sweet-tempered feline.

The marriage to Pepperdon had done its damage, but she refused to allow it to ruin what remained of her life. Nor would she cling to the belief that her heart was so battered she would never feel again. She had believed she was unworthy of love, considering no one had showed her any different. But that was a self-pitying path she no longer wished to travel—Riordan had showed her another way to journey. As did Mary.

Embracing life and what lay ahead would be her new focus. Damn Pepperdon, and her father. Damn every horrid memory those terrible men perpetrated.

"My lady?"

Mary's voice brought her to the present. "Sorry, I was woolgathering."

"Would you like another piece of raisin pie?"

Sabrina placed her teacup on the table. "No, thank you, but cut a slice and wrap it in brown paper. I'll take it to Riordan. He still has thirty minutes of his luncheon break remaining. I will walk with you as far as the school." She glanced at the sleeping Mittens. "Will she be all right alone for awhile?"

"I believe so, my lady. The kitten has settled in fine. Though my duties at the inn do not include the kitchen, I'll see if I can collect a few scraps of meat and fish and bring them with me tonight."

"Wonderful."

Mary halted in clearing the table and gazed at Sabrina intently. "You seem different this morning, my lady."

"Do I? In a good way, I hope." Mary nodded and smiled. "I've had enough of allowing miserable excuses for men to rule my life."

"Good for you, my lady. And Mr. Black?"

"Gaining my independence means I will make my own decisions. I trust Riordan. He has not lied to me, not once. I care for him; I will not deny it any longer." Sabrina stood and gathered up the remaining luncheon dishes. "Will you show me how to make an apple pie tomorrow?"

"If you wish, my lady."

"I do. And Mary, please call me Sabrina. I'm not married to an earl any longer, and I'm blessedly thankful for it. I want to dismiss Lady Pepperdon forever."

Mary's brows furrowed. "But as a widow you're permitted to continue to use the title, even if you remarry, which you did, however temporarily."

"I'm entitled, but I've decided to put the past behind me, and I will put the title there as well. Besides, we *are* friends, Mary. Well past time we acknowledged it." She laid her hand on her maid's shoulder. "Let us toss away the lady and servant roles we wear. If you wish, tell anyone who asks that you are my companion and friend, which is the complete truth."

Mary remained silent, her face showing myriad emotions. "I would like us to think of each other as friends…Sabrina."

Sabrina smiled. "Excellent. We move forward together, come what may. Now, we had better depart."

Mary took the dishes from Sabrina's hand. "I'll wrap the pie and gather my cloak."

"And I will fetch my own cloak. See? Independence," Sabrina said. Mary laughed and hurried toward the kitchen.

Moments later, they headed toward the school. Mary waved goodbye as she continued toward town. Entering the school, Sabrina passed through the alcove into the main room. There sat Riordan at his desk, a pile of papers and slates before him. Her heart swelled at the sight of him, his thick, black-as-midnight hair falling across his forehead as he bent over his work. "Good afternoon, Riordan."

He glanced up, and a broad, warm smile curved about his sensual lips. And they were sensual—the bottom lip a little plumper than the top. Ideal for kissing. "To what do I owe this distinct pleasure?" he asked.

She held up the wrapped bundle. "Pie. And I longed to see you."

A look of genuine surprise flashed across his attractive features. He tossed aside his pen and stood. Sabrina was drawn closer to him, as if an invisible thread held them together. He took the pie and set it on his desk, then, without any warning, cupped her face and kissed her. Deeply. She opened and let him in and their tongues clashed. Sabrina grasped the lapels of his coat, pulling him closer.

For once, she held nothing back, kissing him in return with great relish. When a husky moan left the corner of his mouth, the glorious sound caused her to moan in return. This ignited the simmering passion between them. Riordan moved his hands down to her waist, cupped her buttocks, and brought her in against his erection.

She gasped in surprise, pausing to savor the feel of his hard body. Desire flared within as she continued with her thorough and complete exploration of every part of his hot mouth. He rotated his slim hips, and she could feel his hard shaft through the layers of clothes. Following his lead, she rubbed against him, causing another moan to slip from his throat. Her insides were on fire, her breasts heavy, and a distinct yearning throbbed in her feminine core.

Riordan broke the kiss, resting his forehead against hers. His breathing was as ragged and uneven as hers. "I am tempted to push everything off the desk, lay you upon it, and kiss and caress every part of your body." He exhaled. "Forgive me."

"No."

He pulled away and caught her gaze. Arching an eyebrow, he said, "No?"

"I mean no, do not apologize. I want this. I want more. Tonight, we should talk. Can we?"

"Yes." He kissed the tip of her nose.

"I should go; your students will be returning shortly."

Riordan chuckled. "Quite the condition you are leaving me in."

Sabrina buttoned his frock coat. "There. No one will guess. If you come home for lunch tomorrow, perhaps you can steal another kiss."

"With Mary there?" he laughed.

"I believe she will leave us alone. Riordan, this is all new to me. Can you bear with me?" She glanced up into those beautiful blue eyes—they glistened with deep emotion.

He stroked her cheek. "For you, I can wait an eternity."

"Good answer, Mr. Black." With a sigh of contentment, she stood on the tips of her toes and kissed him. She nibbled on his delicious full bottom lip before stepping away. "I'll see you tonight. I hear roast chicken is on the menu for supper. Enjoy your pie."

Sabrina turned, hurried out of the schoolroom, and, lifting her skirt, ran to the side of the building where she'd first discovered the passionate schoolmaster. She waited patiently. The window was open far enough to hear the happy voices of children as they filed into the room after their luncheon.

Riordan's deep, melodious voice filled her hearing, causing shivers of awareness to cascade along her spine. "Children, let us pick up where we left off before the break: English folk music. Now, much of it originated during the medieval period. Anyone remember when it was? Yes, Becky?"

"Between the fifth and fifteenth centuries?"

"Yes, well done. We refer to it as The Middle Ages, as it is the middle period of three divisional eras of Western history. One popular melody that has stood the test of time is "Greensleeves." Does anyone know of it?"

There were mixed answers, most saying no. A young lad called out, "Sing it for us, sir!"

Other voices joined in encouraging Riordan. "Very well," he said. "I'm not sure I will do it justice." He cleared his throat, then sang: "Alas my love, you do me wrong, to cast me off discourteously. And I have loved you oh so long, delighting in your company…."

Riordan's voice was clear, pristine, and harmonious. His deep tone gave the tune vibrancy and, to her, a decided sensual cadence. Tears formed in her eyes. He could sing. In her mind, he was close to perfection. However, no one was perfect. If he harbored any dark secrets or serious flaws, she'd yet to discover them. There must be one, for that nagging sensation he was keeping secrets had never left her.

But any man who could stand before a room full of children and encourage them to learn and envision the world around them and inspire and shape their minds…she could not imagine a nobler calling, nor a more honorable man. How she admired and respected Riordan. And here, outside his classroom window, listening to his voice as it rose in song, she fell irrevocably in love with him.

* * * *

It was not ideal to teach a class of students when aroused. Thankfully, Riordan had managed to dismiss his desire before his students returned. The teasing minx, showing up in his schoolroom with pie and devastating kisses. What had come over her? Whatever it was, he liked it. And when he sang "Greensleeves," the lyrics held a deeper meaning to him personally.

Riordan did not waste any time packing up his papers and hurrying home after ringing the dismissal bell. No lingering about the schoolroom to correct tests tonight—he wanted to know what Sabrina wished to talk about. Once he entered the cottage and ensured Mrs. Ingersoll was not lurking about the kitchen, he pulled Sabrina into his arms and kissed her fiercely, not only because he yearned for it, but to see if she would kiss him in return as passionately as she had earlier.

Riordan was not disappointed. They broke apart after several searing moments. "We should eat," Sabrina said breathlessly.

Food? Who could think of food? "Yes. Roast chicken, you said?"

"Mrs. Ingersoll departed not ten minutes before you arrived. Allow me to serve you before the food cools off any further." Sabrina scurried to the kitchen area.

Hell. He was hard again. Taking his seat, he winced and adjusted himself. Being in a perpetual state of arousal was damned uncomfortable, and embarrassing. So much for his self-control in most situations. It had certainly abandoned him here.

Sabrina reentered the parlor and set a hearty meal before him. Mittens meowed loudly, no doubt smelling the food. Riordan reached down and scratched the kitten on the head. "How is Mittens fitting into your routine?"

"We're managing well. You were correct."

"About?"

"Nothing like having a pet curled up beside you as you read. It is how we passed part of the afternoon."

"Were you reading *Wuthering Heights*?" he asked.

"No. It's a book Mary gave me, *The Bold Seduction of Miss Featherstone.* Perhaps we can read from it when we've finished our meal."

Bold seduction? Sabrina was full of surprises.

"Excuse me, Mittens is insisting I serve her next." Sabrina disappeared, and when she returned she carried her own plate, then lowered a smaller one to the floor, which the kitten immediately ran for.

Sabrina chuckled at the feline's enthusiasm. Taking her seat, Riordan took in her flushed, happy face. He'd never seen her like this. Relaxed. Content. "I cut up a little chicken, mixed with potatoes I mashed with a fork, a little squash, and water. Look how she is devouring it."

Riordan took a bite of his own food. "I agree with Mittens. Delicious."

During most of the meal, they exchanged small talk. He told her of his afternoon as a little smile curled about her lips.

Pushing his empty plate away, he said, "You wished to talk? May I ask about what? Or would you rather we read first?"

Sabrina dabbed her mouth with a napkin and laid it on top of her plate. "Talk first. Last night, I mentioned that I used to find a man in an aroused state abhorrent. I'm ready to tell you why, because I want you to understand about my past, and perhaps then you will be willing to discuss yours." He winced inwardly at the direct hit.

"The marriage to Pepperdon was arranged. I was eighteen, innocent beyond measure, with no mother or female relative to give me any instruction on what to expect on the wedding night." Sabrina sighed. "Who could I turn to? Not my father, though he barked I must submit to my husband in all things. I was not given a season, and as a result, my experience with men was nonexistent. The marriage took place within ten days of my first meeting Pepperdon."

"Good God," Riordan said. He didn't like the direction of this, for he had an inkling of what would come next.

"Imagine my disappointment at finding a gray-haired man of fifty-five years waiting to greet me. The earl had a pleasing enough face, along with a slight paunch and hair thinning on the top. My father wished me to marry this peer; how could I say no? If he was kind, we might tumble along well enough. Or so I thought." Sabrina snorted, her expression darkened. "Charles Lakeside, Earl of Pepperdon, was the furthest thing from kind. After an elaborate church wedding and a brief breakfast reception, he dismissed the guests, dragged me to his bedroom, ripped my wedding gown from my trembling body and brutally raped me."

Riordan banged the table with his fist, the fury building in him dangerous and potent. Blast her father and Pepperdon to hell!

"He left me crying hysterically and all alone. No one came to my aid. Mary was not yet my maid, not until a couple of days after. Pepperdon returned twice more. I'll not go into details, as you can well imagine them. The first few months were horrible. He wanted an heir, and spent his free time, when he was able to perform, trying to accomplish it."

"Jesus. Sabrina..."

She held up her hand. "No pity, please."

"It's not pity, but empathy. There is a difference." His blood boiled. "The damned arrogance of men. The mistreatment women endure, with no legal rights to see its end, is a blight on society." He banged his fist again, and his water glass tipped over. Sabrina flinched at the sudden movement. "I didn't mean to startle you; I am furious you were treated in such a vile manner."

"It took me several months to realize that my fighting and screaming as he pounded into me merely stoked his lust. Eventually I lay still and did not utter a peep. After the first year, it became obvious I would not become pregnant easily, and his trips to my bed gradually lessened. But not his frustration."

"What do you mean?"

"Pepperdon decided humiliating me would be ample punishment for not allowing his ancient seed to take root. He subjected me to acts…." Sabrina crammed her fist in her mouth.

His heart ached for her. He started to reply, but Sabrina said, "Let me finish, while I have the courage. By the end of our fifth year of marriage, he stopped coming to me. My indifference with the sex act finally caused him to lose all interest in me, thank God. I was left in peace at last. Weeks would go by without seeing him, which was fine with me. But the damage was done."

Sabrina clasped her hands in her lap and met his gaze. "The remaining six years of my marriage allowed me to…heal. Physically and emotionally. Mary assisted me. I crawled out of the abyss, rebuilt my confidence, but built a wall about my heart, for I vowed no man would ever hurt me again. In any way. For if any man does hurt me, it will be an unforgiveable act."

A definite warning. Here was the opportunity to confess about the settlement. There was still a chance she would choose to leave and live her life free and clear of him—and because of that, the lie remained, in order for her to have money for the future. This was all for her future, her protection—yet an uneasy feeling settled deep inside him.

As far as her marriage, it explained why she had shrunk from his touch when they first met. If her foul excuse for a husband wasn't already dead, he would have seen it done.

"For six years I held a death watch. Imagine my surprise when Pepperdon actually did die. I don't know from what; I was never told. Regardless, I was relieved and happy—until the reading of the will. One last humiliation, to leave me with nothing. His toad of a nephew, his heir, could not show me the door quickly enough. I had no choice but to return to my father. You know the rest."

"Sabrina, saying that I'm deeply sorry you were subjected to the worst instincts of man is hardly adequate. Most men do not act in such a vile way. Well, at least those in my acquaintance." But he knew there were men like her father and late husband; he'd heard stories from his father and grandfather of their many dealings with such entitled, arrogant men in London.

"Thank you for saying sorry; it helps." Sabrina exhaled. "I'd like to put this behind me, starting tonight. Shall we read?"

"Of course, if you wish."

She hurried from the room, leaving him stunned. And humbled. She trusted him enough to reveal her past. Guilt also took hold, for he was not being honest with her about a number of subjects. Distracted, he placed the wooden chairs close to the fire.

Sabrina returned and handed him the book. "I have a piece of paper marking the page." Taking her seat, she gazed at him expectantly.

Considering Miss Featherstone was plain of features, she fairly sparkled when she smiled. Her large, expressive eyes reflected her changing emotions. Never had Sebastian been drawn to a woman like this before. Perhaps it was her inner beauty, which attracted him most of all—though she did possess glorious curves and full breasts. Enough with stolen kisses; he wanted more. As he pulled her toward the darkened balcony, the sounds of the ball they'd just deserted faded to the background.

Riordan glanced at Sabrina. She hung on his every word. Should he continue? Why not?

"My dearest, I must touch you." Riordan read, as he deepened his voice to a husky whisper, acting the part of the hero. *Sebastian tunneled his hands under the layers of silk, groaning when the tips of his fingers brushed by the slit in her drawers. "You are passionate, ready for my touch." Pushing two fingers deep inside her, Miss Featherstone gasped at the invasion, then sighed contentedly. Faster he thrust, his thumb stroking her arousal. "Come apart in my arms. Come for me, my dearest." God, he was hard, his shaft throbbing with want. He wanted inside her, but surprisingly, he found he wanted her heart more.*

Hell. He was aroused as well. He caught Sabrina's gaze. Her breathing was shallow, clear proof of her own arousal. If he read any more, he'd explode.

"Reading this book has taught me much. The touch of a man does not have to be abhorrent," she stated breathlessly.

"No. It does not."

"I believed I would never enjoy the touch of a man. But I enjoy yours. And your kisses. There *is* something between us."

Once more, those sparks ignited and burned with an intense heat. "Yes. There is. With patience and care, it could be quite wonderful," he replied, his voice hoarse.

"Will you be patient with me? Understand if I shrink away that it is not because of you, but because horrible memories are intruding on the present?" Her hazel eyes held him in thrall, almost pleading. He could not refuse her anything. "You see, I wish for what I revealed to you to become a firm part of my past. I don't want my late husband or father to have control over my life."

Riordan's heart beat fiercely against his chest. "Yes to both questions. Together we will banish those lingering memories. I yearn to show you what bliss can be found in lovemaking. I can teach you…how to love."

Chapter 20

The air was thick and heavy with emotion from their intimate conversation. '*I can teach you...how to love.*' His huskily spoken words reverberated in her heart, causing it to beat faster. She'd been bold, first by asking him to read from the book, then inviting him to move beyond kissing. Could they do this and part when the annulment was final? To be honest, she wasn't sure she still wanted the annulment. Why not explore their feelings and see where it would lead?

Mittens remained oblivious to the intense emotions swirling about the room, since she was fast asleep on the rug in front of the fire. Sliding her gaze to Riordan, Sabrina met his smoldering look. "How will you teach me? Where do we begin?"

He closed the book and set it aside. "Tonight. Here. I'll be taking a bath. Stay in the parlor with me." Previous nights, she'd retired to her bedroom. But it did not stop her from imagining him. To actually witness him bathe caused another blast of heat to settle in her feminine core.

"And do what?" Her voice was raspy, her breathing uneven.

Riordan hooked his boot under the chair rung and pulled her closer. The legs of the chair scraped noisily across the wood floor. "We'll fill the tub. Then, you will undress me. Slowly. As you remove each piece of clothing, you will touch me, become used to my body. Observe how I respond to your touch." His eyes were half lidded, his look entirely sensuous. "I wish for you to understand that I will never harm you. I respect you too much. I care for you…more than I should." He repeated the movement with his boot, pulling her chair nearer until they were inches apart. "I'm falling for you, Sabrina."

Words failed her. His light blue eyes glowed with sapphire fire. She nodded, her breath coming in short gasps as every part of her body throbbed with yearning. *Heavens.* He was falling for her. The prospect thrilled her to her toes. She returned the sentiment a hundredfold, but could not put voice to it yet, for her deep-rooted vulnerability bade caution.

"We must trust each other. Without trust, there cannot be...love." He took her hand and laid it flat against his chest. His heart pounded fiercely under her palm. "Do not allow my confession to scare you. Let us discover. Open our hearts. Bare our souls."

A lump of emotion lodged in her throat as her eyes welled with tears. His passionately spoken words moved her. "Yes," she whispered. "Discover."

"Once I climb into the bath, I wish for you to continue to touch me," he murmured. An image formed in her mind, of him standing before her completely naked. What was the word in the bold seduction book? *Resplendent.* How it fit Riordan. "And wash all my bits," he winked, using her jesting words from their marriage night. "If you wish, grab my shaft and stroke me to completion." His heart sped up, as did hers. Her cheeks flushed red-hot. "Have I shocked you? Disgusted you?"

How surprising to find he hadn't. "No. Not at all."

Still grasping her hand, he slid it down his torso until it lay on his erection straining against the fall of his trousers. "This part of me is not a weapon, nor a means to hurt and humiliate. This part of me will bring you pleasure. I will not brutalize or hurt you. Instead, I'll show you how desire can enhance existing emotions. We'll move forward at *your* pace. Any time you wish to stop, say the word." He squeezed their hands, and the thickness of him caused her to moan. "Shall we begin?"

"Yes. Begin."

Riordan kissed her hand, then stood. He turned on his heel and headed to the door, opened it, then stepped outside, no doubt to fetch the copper tub. She quickly gathered the dishes and hurried to the kitchen. After placing them on the sideboard, she grasped the edge of the counter, trying to catch her breath.

Sabrina was aroused, and relieved to find that what Riordan described had not filled her with abhorrence. Images of the past tried to push into her mind—Pepperdon's cold hands roughly grasping her breasts. Him forcing his...his—he called it a cock—into her mouth until she choked. No. The contemptible earl would not ruin this evening, nor dominate her thoughts. *Be gone, you miserable reprobate. I no longer fear you.* Taking gulps of air, she exhaled as she primed the pump. Locating the kettle, she filled it with water and placed in on the stove.

Unfortunately, she did not know how to light it yet. Riordan entered, efficiently lit the stove, filled a bucket, and carried it to the parlor. Together they filled the tub with a mixture of cool water from the pump and hot water from the stove. The copper tub stood in front of the fire. Mittens, who had awakened during all the activity, sauntered off to Sabrina's room, no doubt to continue her nap undisturbed.

They faced each other. "Take off my clothes," Riordan said, his voice as rough as sandpaper. Sabrina stepped closer. He'd already removed his frock coat before supper. Her trembling fingers fumbled with his neckcloth. Once unknotted, she tossed it aside.

Next, his waistcoat. After slipping the brass buttons through the holes, she pushed it from his shoulders, but not before trailing her hands across his broad chest. Muscle flexed under her touch. The garment dropped to the floor. Then she concentrated on his shirt. It was finely made, with porcelain buttons and a high collar. The material soft to the touch. Cotton perhaps?

Pushing the sides of his unbuttoned shirt, she gazed at his bare chest. He did not wear an undershirt—how scandalous. How delicious. Delineated planes of taut muscle hugged his torso, swirls of curly black hair spread across his chest and around his nipples. They were as hard as hers. She flicked one with the pad of her thumb and Riordan shuddered, a low groan escaping his throat.

Slowly and with concentrated purpose, she slid his shirt from his shoulders, her hands moving across his muscled biceps. With the tip of her finger, she followed a prominent vein that ran along the length of his arm. His skin, silky and warm to the touch, made her insides flutter with anticipation. "You are…well-made." Sabrina took her time, trailing her hands across his chest and down his arms. Pulling his shirt from his shoulders, she admired the view. Never had she seen a man her own age in such a state of undress. She'd had no idea a man could look like this: masculine, muscular. Enticing.

The garment hung at his elbows, then Riordan straightened his arms and allowed it to fall to the floor next to the waistcoat. *Stunning specimen.* Thankfully, he looked nothing like Pepperdon, which helped to further banish past memories.

Once she looked her fill, Sabrina all but threw herself at him, giving him a fierce embrace as she'd done before. Her breasts, already full and heavy, smashed against his bare chest. He stood absolutely still, but took sharp breaths as she reached behind him and traced the valley of his spine and explored his muscled back. Inhaling his masculine, musky scent, she moaned, completely lost in sensations.

His trousers were next. *Not a weapon. He will not hurt me.* Repeating the phrases over and over until she gathered her courage, she released Riordan and took two steps in reverse.

As she reached for the waistband, he clasped her hand, halting her. "Wait."

Sabrina gazed up at him. "I'm ready to do this."

He gave her a sensual smile. "I am gratified to hear it. Only I should remove my boots and stockings first."

"Oh. Of course." She returned his smile with a shy one of her own. Riordan sat on the chair and quickly removed the items. Lord. Even his bare feet were elegant, if feet could be described as such. He jumped up and faced her. "Please, continue." He lifted her hand to his lips and kissed it. "Please." The pleading tone in his voice sent sparks along her nerve endings.

"Since you asked politely." She pulled her hand from his and with rapid efficiency undid the buttons of his fall. *Steady on.* Without hesitating, she gave his wool trousers a tug until they dropped to the floor. All he wore was his drawers. There was no denying his arousal, as his shaft lay thick and heavy and clearly outlined against him. Curious, she grasped him, and he released a low rumble sounding suspiciously like an animal growl. The heat emanating from his shaft set the palm of her hand on fire.

Oh, she wanted to hear that wild sound again. She squeezed him and ran her hand along his length and was rewarded with another husky groan. His bath was growing cold. Grasping the waistband of the silk drawers, she gave them a yank and they pooled at his feet. Riordan stepped out of them and kicked them aside.

Every nerve ending in her body crackled with awareness. Drinking in his form, Sabrina's intense gaze scanned him head to toe and back again. How wonderful it must be to be completely confident in one's own skin. Broad shoulders tapered to a slim waist and lean, muscular hips.

Shamelessly, her gaze slid to the most masculine part of him. He was hard; his shaft stood straight up on his stomach. It was part of Riordan, and because of that she did not fear it. "Shall you climb into the bath so I can...wash you?" Her own voice was hoarse, her own arousal plain to hear.

"All is well, Sabrina?"

Bless him, he looked genuinely concerned. "More than well."

He sat in the tub, leaning against the back of it. Though the tub was large, he could not stretch out his long legs. Instead, he bent them at the knees. Resting his arms on the sides of the tub, he motioned his head toward the table. "The soap and flannel are there."

She lifted the soap to her nose and inhaled. *Yes. All Riordan.* The lime and bergamot scent she adored. Sitting in the chair Riordan had placed next to the tub, she dipped the soap and flannel into the warm water. Already her body thrummed with sensual alertness; if she continued to touch and caress him she would surely combust. Besides a lone oil lamp, the fire cast the only illumination in the parlor, making Riordan's skin glow with a golden luminescence.

With slow circles, she scrubbed his chest, trailing the lathered cloth across his shoulders and down his arms. Riordan closed his eyes, as if reveling in her touch. Sabrina continued for several moments, enjoying the quiet intimacy they shared. "Lean forward."

He did, and she continued her journey across his shoulders and down his back. For a schoolmaster who sat at his desk a good portion of his day, he was athletically built. Holding his arm, she trailed along it to the faint ink stains and calluses on the tips of his long and elegant fingers. A hazard of his occupation. He opened his eyes. "Touch me."

Innately she understood what he meant. Part of his shaft lay exposed above the water line, standing straight up against his flat stomach. Sabrina rolled up her sleeve, reached in the tepid water, and grasped him.

"Jesus. Yes. Tighter," he pleaded.

She obliged, and gave it a tentative caress, the head disappearing under the hood of skin. A long, ragged groan tore from Riordan's throat. "Here, allow me to show you." He laid his hand on top of hers and demonstrated the way he wished for her to stroke him. "It will not take long, I assure you."

Nodding, she bit her lower lip and gave his shaft short, quick strokes, twisting it as she did. He let go of her hand, his eyes closed, every cord in his neck strained. A deep red flush spread across his chest. He did not remain quiet, he groaned and said, "Yes. Faster. Grip my cock, tighter. More."

Regardless of the fact that he'd used the same naughty word as her late husband, her insides tumbled with desire. How satisfying to learn she had truly put the past behind her. With his head thrown back, he cried out, the sound ending on a moan that caused her heart to beat at a fast pace. He clasped the top of his shaft, his body shuddering with his release. How magnificent he looked. Fetching the cloth from the water, Riordan took her hand and wiped it clean, then cleaned himself. As he stood, the water sluiced across his muscled body.

He pointed to the towel on the nearby table and she handed it to him. Keeping her gaze on him, Sabrina observed the play of muscles as he dried his body. With the towel wrapped around his waist, he stepped out of the tub. Heavens. Now what?

As if reading her mind, he held out his hand. She took it and stood. Pulling her closer, he smiled at her, his eyes hooded, his expression sultry. "This is just the beginning," he murmured.

The beginning of what, exactly? How could they share such closeness and part ways in a little more than two months' time? Perhaps they *could* make this arrangement permanent. He'd not mentioned it since their wedding day. But it was worth discussing, especially if her feelings continued to deepen and grow. After the cruel, cold men in her life, why not embrace a good, honorable man? One she respected, admired, desired...and loved.

Yes, she loved him. Her heart soared with the knowledge.

* * * *

The next morning, Sabrina woke early, gathered pen, ink, and paper, and made her way to the dining table in the parlor. Riordan was still asleep, sprawled across the chaise longue, his bare chest exposed, blankets pooled around his waist. Was he completely naked beneath? She watched him for several moments, his chest rising and falling as his breath exhaled in short puffs. He looked like a dark angel with his black hair tousled and his fine form on display.

Staring at him, drinking in his beauty, caused her to recall every heated moment of the previous night. For years she'd thought herself dead inside because her late husband did not stir passion in her. Why would he? He was a rapist. A violator of innocence. Sabrina understood that for means of self-preservation she'd buried her emotions deep; Riordan had set them free. For once in her life an actual choice lay before her: leave with Mary once the annulment comes through, or build a life with the schoolmaster.

Sighing, she dipped the pen in the ink. Sabrina had decided to write an anonymous note to the second daughter of the Duke of Carlton, her father's innocent target. Mary had informed her the young girl's name was Irene.

With long, cursive strokes she wrote: *To Lady Irene, I begin this letter to inform you of the character of Baron Thomas Durning, who I am told is presently courting you. I wish to warn you, my lady, of his true character.*

Mittens meowed loudly at her feet. "Oh, precious." She picked up the kitten and nuzzled it. "You're hungry."

"As am I," a deep voice rumbled from across the room. She turned. Riordan sat on the edge of the chaise wearing nothing but his silk drawers and rubbing his eyes.

"For food, I take it?" she teased.

"I will settle for food." He winked as he stretched his arms above his head. Such was the closeness between them that he did not cover himself and she was not the least bit offended—quite the opposite. A frisson of awareness shot through her as she stared at his stunning form. "God, is that the time? I've slept later than I intended." He stood and strode to the small cupboard. Opening the door wide, he pulled pieces of clothing from it. As he dressed, he asked, "Whom are you writing?"

Writing? Oh, yes. He had distracted her from her letter. Placing Mittens on the floor, she replied, "I'm writing an anonymous letter to the young lady my father is courting, to advise her of his true character. Of course, I will not sign my name."

Riordan buttoned his shirt. "Do you think it wise?"

She frowned. "I cannot sit here and do nothing. Subject another innocent young girl to my earlier fate. I could not live with myself if I did not at least warn her."

Riordan rushed about the room, gathering his frock coat, hat, and muffler. "I agree. I suggest you keep it brief, reveal nothing that will hint at your identity."

"Good advice. Wait, you must have food."

He leaned down and kissed her cheek. "There are biscuits and an apple in my desk drawer. Enough to get me through to the noon break. I'll be home for lunch…and a proper kiss."

"I can give you a proper kiss now," she teased. How easily she could tease, when mere weeks ago she did not have the wherewithal to go about it.

"Minx. You do and I will not be in a fit state to teach children." A loud knock caught his attention. "Must be Mary, I *am* late. Goodbye." He trailed a finger down her cheek and gave her such a tender look that her heart skipped a beat. Riordan flung open the front door, said good morning to Mary, and dashed outside.

"Goodness, it's as if flames licked at his heels," Mary marveled. "Mr. Black is usually gone before I arrive."

"Yes, he is running late."

Mary closed the door and removed her cloak. "You look happy this morning, Sabrina."

How wonderful that Mary used her name. "I am. It is utterly marvelous to have choices in one's life. Women have no power at all in this suffocating society; it is gratifying to know I alone will choose the path I wish take."

Mary folded the blankets from the chaise and placed them in the cupboard. "Things are progressing with Mr. Black?"

Sabrina turned to face her. "Yes. I believe I am in love with him."

Mary's eyes widened. "You're seriously considering keeping this arrangement permanent?"

"Yes...I'm considering it. No matter what I decide, I want you with me. Of course, you may make your own decision. Your life is your own as well, Mary." She sighed wistfully. "But first, I must discover more about Riordan's circumstances. He reveals little, and it concerns me." She crossed her arms. "The quality of his clothes, for example. The fine greatcoat—tailored, to be sure, the way it fits his broad shoulders and tapers in to his slim waist. The top hat is of the finest beaver, not usually worn by those of the lower and working classes. Then there are the shirts and waistcoats with brass buttons, his silk drawers—"

"Silk drawers?" Mary's eyebrows shot up in surprise.

Sabrina slapped a hand over her mouth as a giggle escaped it. "Good heavens. You see, I assisted him with his bath last night."

"That's a discussion best had over a cup of tea. I'll make us a pot, along with toast and cheese." Mary stared over her shoulder. "Writing someone?" Sabrina explained about the recipient and why she was writing it. "Well done. Only, allow me to write it. What if the girl shows your father? He will recognize your handwriting. And we will pay to have it personally delivered, not sent through the post. It will save time and ensure it arrives in her hand."

"You are clever." Sabrina smiled.

"Devious, more like. We'd better put off making the apple pie until tomorrow or the next day. Now, for tea." Mittens rubbed against Mary's skirts, purring loudly. "And feeding the little beast."

"What I said, about Riordan being middle class? In the end it does not matter. I would love him even if he was penniless." If only he was more forthcoming. Yet she hadn't told him about meeting her father in town. There were secrets between them on both sides. Until they were revealed, how could they have a future?

Chapter 21

His grandfather's words filled his thoughts of late. *The curse.* If nothing else, it had made his family infamous. It had also brought unwanted attention. Their blood ties to the late Mary Wollstonecraft and her daughter, Mary Wollstonecraft Shelley, were removed by several generations. How did the connection go? His grandfather was fourth cousin to the author of *Frankenstein?* Or was it third?

Riordan had never met them, as the two branches were not close. Though they shared a number of progressive causes, his grandfather couldn't abide William Godwin, Mary Wollstonecraft's husband. He leaned toward anarchism—far too radical for the earl. Besides, the man contacted the earl more than once before his death in 1836 looking to borrow money, as did his wife before him. To Riordan's grandfather, that was well past enough, and he decided to have no further dealings with them.

Did a version of the curse touch the other branch of the family? There was solid evidence. Mary Wollstonecraft died in childbirth at the age of thirty-eight. One of her daughters reportedly committed suicide at age twenty-two. Mary Shelley's first child, a daughter, did not survive birth. Then Mary found herself a widow at twenty-five when her husband, the poet Percy Shelley, drowned in Italy. But death touched all families. Riordan remained dubious, yet cautious about the curse.

As an educator, he was open to interpreting and learning all he could. The curse could *not* be completely dismissed. Once, when he and Aidan played in the dusty attics of the ancient Wollstonecraft Hall, they came across a neglected trunk. Locked, of course, but that would not deter fourteen-year-old boys filled with curiosity. Once they broke the lock, the insides turned out to be a disappointment. No gold coins or other treasure, just moldering ledgers. Aidan had stomped off in disgust, but Riordan stayed behind to investigate.

As Garrett had stated, generations of Wollstonecrafts suffered devastating losses of loved ones, mostly female. All were meticulously catalogued in the ledger, but one entry stayed with Riordan. It was written in 1704, by the ancient Earl of Carnstone. In visiting an infamous Scottish sorceress, he begged her to remove the curse, as he had lost his second wife to illness. The woman claimed only a love bond by all the living men of the family during a lunar year would break the curse.

What could it mean? That every living Wollstonecraft man must fall in love within any twelve month period? Unbelievable. And unrealistic. Regardless, the sobering proof of the endless rows of gravestones dating hundreds of years back would give any man cause to believe. Should he live his life as Garrett does, far removed from romantic entanglements, or instead embrace the overwhelming feelings of love coursing through him?

Three nights ago, he shared something rare with Sabrina. A desire he'd never known. Since losing his virginity at seventeen, he'd gained knowledge in the art of love. With each affair he learned a new technique; when to love with slow purpose and when to engage in wild sex. He enjoyed both equally and believed that in any intimate relationship there was room to explore both aspects.

But he was also a considerate lover, mindful of a woman's pleasure. And her trepidations. Sabrina had plenty. Over the next several weeks he would show her that sex did not have to include the violations she'd been subjected to. His anger flared at the thought of her miserable husband.

Riordan glanced down at his beefsteak sandwich. He'd decided at the last minute to not go home for luncheon break today. Instead, he stayed at the school in order to make up lesson plans for the coming week, leaving Saturday and Sunday free. Spend it with Sabrina. He yearned to move beyond sizzling kisses and her touching him. God, how he wished to see her lying flat, her legs spread, him feasting as she writhed and moaned, culminating in her release.

They would get there. The vision formed in his mind, and he was lost in the erotic fantasy and did not hear a young lad enter the schoolroom.

"Are you Mr. Riordan Black?"

His attention returned to the present. "Yes, I am."

The lad touched his forelock. "Delivery for you, sir." Riordan fumbled in his pocket, found a shilling, and passed it to the boy. "Thank you, sir."

He handed an envelope to Riordan, turned on his heel, and departed. There, on the reverse of the sturdy envelope was the wax seal of the

Wollstonecrafts; a large wolf standing on a stone, howling at full bore. Breaking the seal, he pulled out the papers.

From his father. Riordan frowned as he read: *Do not become angry, Riordan, but I have set a tentative date for the annulment hearing, with the understanding that if Miller Kenworth does not hear from you by the end of November the appointment will be henceforth cancelled.*

The option is there if you wish. I did say I would not interfere, but I wanted to use our family's influence to our advantage in order to procure a date as soon as possible. As you stated, you are of age, and the decision is ultimately yours. Regardless of my initial reaction, I will abide by and respect your judgment.

As I respect and love you. Forgive my harsh words. Riordan paused, his annoyance dissipating. A lump of emotion lodged in his throat. *You are not your brother. Chalk up my irrational and emotional behavior to worry and concern, not only for you, but for Aidan's mysterious disappearance.*

Love, Papa

Julian Wollstonecraft had not used "Papa" since Riordan and Aidan were small boys. The affection and love in this note touched him. Leave it to the inventive Viscount Tensbridge. Did his father believe him not capable of handling this situation? The note stated the decision was his. However, he now understood why Aidan bristled under their father's firm hand and high expectations.

A postscript he'd missed: *Garrett has hired an investigator in London, a former Bow Street Runner by the name of Edwin Seward, to begin the search for Aidan. I will keep you apprised of any updates.*

Folding the paper, he slid it into the envelope. He had at least two weeks to decide when to inform Sabrina of this. It would be an early exit. He would not keep this information from her. Enough secrets lay between them already. As soon as she learned his true identity, and the fact that her father had not put up a settlement, she would know the money had come from him.

How would she react? Anger for his high-handed interference? Another man controlling her life? Or would she look beyond and see that all he wished was to give her what she most desired: her freedom. A chance to live an independent life. He'd wanted to protect her from the hurtful knowledge of her father selling her. For when it came down to it, he wanted Sabrina to choose between a life with him or the life she originally planned.

Not that a life with him would be stifling. He would give her freedom, property, money, anything she wished. For he truly believed all women should have rights, own property, and not be chattel to heartless, soulless fathers and husbands.

In the interim, they would continue on. Investigate this attraction. These passionate emotions. The unspoken love pulsed between them with a force of a gale storm. He must know what her feelings toward him were before suggesting they make the marriage permanent, or before revealing about the money. When he mentioned the idea at the registrar's office she'd been horrified. He wanted her to be thrilled at the prospect. Happy.

Exhaling, he turned his attention to his schoolwork.

* * * *

Riordan no sooner arrived home when he swept Sabrina into a crushing embrace and a hot and fierce kiss. A smile curved about his mouth when she threw her arms around his neck and returned the kiss with equal passion. How gratifying that she'd lowered her defenses and accepted the desire within.

Clasping her face, he laid kisses on her temple and cheeks, while her alluring citrus scent surrounded him. Hell, he was hard. To the point of pain. She gazed up at him, a look of complete trust and warmth. "What did you do today?" he murmured.

"Oh, Riordan. I made a pie. With Mary's help, of course. We sat and peeled the apples, she showed me how to make a crust and roll it out. Flour was flying every which way! She had to return to the inn, so I assembled it and baked it myself." She hugged him. "I learned to light the stove, and I followed Mary's directions closely and the pie turned out wonderfully."

He lifted his nose and inhaled. Apple and cinnamon. He hadn't noticed it when he first entered the cottage, for he was too wrapped up in feminine softness and luscious lips. "Let's have a piece while it is still warm."

Her brows furrowed. "It might spoil supper, but it isn't much, a chicken and potato soup…."

He kissed the tip of her nose. "Won't spoil my supper. I love apple pie. Let's see this wondrous achievement."

With a broad smile, she hurried to the kitchen. Riordan removed his coat and rolled up the cuffs of his shirt, then removed his neckcloth. In such a short period, they'd become comfortable in each other's company, enough that he could relax like this. Or walk about the room in nothing but his drawers. A smile tugged at the corner of his mouth.

Sabrina laid small plates and forks on the table. Nothing matched, for they were donations from various households in the town. Finally, she brought out the pie and a knife. Never had he seen her smile as broadly, and his heart hitched in his chest at the sight. She sat the pie on the table. It did look delicious; the crust was golden and small wisps of steam swirled from the slits on the top.

He took his seat, eagerly anticipating the treat. God, he could become used to this. There was a lot to be said for domesticity and all the benefits it brought.

Sabrina served him a generous slice, then waited for him to taste it. His fork cut through the flaky crust with ease. He lifted the fork and placed the pie in his mouth, savoring the warm apple and the tang of the cinnamon and nutmeg on his tongue—then his throat closed over and he choked. He couldn't swallow, so he spit the half chewed pie on the table.

"What is it? What's wrong?" Sabrina cried worriedly.

"Salt," he croaked. "You added salt instead of sugar."

She grabbed his fork, cut off a small piece and brought it to her mouth. Her pink tongue darted out to taste it and she grimaced. "Oh, no. You see, they're in glass containers, I must have mistaken…." A giggle slipped from her throat as she laid the fork on the table. "Salt instead of sugar." Sabrina did the most wondrous thing: she began to laugh. Not her usual rare and brief giggle, but a full-on laugh. She pointed at him while holding her stomach with her other arm. "You…you should have seen your face." Another peal of laughter escaped her.

She was beautiful. Happy. By the time he'd vaulted from his chair and came to face her, she was already wiping tears from her eyes. Riordan clasped her arms. "I've never heard a more beautiful sound. Do you remember what I said, about how I longed to see you laugh for the pure joy of it?" She nodded. "You're doing it now, and it is music to my ears."

"I ruined the pie…."

"Ruin a hundred pies and it would not matter to me. I would rather see you happy and taking delight in life." He kissed her. It didn't take long for the heat to flare between them, and he took the kiss deeper, tangling his tongue with hers. All thoughts of taking things slowly dissipated into nothingness. He trailed his lips across her cheek, down her supple neck, and up again to nibble on her earlobe. "When Mary comes later, inform her she will not be needed tomorrow night," he rasped.

"Why?" she asked breathlessly.

"I'll be preparing you for bed. And if you ask me politely, I will be joining you in it."

A moan escaped her, which merely stoked the roaring flames within him. Riordan pulled her close and she softened all around him. "I want to be patient, and I will if you ask me." He clasped her breast, his thumb running across her erect nipple. "Come with me to the bedroom. Let me give you pleasure like you gave me. If you like it, tomorrow night we will do more." He cupped her rear and brought her in tight against his erection. "But only if you wish it. Tell me, Sabrina. Put voice to your desires."

To his utter surprise, she reached behind him and grasped *his* ass, squeezing it until he moaned. "Come with me to the bedroom. Give me pleasure."

Riordan did not need any further encouragement. Sweeping her up into his arms, she squealed as he ran into the bedroom. Mittens, curled up on the rug, lifted her head to give them a nonchalant look, then continued her nap. Riordan slowly lowered Sabrina to the floor, keeping her close against him. She stared into his eyes searchingly, as if asking what comes next.

"I'm going to slowly remove your clothes. How many layers is up to you. Agreed?"

She nodded, biting her lower lip. Sabrina wore a large apron over her light gray wool dress. He moved behind her to work the knot free. Considering what she'd revealed about her marriage, it was a safe bet she'd never reached a sexual peak. Why would she? Her husband was a reprobate and a rapist. "I am going to caress and kiss every bit of exposed skin. Suckle your breasts, and as I do, insert my fingers inside you and stroke." Sabrina gave a sharp inhalation of breath at his wicked words.

The apron fell to the floor. Riordan encircled his arm across her chest, leaning her against him. "Tell me to cease and I will. You have my promise. Any time you're uncomfortable, let me know."

"How experienced are you?" she asked, her voice breathless.

"Not as much as you may think. But I'm a quick learner. I have learned this: sex is an intimate act, and when emotions are in the mix it makes the experience all the more intoxicating. When you touched me the other night? I've never experienced such soaring heights before. Not with any woman. Only with you."

"Oh. How wonderful," she whispered.

He kissed the crown of her head. "It will be for you as well. I know it."

"I wish I had your confidence." She laughed brokenly.

"I will say this once and never mention it again: your relations with your brutal and cruel husband were not based in intimacy or emotion, but in hatred and humiliation. Let us banish those memories forever."

A great sob left her throat, and he hugged her tighter, holding her close as she calmed and softened in his arms. He turned her about to face him and kissed her tenderly.

Breaking the kiss, she gave him a tremulous smile. "Yes. Let us banish the memories."

Nodding, he slowly unbuttoned her dress down to her waist. Already the creamy mounds of her breasts were visible, peeking out from the top of her corset. The sight caused him to harden further. He pushed the dress off her shoulders, then pulled it down past her waist until it pooled at her feet. Her corset was not the heavily boned one that women in the upper classes wore, but of a malleable linen. It had front laces, and small blue roses sewn into the stays.

He next removed her two petticoats. Sabrina stepped out of her shoes. She wore blue knee-length drawers and white stockings. He got down on one knee and glided his fingers up her shapely leg to untie the strings of her stockings. Placing her foot on his thigh, he pulled off one stocking and tossed it aside. Sabrina curled her toes and kneaded his thigh. He did the same with the other leg.

"Shall I remove more?" he questioned.

"Not tonight. Mary will be by soon. Will it be all right? Are you able to…to…"

"Gain access to your most feminine attributes?" He moved his hand up her leg and slipped it between them. She gasped at the contact as his fingers delved into the slit in her drawers and brushed by her curls. "I will manage."

He stood and led her to the bed. It was not wide at all, barely room for the both of them. But if he lay on his side, it could be accomplished. Once they were on the bed, he skimmed his fingers along the top of her breasts, across her bare shoulders and down her arms. Her breath caught and held as he tugged at the laces at the front of her corset, loosening them. When he kissed the tops of her breasts she exhaled, and it ended on a sensual moan. He kissed the hollow of her throat, moving upward until their lips met. Heat flared and he plundered, giving all he had, everything he felt.

Already this had moved beyond any experience with other women. The desire was inexplicable. Never-ending. Complete.

Breaking the kiss, he started removing the pins from her hair. Sabrina gazed up at him, her expression, though tense, also showed trust. Again he was humbled. Gathering the pins and laying them on the small table next to the bed, Riordan ran his hands through her golden-brown locks. As silky as her skin. He laid the strands across the pillow. "You are beautiful," he murmured.

Her eyes glistened. "Thank you. Though I'm not as firm as I once—"

He laid the tips of his fingers on her lips. "That you are four years older means nothing to me. Nothing should matter in this bed but you and I. The pleasure we give each other."

Trailing his fingers downward, they tangled in the laces once again. With slow deliberation, he pulled them apart. Sabrina's ample breasts rose and fell with each exhale. Dear God, they were stunning. Large enough to fill his hand and more. The nipples were coral pink and pebbled.

He cupped one gently, his thumb brushing past her nipple again and again. Sabrina moaned, her back arching slightly. The sight of her pleasure was more than he could bear. He leaned in and suckled her, squeezing her ample breast as he did.

"Oh!" she gasped. His heart nearly burst when she slid her hand at the nape of his neck and pulled him in closer. His free hand trailed down her side, taking a leisurely journey across her curves. Her legs parted, and a smile curved across his lips as his fingers found her dampened curls. Parting her folds, he inserted two fingers. *Tight. Oh, so tight.*

Sabrina writhed and he stilled—had he hurt her? When another moan escaped her, he continued his ministrations. As he stroked in and out of her, his thumb rubbed her sensitive nub while he continued to lick and suckle her breast.

"Heavens…what…"

"Let yourself go, Sabrina. Embrace the sensations. Own your desire."

The words must have been what she needed to hear, for she relaxed and the moans increased in volume. He watched her, committing this to memory: her eyes closed, her hips slowly undulating with each stroke of his fingers. Yes. She was close.

With a final arch of her back she cried out, her body shuddering as ripples of pleasure moved through her with her release. God, he was ready to explode. He pulled his hand of out her, unbuttoned the fall of his trousers, reached in and stroked himself, once, twice, three… He groaned, his body shook. The damned intensity of this. What would it be like to be deep inside her heat? His head hit the pillow and he pulled Sabrina next to him. She still shook, her breathing as harsh and raw as his. He kissed her forehead. "Are you all right?"

Chapter 22

All right? How could she ever be all right after this? Tears formed in her eyes. She'd had no idea, no inkling, that it could be like this between a man and woman. There was such tender concern in his voice. She laid her head on his chest, his heart beating rapidly, matching the rhythm of her own. "I am in awe," she whispered.

"As am I," he replied, his tone husky.

"Did you..."

"Make myself come? Yes. Watching you reach your peak aroused me like never before. It is the most beautiful thing I've ever seen."

She hugged him. "Oh, Riordan."

They lay in each other's arms, and Sabrina was content as never before. Safe. Treasured.

"We had best clean up. Mary will be here before we know it." She moved to sit up, but Riordan laid a hand on her shoulder.

"Stay, I'll return in a moment."

"Could we wait a couple of nights before asking Mary not to see to me in the evening?" His brows furrowed. "I want to savor what happened tonight, before we continue. Perhaps do this again"—she gave him a sultry smile—"for I enjoyed it immensely."

A smile touched his sensuous lips. "Whatever you desire."

Sabrina clasped his hand and kissed it. "I desire *you*, sir."

Riordan groaned. "Minx."

Laughing as he left the room, Sabrina burrowed into the blankets, a contented smile firmly in place. Was it always like this? The pleasure they had given each other from touching...what would actual sex bring? She wanted to know, but wanted to learn in a deliberate manner. Riordan would agree. Some men wouldn't. They would simply take…as Pepperdon… No. She dismissed him outright. *Rot in hell. Stay there. Never enter my thoughts again.*

How many minutes passed, she'd no idea. Riordan entered the room carrying a small basin and a flannel cloth. "I placed the soup on the stove. We will eat once we put ourselves to rights."

He made room for the basin on the small table, sat on the bed, dipped the cloth in the water, and placed it between her legs. The warmth of the flannel caressed her folds. He'd heated water for her. How thoughtful. She sighed with pleasure as he stroked her between the slit in her drawers. He leaned in and kissed her. Deeply. Stirring the passion between them. But before it galloped out of control, he ended it.

When he assisted her to stand, Sabrina was surprised to find her legs still shook. Leisurely, and with great care, he dressed her, leaving off the petticoats. As she reached for the hairpins, Riordan shook his head. "Leave it down. Please."

"Mary will know…."

"Let her." He winked.

They were sitting at the table eating when Mary knocked and entered. "Good evening. My, you're having supper late, what—" Stopping in her tracks, she looked back and forth between them. She smiled, and Sabrina could not stop the blush from spreading across her cheeks.

What Riordan had read to her about Miss Featherstone's seduction on the balcony had just happened to her not an hour before. Last night she'd read that the ex-soldier hero also…kissed her there. Between her legs. "Feasted," the book said. How deeply intimate. Would she enjoy it as Miss Featherstone did? She glanced at Riordan, and he winked once again. Oh, yes. Without a doubt.

"Join us, Mary. Have a cup of tea and a buttermilk biscuit," Riordan said.

"Oh no, sir. I couldn't."

"Mary, please?" Sabrina asked. She wanted her friend and Riordan to know each other better.

"Very well." Mary removed her cloak and sat at the table, making herself at home. She poured a cup of tea, and refreshed theirs. Once she finished, she spread apple jelly on her biscuit.

"I've asked Mary to call me by my first name. We have moved past the lady and maid roles into a far more satisfying bond. I'm also leaving behind the 'lady' designation permanently. It belongs in my past. For now, I am Sabrina Black."

"By law, you can call yourself Lady Pepperdon for the rest of your life," Riordan said.

"I could." She sipped her tea. "I choose not to."

"And what of your future?" Riordan asked.

She stilled. Both Riordan and Mary stared at her, waiting for her response. Why would he bring this up here? "I'm not sure yet." Before she could stop the words, she blurted, "Tell me what your salary is?"

Mary took a sharp inhale of breath; no doubt sorry she'd sat at the table. Yes, Sabrina was being unconscionably rude.

"I'm university educated, as I told you, and my yearly salary reflects such. The board is paying me forty-six pounds per annum. About the salary of a clerk at a prestigious firm. I have this cottage rent-free. Also the use of a part-time housekeeper-cook, Mrs. Ingersoll, free of charge. It's an ideal situation for a middle class lad such as myself." His words were clipped, his expression annoyed.

"How tactless of me. But I'm curious about you. Your past. You've told me next to nothing even though I have asked before this."

"There isn't much to tell." He shrugged. "There is time yet to consider all options."

She met his gaze. "What options?" She shouldn't have started this discussion on his salary, but blast it, she was tired of him revealing next to nothing about himself. Also, she longed for him to mention staying married as he'd done at the registrar's. *Say it, please.*

Riordan reached for another biscuit. "It's your future, Sabrina. Your choice. The end of the three month period may be a better time to discuss it."

How embarrassing. She'd made a fool of herself. Biting her lower lip to stem any tremor in her voice, she tossed her napkin on the table and rose to her feet. "I believe I'll retire." She hurried from the room. Mary followed right on her heels and closed the door behind her.

"Oh, Mary. I feel entirely stupid." She sat on the edge of the bed.

"What happened between you?" Mary asked gently as she sat next to Sabrina.

"Something wondrous. I'm caught up in emotions that are carrying me in four different directions. I love him. I'm beginning to believe he does not feel the same. Not completely. There are secrets, I know it."

Mary took her trembling hand. "I've seen the way he looks at you. Even tonight, when I first entered the room. If it's not love, it is very close to it." Mary sighed. "Let me explain an important fact about men: for the most part, they are confused by their emotions, reluctant to acknowledge them, as if doing so would make them weak and vulnerable. I'm not sure such is the case with Mr. Black, for he appears all confidence in most situations."

Mary slipped her arm about Sabrina's shoulder. "Perhaps he is simply allowing you to come to your own decision. You've been through so much. Why not allow things to unfold naturally? Do not worry for the future. I'm positive he will tell you all you wish to know soon. Let's say you wish to stay married. With his income and your settlement, you can both live comfortably enough."

"What about you?"

"My dear, your late husband was a complete rotter, but he did pay his servants well. I've saved a pretty penny the past decade. A cottage by the sea for the two of us? Good. Staying with the fine looking schoolmaster? Even better. How thrilling to actually have a choice. Know that I'm with you whatever you decide. For that is my preference. *My* choice."

The tears came. Sabrina could not stop them. Mary held her close, rocking her, humming a quiet tune.

As a loving mother would.

* * * *

For two days, Riordan admonished himself for his curt reply at supper. Sabrina asking about his salary had caught him unawares. And in front of Mary. Forty-six pounds was mere pocket change to him. The truth of it was, most people got by on much less. A farmer or laborer would be lucky to earn nineteen pounds per annum.

Referring to himself as a "middle class lad" wasn't a complete lie, for he was such at this point in his life, since he lived within the means of his teaching salary. The more intimacies he and Sabrina shared, the more questions she would ask. Riordan could keep his distance, but after observing her come apart in his arms, he could no more stay away from her than not draw his next breath.

They sat at supper, barely speaking. Riordan pushed the sausage about on his plate, for he had little appetite tonight.

"The pork sausage not to your liking?" Sabrina asked.

He looked up. "No, it's tasty enough." He cut a piece, placed it in his mouth, chewed, and swallowed.

"I…I asked Mary not to come tonight," she stated shyly.

He stopped cutting the meat. His heart slammed against his ribs. "You wish to continue with…"

"Making love? Yes, I do." She paused. "Are we moving too quickly? Am I being too bold?"

"Please, be bold," he croaked.

"In your best, sensual, schoolmaster voice, explain what you're going to do to me. And with me." Her eyelashes batted coquettishly and he grew hard.

Damn, he did like it when she acted audacious; he would as well. Placing his utensils across his plate, he gave her his full attention. "We will remove every last piece of clothing from each other. Touch and caress, lie on the bed, and continue to explore. Taste, kiss, lick every inch of skin. Then I will prepare you."

Sabrina smiled. "Prepare…how?"

"As I did last night. Suckle your luscious breasts, stroke your folds until you're soaking. Next I will grasp my…" God, he was aroused beyond all imaging. Hard as oak. Sabrina's lips parted, her cheeks flushed, and her breathing came in short bursts the same as his. His emotions were raw, exposed. As will his words be. "Grasp my cock, place it at your heated center, stretch you wide, fill you…." Swiftly vaulting from his chair, it fell to the floor. Scooping her up in his arms, he marched the few steps to the bedroom.

"Enough talk," he growled. He'd planned to bring her along slowly—those plans had been ground to dust. Once in the room he lowered her, clasped either side of her head, and kissed her savagely. Hungrily. Sabrina returned every stroke of his tongue. Without needing to vocalize it, their hands started to tear at each other's buttons as they continued to kiss. Frenzied movements. He must slow this down, a least by a notch or two.

Breaking the kiss, he pulled away, far enough to capture her gaze. Never had he seen such heated desire in a woman's eyes. Without breaking eye contact, they peeled the layers away, kicking aside petticoats, skirts, shirts, and trousers, until they were completely nude. Sliding his gaze downward, he drank in her curves, her plump breasts, the curve of her hips, her long legs. "You're beautiful. Every part of you."

Sabrina smiled. How readily she did it now. Boldly, she drank him in, her gaze lingering on his erect cock. "As is every part of you. Is this where I ask shyly if that will fit inside me? Because surely it cannot." She gave him a wink and a deep-throated laugh. "Miss Featherstone said the same to Sebastian."

"You've become such a tease. A vixen. And I love it." He fisted his prick. "This is yours. To bring you pleasure. Never to hurt or humiliate. I mean it, my darling."

She stepped forward, laid her hand on top of his and gave him a squeeze. "My darling."

He kissed her again as they both stroked him, inching closer to the narrow bed. One day, if all worked out according to his deepest hopes and desires, he would have her in his large bed at Wollstonecraft Hall.

They lay upon the bed, kissing, caressing, and stirring the passion to full boil. One of his hands slid between her legs. *Wet.* Damn it all, he couldn't wait. He rolled on top of her, raising himself up by his arms, and gazed down at her. Skin against skin. Heat. Fire.

First, he wanted her to come. Cry out, writhe under his ministrations. Riordan began at the curve of her hip, laying kisses up her torso until his mouth locked onto her erect nipple. His other hand caressed her inner thigh, moving ever closer to the heart of her. Inserting two fingers, then three, he stroked, rubbing her nub while suckling madly at her breast.

Already she moaned, her face flushed. He pulled his mouth away far enough to say, "Do not suppress it, Sabrina. Demand I give you more." He returned his attention to her breast, his tongue flicking the nipple and he stroked her faster.

Sabrina groaned, her hips rising off the bed. "More. Faster."

That she vocalized her demands nearly made him come. He liked to talk during sex, always had. Perhaps it was the teacher in him. Describing and explaining what he wanted. What he would do to her. Then to follow through with a thorough demonstration.

With a widening of her eyes, she cried out, gasping for breath. "Oh, God, Riordan…" Her feminine core tightened and spasmed, her entire body shuddering with her release. Removing his fingers, he grasped his shaft and teased her entrance, then thrust in. Filling her as she still trembled with her release was damned astonishing. Her climax vibrated through him, to his very soul.

Starting with a slow pull and push motion, he increased the speed of his thrusts. Leaning forward, he wished to give her swollen nub the friction it needed to make her fly apart once more. The sounds and smells of sex filled his senses. The air fairly crackled with life and vibrancy. Colors swam in his vision.

With a moan, Sabrina trailed her hands down his arms, reached behind him, and grabbed his rear, pulling him in deeper. They moved together in perfect rhythm. Faster, until she cried out his name over and over, shuddering once again.

He was damned close. He was about to pull out, but Sabrina clutched him tight, holding him in place. "Don't leave me. Stay."

"If I do, we must stay married, do you understand?" Her father had crudely claimed she was barren, but he didn't care one way or the other. But in case she wasn't, he would not take the chance of getting her with child without the promise of his name and protection.

Leaning up, she bit his shoulder. "I understand. Come inside me."

With a hoarse cry, he did, giving her all he was and ever hoped to be. Every muscle in his body contracted as the powerful force of his release made his heart pound. Gasping for air, he fell to her side, pulling her close into his embrace. He still shook and shuddered, completely awed by the experience. Completely in love with her.

They didn't speak; they merely held each other until they both drifted off into a blissful sleep. When Riordan awoke, he gently positioned himself between her legs, bringing her awake with gentle kisses to her inner thighs.

"Riordan, what are you…oh!"

He licked her, then spread her folds. "If you do not like it, I will stop."

"Is…is this the feasting?"

He laughed. "Let me guess. Sebastian did this to Miss Featherstone." Sabrina nodded. "It most certainly is, my darling vixen." He pushed his tongue inside her and she gasped. With a contented sigh, Sabrina grasped a handful of his hair, her hips rising with each stroke of his tongue. She was close; he recognized the signs. He rose to his knees and plunged inside her as she screamed his name over and over. Again he rode the waves of her pleasure, which fueled his to fiery heights.

He lost all control. Pounding fiercely, an animal growl escaped his throat as he reached his peak. Riordan collapsed next to her, taking great gulps of air.

"Is it always like that?" she asked.

"No. Only with you."

Sabrina lay partly on top of him, stroking his damp chest. "Stay with me tonight. Sleep with me. I've never slept with a man before."

Good. He would be the first to hold her through the night. A fleeting thought of the dead earl crossed his mind. *Glad he's dead.* How dare he misuse and abuse this glorious woman? No one would ever harm her again. And if he had his way, they would spend every night lying in each other's arms. "I love you," he whispered in her ear.

Chapter 23

When she awoke in the morning, Riordan had already departed for school, but he'd placed a note on the pillow: *I owe you another kiss, my darling vixen, in a most intimate place.* He had drawn a heart next to the words. Once Mary left after lunch, Sabrina carefully folded the small piece of paper and placed it between the pages of *The Bold Seduction of Miss Featherstone.*

She may not have said the words last night in response to his declaration of love, but she'd showed how she felt with her body—and the fact she'd allowed him to spill inside her. Before they fell asleep, he told her they had much to discuss tonight, hinting that, at last, he would reveal more about himself. She couldn't wait.

With tea steeping on the stove, she tucked the book under her arm and settled on the chaise longue, curling her feet under her. Mittens meowed loudly, and Sabrina picked her up. The kitten settled in next to her, as she'd done the past few afternoons. Sabrina had no sooner read three pages when a pounding at the door interrupted her peace.

Sliding off the chaise carefully, so as not to disturb Mittens, she smoothed her skirt and headed toward the door. Opening it, she gasped in shock.

Her wretched father.

She tried to close the door, but the baron stuck his booted foot across the doorjamb. "I have need of you once more." He pushed his way into the cottage and slammed the door behind him.

"We have nothing to say to each other," Sabrina sniffed.

"I beg to differ. Remember that I said there would be consequences." He pulled a small bottle out of his coat pocket. "Drink it."

She raised her chin in the air. "I will not."

Her father glanced around the room, and his cruel gaze settled on the sleeping kitten. "Yours?" He stepped toward the chaise.

"Do not touch her!" Sabrina cried, remembering the threat he had made toward the kitten she'd wanted years past.

"Drink what is in the bottle or I will wring the mangy creature's throat," her father snapped.

Panic began to set in. Why was he here? Oh, why hadn't she told Riordan about her father's threats? Why hadn't she taken them seriously? All she wanted was to place all memory of her father in the past, and because of that she'd placed herself in danger. "What is it?"

"Enough laudanum to keep you quiet on the journey. Sutherhorne has made an offer I cannot and will not refuse. He wants you still, and for what he has offered, I will deliver you to him. This very day."

Sabrina's heart chilled. "No. Do not do this."

He slammed his fist on the table, knocking the teacup to the floor. It smashed into pieces. "I. Have. No. Choice."

"We all have choices." Sabrina vaulted toward the bedroom. There she could lock the door, perhaps escape through the window. But her father moved too quickly. He grabbed her arm, wrenching it and causing her to cry out in pain. She bumped against the table and the saucer joined the cup on the floor, shattering on impact.

"The sooner you drink this, the sooner this will be over with. My carriage awaits."

"But I'm married—"

"I don't think Sutherhorne much cares. When the marquess has his mind set, he is determined to have his way. Now, drink the contents of the bottle or I will snap the cat's neck."

She gave her father a deadly look; she knew him well enough to know he would do it. "This could poison me."

"I measured the correct amount. I would not damage the goods."

Goods. Chattel. Property. That is all she ever was to her father. Snatching the bottle from the table, she pulled out the stopper and drank. The bitter taste made her shudder.

He pulled her toward the door. "Then let us depart."

"You're a hateful man." Already her words were slurred.

"You don't know the half of it."

Next she knew she was bundled into the carriage. Her surroundings spun at a rapid pace as the horses lurched forward. All turned to darkness.

* * * *

Riordan was having an incredible day. To wake with Sabrina in his arms was heaven on earth. Because she slept contentedly, he did not disturb her when he rose from the bed. Leaving the naughty note would give her a smile, he was sure of it.

The children were working diligently on their geography assignments when a frantic knock interrupted the quiet. His students all raised their heads questioningly. "I will see to the door, continue on with your work."

He opened it and Mary stood there, a worried look on her face. She clutched his arm and pulled him outside, away from the children's hearing. "Mrs. Ingersoll came to fetch me. She arrived at the cottage at two o'clock to do the housekeeping, but Sabrina was not there. She thought at first she'd gone for a walk, but when she discovered the smashed teacup and saucer, she became worried."

Mary took a deep breath and exhaled. "She also found the teapot. The contents had boiled away. The kitten was in an agitated state. Sabrina would not go out and leave the teapot boiling on the stove. Besides, her cloak is still on the hook. It is too chilly to go walking without it. Something has happened. There are carriage tracks and hoofprints by the door. More than one set of footprints in the mud. A man's boot, to be sure."

Damn. Alarm bells pealed inside him. Her father? The marquess? Who else could it be? "Can you stay here until dismissal? Or better yet, when they finish their assignment, have them pass it in and allow them to go home. Once the last student is gone, make haste to the cottage and wait for me." Jesus, he'd have to run to Walsh's farm for his horse. "I'm heading to Durning's."

Mary gasped, covering her mouth with her gloved hand. "You don't think..."

"I know the baron's finances are in precarious shape. God knows how desperate he is." Damn it all for not realizing the man would pull such a stunt. Did he think to still marry her off? Collect the money? Never in his wildest imagination did he believe her father would snatch her away. Unless this is entirely innocent—his gut, however, said different. "Will you stay here?"

Mary nodded and followed him into the schoolroom. Riordan had already gathered his coat and gloves. To hell with the hat. "I have an emergency," he announced to his students. "Miss Tuttle will stay with you. Behave." He whispered in Mary's ear, "I'll meet you at the cottage."

He was out the door and running across the field toward Walsh's farm, admonishing himself the entire way. Serves him right for thinking men of the peerage had any remnants of honor. He should have told Sabrina what her father was capable of. Damn and hell, after last night, he should have told her everything, right then and there. That the settlement did not come from her father. That his real name was Wollstonecraft. He'd planned to tell her tonight. *Too bloody late.*

He reached the barn. Out of breath, he saddled his horse. Farmer Walsh stepped into the stall. "Is something amiss, Mr. Black?"

"I need Grayson, not sure how long I'll be gone. Family emergency." By God, Sabrina *was* his family. All he wanted in this life. If anyone harmed her, he would commit murder. With a fluid motion, he was seated. Kicking Grayson's flanks, they were off, heading toward Durning House.

Once they arrived, Riordan tethered the reins to a post, then gave the gelding a pat. He vaulted up the stairs and banged on the door. The footman answered—what was his name? *Bugger it.* He grabbed the lad's livery and twisted as he stepped across the threshold. "The baron, where's he gone?"

"I don't...don't know," the footman sputtered.

"Why is there no butler?"

"Left last month. Hadn't been...paid."

Ah. Riordan twisted tighter and the footman gasped for air. "Your name again?"

"George," he croaked hoarsely.

"Right. George. I'm going to release you, and you're going to tell me everything you know. Where is the baron, and where is my wife, Sabrina?"

Riordan let go and George coughed, trying to regulate his breathing. "All I know is the baron is in a bad way, moneywise. He's been in a rage for the past three days, cursing his daughter." George paused; anger radiated in his eyes. "He owes me wages as well. Why protect him? I'll tell you what I know...give me a minute." He coughed again, rubbing his throat.

"Hurry up, man."

"He received a letter from the marquess, the old one who was here weeks ago. It made his eyes light up. I delivered the response myself."

Riordan crossed his arms. "And you read it."

"Yes, I bloody well did. The baron said he would deliver his daughter to the marquess for no less than thirty thousand pounds. I figured I'd get me pay at last. I figured you lot all came to an agreement or some such. None of my business what toffs get up to." George's accent was slipping. "Guess he took her against her will, if you're here. Wouldn't put it pass him. He's a nasty bit of work, is the baron."

"Where did you deliver the note? Is it where he's taking Sabrina?"

George shrugged as he continued to rub his throat. "Maybe. It was in London. In Mayfair, at Ten Duke Street."

Riordan grasped the neckcloth again and twisted. "This had better be the correct address, or I will hunt you down and—"

"'Tis, I swear!" George cried.

Riordan pushed the trembling footman away. Turning on his heel, he exited, then immediately mounted Grayson. First he would see Mary, pack a small kit, and stop at Wollstonecraft Hall on the way to London—he would need Garrett. Giving the gelding a swift kick, he galloped off toward the cottage.

Minutes later, he arrived. Slipping from the saddle, he patted Grayson's neck once again. "Sorry, my lad. I'll have to push you hard all the way to the hall." The horse nickered, his hoof pawing the dirt in reply. "Good boy."

He entered the cottage, and the emptiness of the place struck him hard. Her absence was keenly felt. Riordan spied the smashed cup and saucer. Over on the chaise, a book lay at a strange angle. As he picked it up, a piece of paper fluttered to the floor. He bent to pick it up. It was the note he had written her this morning.

Mittens came from the bedroom, and when she spotted Riordan she sprinted toward him at an awkward gait. The kitten rubbed against his legs, meowing loudly, sounding forlorn. Riordan gathered the distressed feline into his arms and petted her. "There now, it will be all right."

But would it? God knows how much of a head start they had. Was Sutherhorne in London, or at his country estate? Perhaps he wasn't at his residences at all. Then how in hell could he locate Sabrina? Once the kitten had calmed, he lowered her to the floor, then commenced gathering a few items to place in his pack.

Mary entered the cottage. "The children are on their way home. What did you find out?" Riordan relayed everything George the footman had told him. Mary frowned. "The lad was always an unlikable sort. But I believe he's telling the truth. As he said, he hasn't been paid; why lie for the baron? What will you do?"

"Head for London with all speed. My family home is on the way. I'll be collecting my uncle to assist."

"The flame-haired Viking? Good choice."

Despite the circumstances, Riordan smiled. "I do like you, Mary. Garrett is half Scottish, always reminded me of a medieval Highlander. Please stay here. Look after Mittens, make use of the food, and make yourself comfortable. I'll send word when I locate Sabrina."

Mary clasped his arm. "You love her."

"With all my heart. I think I have from the beginning." He patted her hand. "I *will* find her."

"I don't doubt it, Mr. Black. I've every faith in you. Godspeed."

Nodding, he reached for his bundle and dashed outside. After securing it on the saddle and giving Grayson another encouraging pat, he mounted his horse and started off with a trot. How tempting to push Grayson at full gallop the entire way, but he knew his horse well, what he was capable of.

Two hours later, he arrived at Wollstonecraft Hall. Martin opened the door and could not keep the look of surprise from his face, though he quickly settled his features into a passive expression. "They are all in the library, Master Riordan."

They? Damn it, his father and grandfather were here. Well, that couldn't be avoided. He marched into the library. Garrett, his father, and grandfather were looking at maps spread out on the desk. "I need assistance. Sabrina has been taken by her father to be sold to Sutherhorne. I pray I'm not too late."

The men all started talking at once, peppering Riordan with questions. He held up his hand to quiet them, then quickly filled them in on the situation.

The earl shook his head. "Sutherhorne? He keeps his life private. Who is to know what a man is capable of?"

"He's obsessed with Sabrina. Has lusted after her for years. Her father held an auction for her when she was but eighteen. Pepperdon outbid Sutherhorne."

"A repulsive act, and one that can be prosecuted in court," the earl spat. Then his eyes widened. "Julian, do you recall the invitation we received from Durning about ten or eleven years ago? He was vague on the grounds for the invite, claiming our complete secrecy was needed, and since we did not know him, we declined."

Riordan's stomach lurched. His father and grandfather had been invited to the auction?

Julian's lip curled with disgust. "Yes, I do. Now he intends to try and sell his daughter for a third time."

Riordan turned to his uncle. "Garrett, will you come with me to London?"

"I will. And before we leave, I'll send a message to Edwin Seward."

"The ex-Bow Street Runner looking for Aidan?" Riordan asked.

"The very one," Garrett replied. "He's in London. He can watch Sutherhorne's residence in Mayfair, or have one of his lads do it until we arrive."

Julian crossed his arms. "We will all go with you. Make a united front."

His grandfather nodded. “We’d better prepare to depart. Best bring weapons.”

Jesus. Weapons? Absolutely. He was going into battle to rescue the woman he loved, but he did not think of himself as a hero—didn’t possess enough of an ego. For Sabrina, the woman he loved to distraction? He’d wear armor and ride in on a white horse in a heartbeat.

Chapter 24

Opening her eyes, Sabrina was met by hazy images. She blinked several times to try and focus. A room at an inn? It was not an expensive one, if the sparse furnishings were any indication. The bed was narrow and uncomfortable. She wrinkled her nose. This place reeked of horrible odors she did not want to guess at the origins of. With great difficulty she sat upright, the bedframe squeaking with her efforts.

"You're awake."

Her loathsome father. She remembered all of it. How he made her accompany him after taking the laudanum. Her mouth was dry and tasted bitter and her stomach churned. "Explain what you mean by Sutherhorne is willing to pay," she said.

The baron crossed his legs. "A railway scheme I was involved in has collapsed. I'm close to ruin. There may be an investigation by parliament, as there have been many such schemes. I will *not* go to debtor's prison." He reached in his side coat pocket and pulled out a sheet of paper. "And this anonymous letter has destroyed my chances with Lady Irene and her substantial dowry. I've no choice but to sell you. Again."

Her heart froze. "Sell?" The word came out as a croak. Again? *No.* She'd told Riordan her father had sold her to the highest bidder, but she'd used the exaggerated phrase to punctuate a point. Never did she believe she was literately *sold.* "What do you mean?"

"I held an auction when you turned eighteen. Quite a few peers attended, all for the chance of having a young virgin bride. Since there is a chance of being arrested for selling a woman for profit, they all signed confidentiality agreements before I allowed them to attend. The bidding became particularly intense between Sutherhorne and Pepperdon. The earl won, since Sutherhorne's fortune was not as robust as it is now. Though I have to hand it to the stubborn marquess." Her father chuckled cruelly. "When he wants something, he is determined. And he wants you."

Auction. Her blood curdled. Sutherhorne's cryptic statement now made sense. *I have waited eleven years for this, Sabrina, and I have run out of patience. You see, your father chose Pepperdon over me. There was more than one suitor for your hand. Quite the...contest.*

Oh. My. God.

"Imagine my surprise when Sutherhorne contacted me last week, claiming he wished to reopen negotiations." Her father stood and walked about the room. "He met my exorbitant price. It will be enough to see me free and clear from my financial obligations and start again."

"You're the worst sort of man. Selling your only child…a thirty-year-old woman!" she cried.

The baron swung about to face her, his face thunderous. "You are nothing to me but property. I can do as I like, regardless of your age." He stomped toward her, waving the paper in her face. "Well deserved, in light of this. You *owe* me. This letter came from *you*; do not deny it. I showed it to George and he recognized your bitch of a maid's handwriting."

"I don't deny it. Someone had to warn the poor, innocent girl. You would have destroyed her life. As you have destroyed mine." Tears welled in her eyes. "You are my father. You're supposed to protect me. But you never have. You're supposed to love me, but you never have. I still don't understand why you act this way. Why treat me so miserably? What have I ever done to you?"

"You were born a female. I wanted a son to carry on my name. Not a sniveling, grasping daughter. What good are daughters but a millstone about a man's neck? No, I never loved you. But don't take it personally; I am incapable of the emotion." His lips curled. "On top of that, you're an interfering cow for ruining my chances with Lady Irene. For that alone, you deserve this fate."

His words were spoken with cold indifference. Looking into his dead eyes, Sabrina saw the truth in his surprisingly honest statement of being unable to love. For years she thought there was something fundamentally wrong with her. Now it became clear: it was not her at all. She was *not* unworthy of love. Riordan had proved it. Especially last night. It had taken her this long to realize her father was soulless, with no heart, no morals. Evil to the core. The worst sort of man, out for his own selfish needs.

Purchased for Sutherhorne? Sabrina could not allow this to happen. She would do anything to return to her passionate schoolmaster. "I'll give you the ten thousand pound settlement if you release me. I swear I will. No one need ever know what you've done. We will go our separate ways and forget this day."

Her father laughed cruelly, then he sobered. "Here is the truth: there's no money. Never was. Sutherhorne was going to pay for you again once you came out of mourning; it is why he came to Durning House a couple of months past, but that damned interfering schoolmaster ruined the plan. The man had me sign a paper claiming there is money…but there isn't. He lied to you and married you under false pretenses. Why you stir such passions in men that they go to great lengths to claim you is beyond me."

Sabrina did not think this situation could get any worse, but it had. Her heart shattered. Riordan would *not* lie. They sat in a solicitor's office, signed official papers… Yet the solicitor was his friend. Was it all an elaborate plot? To what end? This made no sense whatsoever. She shook her head. "No. He would not lie to me."

Her father shrugged. "Believe what you will, but think about it: if there was money, I would have used it to better my situation, not allow you to marry some upstart. I signed the paper because I wanted you gone. With Sutherhorne out of the picture, I knew I would be stuck with you. I let the schoolmaster have his way." He stared at her. "You left a trunk full of gowns behind. I sold them for over two hundred pounds because I needed the money. Chew on that."

Could all of this be true? She'd seen the proof on display at the dress shop. There had to be an explanation about the money. Riordan would not deceive her. "You've become a true villain. Kidnapping? Selling your daughter for profit?"

He tucked the letter back into his pocket. "Did you not hear me?" he sneered. "I have no choice."

"We all have choices," she snapped. "You will not take mine away ever again. My husband will come for me. I know it."

The baron's eyebrows shot up. "Why, because he's the hero?"

"He is *my* hero. It's all that counts," she sniffed.

Her father snorted. "He won't be for long, I'll wager. Now cease your incessant chattering. I've sent word to Sutherhorne, he should be here presently." He strode across the room and took a seat.

She felt sick to her core. There was no doubt Riordan would come after her, but how on earth would he find her? As far as her father's statement about the money, she would not believe it. Not until she heard it from Riordan's own lips. *Oh, please find me, my love. Be my hero.*

* * * *

They made it to London in record time, Garrett's message arriving only thirty minutes before they did—but Edwin Seward had already sprung into action. Stopping at his small office on the outskirts of Whitechapel, one of his underlings informed them that Mr. Seward had placed men in Mayfair to keep the marquess's townhouse under surveillance, and would they please make themselves comfortable as he would return directly.

"I will not sit around while Sabrina is in her father and Sutherhorne's clutches," Riordan shouted.

The earl laid a comforting hand on his shoulder. "Easy. We have to craft a plan. We cannot move forward until we know where she is."

"I will tear London apart until I find her," Riordan declared.

"Ah, the passion of youth," the earl smiled.

A man strode into the small office. "Edwin." Garrett took the man's hand and shook it. This Edwin had the look of a former Bow Street Runner: tall, imposing, with shrewd eyes that studied his surroundings. A scar ran down the side of his face, from his left temple to the corner of his mouth. Danger exuded from him, but also an aura of confidence and competency.

"Allow me to introduce you. My father, Oliver Wollstonecraft, the Earl of Carnstone. Next to him, my brother Julian, Viscount Tensbridge. And this is my nephew, Riordan, Aidan's twin. They're not identical, but you can ascertain the similarities in features." Garrett turned to face his family. "I gave Edwin the small painted portrait done on the twins' twentieth birthday."

Mr. Seward shook the men's hands. When he came to Julian, he said, "We're doing all we can to locate your son, my lord."

"Excellent. Two days past, I instructed my steward to contact the bank and discontinue Aidan's quarterly payments. If he resurfaces and tries to collect, they will inform me."

Mr. Seward nodded. "A prudent plan, my lord. We will discuss it further soon."

Riordan blew out a breath. Freezing the funds would anger Aidan. But if it helped locate him, all the better. His brother could hardly indulge in his vices with no coin. Riordan's own quarterly payments had sat untouched since he'd accepted the teaching position.

"Now, why we're all here," Mr. Seward intoned. "It's by sheer luck we caught Sutherhorne departing his townhouse. I followed him to a small inn on Cheapside. It's not far from here, a few miles southwest. I've two of my men standing by. I would suggest we head there with all haste."

Racing through the cobblestone streets, they reached the grubby little inn on Cheapside, nestled between a poultry market and a number of brick row houses. Riordan wrinkled his nose at the odor. Apparently the market had a number of live chickens, and the stench of poultry waste made his eyes water.

Riordan was off Grayson before the horse came to a full stop, with Mr. Seward right behind him. The investigator stopped and nodded toward a man standing by the door. "Top floor, Mr. Seward. Room fourteen. He's not alone; I heard voices. Another man and a woman. The man arrived five minutes past."

What luck they were able to locate the marquess. What if the baron hadn't stopped at an inn, but delivered Sabrina directly and the marquess had left the city before they'd even arrived? Riordan vaulted the stairs two at time. The stairway was dark and narrow and creaked loudly under his boots; no doubt they could hear their approach.

Mr. Seward and Garrett were directly behind Riordan. Garrett had his gun drawn, a Colt Paterson revolver from America. With a swift kick, Riordan tore the flimsy wooden door from its hinges. He entered the room, his frantic gaze locking on Sabrina, who was sitting on the edge of the bed. Her expression was shuttered, but he could read the fear in her beautiful eyes.

Garrett raised his revolver and pulled back on the hammer. Mr. Seward stood on the other side of Riordan, holding a similar weapon.

"Ah. What perfect timing. Sabrina, meet Riordan Wollstonecraft," Sutherhorne sneered. The look of shock on her face tore at Riordan's heart. Damn it all, he should have told her everything before this. Last night especially. "You did not know of his true identity? How interesting. I only found out myself two days ago, when I opened an investigation into the men who'd bodily manhandled and threatened me at the Carrbury Inn." The marquess's eyes narrowed as he glared at both he and Garrett.

The viscount and the earl entered the room. Both of them held unsheathed swords from their Malacca walking sticks. "And here is the rest of the venerable clan," Sutherhorne mocked. "On a rescue mission, I assume?"

"Riordan?" Sabrina whispered, her eyes shimmering with unshed tears. "Is this true? Black is not your name?"

"Sabrina, I can explain—"

Sutherhorne grabbed Sabrina's arm and brought her none too gently to her feet. She struggled under his grip, her face stricken. "No explanations are necessary. I've made my acquisition, and you will allow us to leave. I was not going to bother with an annulment, merely keep her as my mistress. But I believe we'd best keep this above board. She was promised to me. Your so-called marriage is forfeit. I will ensure any court will rule in my favor."

"Not bloody likely," the earl hissed dangerously. "You don't have a legal foot to stand on."

"Legal? We will call for the Metropolitan Police and have you both arrested. Mistress? Your slave, is more like it. Women are not chattel to be bartered, sold, or held and used against their will," Riordan yelled. "To hell with being civilized, I'm going to beat you senseless." He vaulted forward, but Mr. Seward grasped his arm. Sutherhorne shrank back, no doubt reading the murderous intent in Riordan's expression.

Julian pressed the tip of his sword against the baron's heart. "Give the satchel to the marquess, Durning. The transaction has been cancelled."

"No. I need this money. I'll be ruined." He clasped the satchel closer. "There is thirty thousand pounds in here."

Sutherhorne dragged Sabrina toward the door, but she managed to wriggle out of his grip. "If you think I will submit to this, you are sadly mistaken. All of you." She faced Sutherhorne, her look determined. "I'm not a green girl any longer. I will not cower in fear. I will fight every step of the way and make your life a misery. You will not own any part of me…ever."

Is it any wonder he loved her? Seeing her standing there, defiant, he fell more in love. How could he not? She was magnificent.

Sabrina turned her resolute gaze to Riordan. "No man shall ever own me."

Ominous words. And directed at him. Perhaps she would feel differently once he explained his logical reasoning for lying. But he could hardly explain himself here. Because of his male arrogance, believing he could protect her from all harm and hurt, he hadn't protected her at all.

Riordan stepped forward. "This repulsive episode is at an end. Baron, give up the satchel or blood will be shed this day."

Durning let the satchel fall to the floor. The container fell open, and numerous notes and gold guineas spread across the dusty wood floor. Garrett whistled at the sight.

"Sutherhorne, retrieve your money. Relinquish all claims on Sabrina. Say it," Riordan barked. His grandfather placed the point of his blade against Sutherhorne's chest.

"I relinquish all claims on Lady Pepperdon."

"Her name is Sabrina Black. Say her name," Riordan growled.

"Sabrina Black, then. Let her be your problem." The marquess's cold, gray eyes held murderous intent. "I shall not forget the humiliation I have borne. Nor shall I forget those behind it." His thunderous look slid from Riordan and landed on Garrett. In a deadly tone so low Riordan could hardly hear it, Sutherhorne said, "This is far from over." Did he threaten Garrett? The entire family?

Edwin Seward gently grasped Sabrina's arm. "I suggest, gentlemen, we take our leave."

Durning scrambled to gather the wayward money and scoop it into the satchel.

"Hand it over to me, Durning," Sutherhorne commanded.

"I cannot go to debtor's prison," the baron sniveled.

"You shall," Riordan yelled. "Or this entire incident will be made public. And you will be going to Newgate Prison instead."

The men backed out of the room and quickly made their way downstairs. Sabrina was trembling. "But…what about Sutherhorne?" she asked.

The earl shook his head. "He is a marquess, above us all, and he has Prince Albert's ear. He is untouchable, and he knows it. Peers are rarely arrested and prosecuted for crimes. It's far from fair, but unfortunately it's how Society functions. The rich and powerful rule, profit, and escape justice."

Riordan motioned toward Grayson. "Come, Sabrina. We will head to Wollstonecraft Hall."

She pointed to Garrett. "I will ride with him."

Riordan took a step toward her, but his father held his arm. "Leave her be, Son. This is not the time." His father was right, but damn it, her expression of disgust, anger, and fear made his heart crack in two. He was responsible for this mess. It was all on him.

After they shook Edwin Seward's hand and the man departed, Garrett helped Sabrina onto his large horse and slid into the saddle behind her. Riordan could not tear his eyes from her; she would not even look at him.

"Lady Pepperdon, my nephew did not mean to deceive you, he—" Garrett began.

"Please, Mr. Wollstonecraft. I would prefer we not speak on the journey, for I shall cry or rage, or both."

Garrett gathered the reins. "As you wish, my lady."

Riordan swung his leg up and over the saddle and mounted Grayson. His heart was heavy, his stomach roiling. He may have destroyed the love and trust they'd built between them. *Idiot.* He should've told her. Everything. All his blather about wanting a partner in life and he had not been honest with her. Life would not be worth living if he lost her.

Following behind Garrett, his father and grandfather mounted their horses, and soon they were all heading out of London toward Kent and Wollstonecraft Hall.

Loving Sabrina was all he wanted. All that remained was to convince her he was worth loving in return.

Chapter 25

"One of the maids will come and prepare a bath for you. Then she will bring you a tray of food." Julian Wollstonecraft pointed to the bed. "The maid, Helen, has volunteered a nightgown and dressing gown."

"Thank you, my lord." Never had she been in the presence of such formidable, handsome men. Gazing at the viscount, she could hardly credit this was Riordan's father; though there were many threads of gray at his temples, he looked more like an older brother. The viscount was a sinfully striking man with a near perfect profile. It was plain to see where Riordan got his dark good looks and athletic build.

Though she did not move about in society much when married to Pepperdon, snippets of gossip did reach her—especially the salacious tale about Julian Wollstonecraft and a disreputable actress caught having sexual relations in an opera box. Even tales of Riordan's grandfather, the earl, and a young baronet's widow reached her.

"No one will disturb you for the rest of the night. You have my word. In the morning, my father and brother will be heading to Carrbury to collect your maid, Miss Tuttle. We've already sent word that you have been recovered and are safe."

"She is not my maid any longer, but my dear friend. I also want my kitten and my belongings, if you please."

"I do beg your pardon. Your friend, then. Should you not speak to Riordan first before making such a decision?" His tone was kind, but she bristled nonetheless at his suggestion.

"You may inform Riordan that I will speak to him tomorrow afternoon. Three o'clock, here in this room. Until then, I *would* like to be left alone, thank you." Her voice sounded cold to her own ears. As the viscount turned to leave, she said in a warmer tone, "I do thank your entire family for coming to…well, to my rescue." She gave him a tremulous smile. "I'm relieved you were able to locate me."

"It is due to providence and the superior investigation skills of Mr. Seward. And Riordan's dogged insistence. Anything you need, please, let the maid know."

She nodded. "I will."

He closed the door, and the handle no sooner clicked in place when the tears came. For hours she had held them in reserve by sheer force. Male voices drifted in from the hallway.

"Father, let me pass. I need to see her. I need to…hold her." *Riordan.* His passionately spoken words made her heart ache with longing, enough that she nearly opened the door and threw herself into his warm embrace. But if she did, she would shatter into jagged shards.

"She's asked to be alone tonight. Honor her wishes. She will see you tomorrow. Come, we'll have a brandy and I will tell you all…." The voices drifted away.

Sabrina threw herself onto the large bed, gathered the pillow in her arms, and cried into it, hoping it would smother her ragged sobs. Her heart was breaking. Perhaps already broken beyond all repairing. Not only from her hateful father selling her—more than once—but to Riordan's betrayal. Her mind swirled, why he would lie about the settlement? And his name? What else had he lied about?

Was all that had passed between them a lie? Her emotions were raged; this was not the time to try and sort through her confused feelings. She couldn't make sense of anything. Oh, how she wished Mary was here. She could always put things in their proper perspective.

Her sobs quieted. She took great gulps of air and exhaled to calm her frayed nerves. If there was no settlement, how would she and Mary survive? Another problem to work through. A knock disturbed her thoughts. Sabrina sat upright and dashed the tears from her cheeks. "Yes?"

"It's Helen, the maid, my lady."

For a moment she'd thought it might be Riordan again, which simultaneously annoyed and thrilled her. Despite all this, she still loved him. *Drat the man.* When he kicked in the door at the inn, her heart leapt with relief and anticipation. He'd come for her. As she knew he would. Oh, why did he lie and ruin it?

"Come in."

An older woman of middling years entered with footmen carrying the tub and a phalanx of maids carrying buckets of water. The tub was filled quickly and slight wisps of steam curled into the air. The maid placed rose petals in the water. How inviting. When had she last received such care?

"The lords, the earl and viscount, said I'm to see to your needs, my lady." Everyone was referring to her as "my lady" or "Lady Pepperdon." She didn't have the energy or inclination to correct them tonight.

"Thank you, Helen."

The older woman nodded and gave her a warm smile. "I'm to attend to you in the bath, then bring a tray of food. Would you prefer a hot or cold meal, my lady?"

Sabrina wanted to scream "leave me alone," yet she did not wish to be left with her thoughts. Her mind raced, her emotions in turmoil. Her heart still banged at tattoo beat; she needed to calm, and a warm bath and a hot meal would assist in such an endeavor. "A hot meal, thank you."

"Master Riordan said to bring you apple pie…."

She shook her head. "No." The memory of them sharing a jolly laugh over her botched attempt at baking an apple pie, and the heated intimacy that had followed, rushed through her mind. Shaking it away, she said, "No, thank you."

"Very well, my lady. You have a good soak and I'll return directly." Helen hurried from the room, leaving her alone. After slipping off her clothes and laying them on the bed, she tentatively stepped into the tub and lowered into the warm rose-scented water. *Blessed relief.* Leaning her head against the high back of the copper tub, she sighed and closed her eyes.

Did she fall asleep? For next she knew, Helen had returned, carrying a tray with covered dishes upon it. Another maid followed, carrying a tea tray with a small decanter. Still another maid followed, with towels and bathing cloths. "I located a bar of rose-scented soap, my lady. Not easy in a house full of men."

Helen saw to the trays and dismissed the other maids, closing the door behind them. She pulled up a chair and dipped the soap and the cloth in the water. "Still warm. I was gone close to thirty minutes. Did you rest, my lady?"

So she had napped. "Yes, thank you." She paused. "I'm curious, why are an earl and a viscount under the same roof? Father and son usually have separate residences."

Sabrina leaned forward so Helen could wash her back. "It's usually the case, but the Wollstonecraft men are a different breed, to be sure. I've been here thirty years, since Master Garrett was a wee one. Seen the tragedy of both men losing their wives. I've seen the earl lose two wives.

He had three, if you can imagine." Helen squeezed the cloth, rinsing the soap from Sabrina's back.

"They decided it was best if the twins and Master Garrett grew up together, seeing there was only six years between them, and as a result the three of them are very close. So the viscount stayed here instead of taking up residence in London. You see, Master Garrett and the viscount are half brothers. The place is big enough to house several families."

Sabrina had been impressed when the moonlit hall had come into view. How late was it? She glanced at the mantel clock. Good heavens—near eleven. What a long and stressful day. Fatigue covered her, but she must eat. She glanced about the room, inspecting it closely. Large and welcoming with the fire blazing. Not feminine in style, but a well-maintained guest room, with its gold curtains and rugs and large wooden bed with intricate carvings of acorns and trees on the headboard.

The Wollstonecrafts were rich. Why on earth had Riordan taken a position as schoolmaster in a small country township? The clothes he wore...of course. She'd chosen to believe they came from a middle class background when in fact he was of the peerage. Was he the heir? Wait... the twins? "Who are the twins?" she asked Helen.

"Why, Masters Riordan and Aidan, sons of the viscount. Master Aidan is away. He is the oldest, and the heir. They are not identical—close enough in looks, but not temperament. Listen to me prattling on, but you are Master Riordan's wife and it all stays within the family." Helen stood and held up a large, plush towel. "Here, my lady. Let me dry you off and get you into nightclothes. Your meal awaits. We've set up a table by the fire."

Oh, how she had missed this. For all her brave talk of adjusting to a simple country life, she was to the manor born. But not on this scale. Goodness, Wollstonecraft Hall must be twice the size of Durning House. Perhaps three times larger.

As Helen assisted her into the nightgown and dressing gown, Sabrina dismissed the doing of the day—at least for tonight. She was emotionally wrung out, and all she wanted was to eat a little food and climb into bed.

Helen escorted her to the table. Once she was seated, the maid lifted the chafing dish cover. Slices of beef and dainty potatoes drizzled with what looked to be a red wine sauce. "Tea, my lady? The viscount thought you might like a brandy before retiring."

"Yes to both." Sabrina cleared her cluttered mind and concentrated on the meal before her. What she would say to Riordan tomorrow? She had absolutely no idea.

* * * *

In his sixty-four years on this earth, Oliver Wollstonecraft had witnessed much tragedy and heartache, along with venal, illegal, and morally bankrupt behavior from people of all walks of life. But never had he witnessed such disregard for the sanctity of human life than he had yesterday. A man selling his only child. And more than once. His lip curled with disgust. Sutherhorne purchasing a woman as if he were procuring a horse at Tattersalls.

Sutherhorne was bad enough, but it was Durning that gave Oliver pause. Only once in his life had he met such a man: emotionless, lacking in remorse, yet possessing a superficial charm that people often fell for. The arrogance and poor judgment, the selfish need to see to one's own comforts. The power to manipulate others. The traits applied to Sutherhorne as well; they were peas in a pod.

How unfortunate that the law would not touch Sutherhorne. A marquess was above an earl; Oliver could do nothing to bring the man to heel. Allowing the story to circulate would hurt Lady Pepperdon's reputation more than the men's—such was the imbalance in Society. The marquess would bear watching.

"Da?" Garrett asked. "Did you not hear me?"

Oliver shook his head. "Sorry, Son. Deep in thought."

Garrett snapped the reins. They were riding in the wagon toward Riordan's residence. "No bloody wonder. My head is still reeling from yesterday. What do you think will be the outcome of this?"

"It's patently obvious that Riordan loves this woman. It will be between them to decide if the ending will be a happy one."

Garrett frowned. "He'd be better off cutting ties and going through with the annulment."

"Ah, the curse. Garrett, you take it too much to heart. And before you start to rattle off statistics, I am fully aware of the death count. I agree caution is warranted, but think on this: If I hadn't taken a chance on love, you, Julian, or the twins wouldn't be here. I would be a lonely old man sitting by the fire, drinking myself into oblivion, cursing the fates with my last ragged breath. Is that the future you wish for yourself?"

Garrett scoffed. "Perhaps it is. At least I would avoid heartache and loss."

Oliver shook his head. "That is the coward's way. Besides, feeling pain and loss lets one know they are alive." He loved both his sons, but Garrett did hold a special place in his heart. Not only was he his true love Moira's child, but the spitting image of her. Looking at him sometimes hurt, but on the whole it gave him comfort. As if she were still with him.

Garrett stiffened beside him. "Don't get your hackles up, Son. You're thirty-two years of age. It's well past time you married and had children. Yes, it is a selfish request. I want your mother and the Mackinnon clan to live on for future generations. I want *you* to live on. Don't let the line end here."

Garrett laughed sharply. "The twins can carry the torch." Then he sobered. "As soon as we locate Aidan and set him on the straight and narrow path."

"What possessed him to disappear?" Oliver asked.

"He's been drifting away from us for a long while, Da. His taste for adventure and vice could be his downfall," Garrett replied sadly. "We've been close through the years, Aidan and me, but not of late. I should have intervened, given him my support. Instead I became angry and disgusted at his behavior."

"As did we all. You feel guilty. Is that why you hired the Bow Street Runner on your own?"

Garrett nodded. "Once Riordan is straightened out, I'll be joining Edwin in London to assist in the search."

And here is why he loved Moira's son so dearly: his generous heart. His capacity for love. If only he didn't keep the curse at the forefront of his mind and allow it to control his life.

The men remained silent for several miles. "There's the schoolhouse." Garrett pointed to a wooden structure sitting alone in a wooded area. "The cottage is but a half mile beyond."

They arrived, and Oliver was shocked to see how small the cottage was. Heavens, it was no larger than a woodshed. Oliver jumped from the wagon, and as Garrett saw to the horses, he knocked on the door.

It flew open. "I told you I would leave once I heard word, stop—oh. I thought you were someone else."

This must be the companion, Mary Tuttle. She stared up at him, waiting for a reply, but Oliver was too busy drinking in her fine form. In her middle years, but still attractive. "Sorry to disturb you. Miss Tuttle, I presume?" She nodded. "I am Riordan's grandfather."

She arched a dubious eyebrow. "Grandfather? I find the prospect highly unlikely. You look far too young. And don't take it as a compliment, it is merely an observation."

A curve of a smile twisted at the corner of his mouth. "I thank you anyway. May we come in?"

She looked past him and her eyes widened. "Good God, it's the medieval Highlander."

Garrett stood beside Oliver. "The Highlander is my son, Garrett, and Riordan's uncle. His mother was Scottish. May we come in?" Already he liked this woman.

She shook her head. "Of course. Forgive me." Miss Tuttle stepped aside and let them pass, closing the door behind them. "Can I offer you tea or a bite to eat? There is stew I can heat."

"Perhaps after we talk. Since you did not ask about Lady Pepperdon, I assume you received our message?" Oliver asked.

"I did. I'm relieved she's been recovered. The baron is a despicable man and deserves all he gets."

"And he will. Debtor's prison is in his future, make no mistake," Oliver replied. "We will see to it." They all took seats in the tiny parlor, with Garrett's large frame precariously perched on a wooden chair. "My name is Oliver Wollstonecraft, Earl of Carnstone. You see, my grandson's full name is Riordan Black Wollstonecraft."

Miss Tuttle covered her mouth in shock. "But why…"

"Why did he conceal his true identity? He wished to take his teaching position without the family name and history becoming a distraction."

She shook her head. "Sabrina had no idea. Oh, dear. When she finds out… She cannot abide deception."

Oliver crossed his legs. "So I gathered. Hopefully, they will work it out. Then perhaps Riordan will return to his position here with his wife."

Miss Tuttle clasped her hands in her lap, a sad expression on her face. "I fear your grandson does not have a position to return to. A member of the education board appeared here early this morning, claiming I'm to vacate the premises by tonight. Mr. Black—I mean, Mr. Wollstonecraft—has been dismissed. 'For abandoning his post and responsibilities.' As if your grandson was in the army. Wretched man. He wouldn't listen to my explanation."

Garrett vaulted out of his chair, his fists clenched. "Allow me to find the man and straighten him out," he barked.

Oliver clutched his arm. "Easy. Diplomacy may be better than fisticuffs. At least initially. Who is this board member and where can we find him?"

"He is Mr. Umlah, the blacksmith." Miss Tuttle slid her gaze to Garrett. "Although he is not as large or imposing as your Highlander son."

Oliver laughed; he couldn't help it. How refreshing to find a woman near his own age sparking his interest. His previous affair of three years past with a young, spoiled, pampered widow of a baronet had left him empty.

In the twilight of his life, he wanted to find a woman whose company he would enjoy. One he could talk to, laugh with, and, yes, have frequent sex with. He may be in his sixties, but he still experienced desire.

"Garrett, regardless of how the conversation goes with the smithy, we should gather all Riordan and Lady Pepperdon's possessions and take them with us to the hall."

"Good thing we brought the wagon," Garrett replied as he sat.

"Miss Tuttle, Lady Sabrina mentioned a kitten?"

"Yes. Your grandson gifted her to Sabrina. I'll pack while you and your son seek out Mr. Umlah, my lord."

"I believe you should accompany me and direct me to the place. Besides, the man owes you an apology; I intend to see he gives it. Garrett will start loading the wagon." They all stood.

"Let me fetch my shawl. Oh, the kitten is asleep in the bedroom. Make sure she doesn't get outside, will you, Mr. Wollstonecraft?"

"Of course," Garrett replied.

Once Miss Tuttle placed her shawl about her shoulders, Oliver gently clasped her arm. Sizzling heat moved through him, settling deep within; what he was about to propose would only stoke the flames. "I'll unhitch one of the horses and we will ride into town together. Are you fine with the plan, Miss Tuttle?"

She met his gaze, and he did not mistake the interest sparking in her light brown eyes. "Completely fine, my lord."

Yes, standing here next to the fetching Miss Mary Tuttle, everything *was* completely fine.

Chapter 26

Forget about sleep; Riordan had none at all. He'd respected Sabrina's wishes and stayed away from her, though he had stopped and listened outside her door shortly before eleven. Water splashed—she was in the bath. The thought of her naked caused him to harden, and he returned to his room and took care of the condition. But the release left him unfulfilled and staring at the ceiling until the sun peeked over the horizon.

He still had no idea how to explain, but he would face her and tell her whatever she wished to know. He knocked on the bedroom door, and she bade him enter. Sabrina stood by the window, engulfed in warm autumn sunshine, which gave her skin a golden glow. She looked as if she belonged here at Wollstonecraft Hall. The lady of the manor.

"Sabrina."

She turned to face him, her expression as impassive and devoid of emotion as the day they first met. With a sweep of her arm, she motioned to the two chairs set up in front of the fire. She wore the same clothes as yesterday, but they looked to have been pressed.

He sat, as did she. "Allow me to begin with an apology. I am truly sorry I did not tell you of my name, especially after we grew more intimate. I was going to…" He stopped. Saying he was going to tell her last night would be a lame excuse. He changed direction. "The main reason I did not tell you was that the false name was the grounds for the annulment. You recall I did tell you it was better if I kept the motivation secret until we appeared before the court. Also, I hid it from the school board, save for one member, as I wished to take the position of schoolmaster on equal footing with the residents of Carrbury. I did not want my family's standing and reputation to interfere with my plan."

She frowned. "You sat there at the inn, the night before our wedding, choking when I mentioned the name Wollstonecraft. You could have told me during that conversation. Or when I lay in your arms after making love. Or when you told me you loved me. Why did you not tell me then? Or, better yet, *before* we became intimate? I feel betrayed. Used. By yet another man for his own selfish reasons."

He was about to reply, but Sabrina continued, "And what of the settlement? Imagine my horror at finding out there never was one. You created an elaborate ruse with your solicitor friend to…to…I'm not sure why. To lure me into marriage for your own base needs? Is the marriage even legitimate?" Her voice rose with each sentence. The hurt in it cut him to the quick.

"The papers we signed are legal, as is the marriage. I was going to say no to your proposal, but your story moved me. It spoke to my progressive soul, as it were. And I realize now that I was already beginning to care for you. I wanted to protect you from hurt." He paused, staring into the fire before meeting her gaze. "There is money, Sabrina. I alone put up the ten thousand pounds. It sits in an account at the law office, awaiting you."

Her eyes widened. "Why would you give such a sum to a complete stranger?"

"I am a Wollstonecraft, raised with liberal beliefs. I spoke the truth when I said women are treated no better than property, with no rights at all. I wanted to give you a fresh start. I did not intend to fall in love with you. But I did."

She looked away, staring out the window once again, as if contemplating what he was saying. "What do you mean by plan? Regarding your position?"

"I originally accepted the teaching position in order to try out my ideas on education reform. Each of us in the family have our own pet causes; education was mine. I did not expect to enjoy teaching as much as I do. God, I don't know how to describe it. Never have I felt as alive as when I am standing before a group of children eager to learn." He paused. "Except when I'm in your arms. Except when I'm deep inside you and you raise your hips to meet my thrusts, taking me deeper. Taking me…to paradise."

She flushed, then stood and began to pace, wringing her hands. "I must speak to your father. Please bring him here at once."

What in the hell? He'd gone too far, bringing up the intimacy they'd shared. "Sabrina…"

"Please!" she cried, clearly distressed.

Riordan stood and inched toward the door. "As you wish."

He located his father in the library, reading assorted papers. "Sabrina asked me to fetch you. I don't know why."

His father followed him upstairs to the guest room. "What is it, Lady Pepperdon?"

She turned to face his father, still wringing her hands. "I cannot stay under this roof any longer." Riordan's heart sank. "At least, not until I think this over. I appreciate your family's hospitality and all you've done for me. But I need a place of quiet, with no…distractions."

Wonderful. Now I'm a distraction. Damn it.

His father took Sabrina's hand. "I understand." Well, Riordan didn't. "You have a lot to process. I believe our neighbor, Mrs. Alberta Eaton, would gladly offer rooms for you and your companion until you are ready to make a decision. Allow me to make the arrangements." He turned and said to Riordan in a low voice, "I believe you should leave."

He was not a petulant child; he would not rant. He was raised as a gentleman. Sabrina was distraught, and that concerned him, but after what she'd endured yesterday, on top of his revelations, he could not blame her at all.

"Of course." He withdrew. Should he take comfort in the fact that she hadn't dismissed him outright? All he knew was he loved her more than his life, but he would give her the time and space she asked for.

* * * *

Julian strode toward the Eaton residence. He had not returned since the hedgehog incident. He'd considered Alberta's place instead of taking Lady Pepperdon further afield, like the inn at Sevenoaks, because it was close enough to Wollstonecraft Hall and private enough for quiet contemplation.

He knocked on the door. As it swung open, the breath caught in his throat. Alberta Eaton wore a dark green day dress, hugging curves he'd no idea she possessed. Hell, she must have bound her bosom when working in the garden, because he'd seen no evidence of such lushness. Her hair was the color of a field of wheat and styled fashionably. Since it had been hidden under her large hat, he'd no idea of the shade.

The smile she gave him made him weak in the knees. "How wonderful to see you, Tensbridge. We're about to have tea. Do come in. Jonas will be thrilled."

He stepped across the threshold and followed her into the parlor.

Jonas stood. The young man wore a brown suit, and was certainly in a neater condition than when they'd last met. He smiled, and the lad's perfect features stunned him afresh.

"Jonas, my dear. Remember what you do when a guest arrives?" Alberta gently urged.

"Right." Jonas stepped forward and held out his hand. "A pleasure to receive you, my lord." Julian took his hand. A firm shake. Blasted pity the lad was mentally deficient; with his looks, he could have made a fine alliance with a young lady of property and prestige.

After she took his greatcoat, they took their seats, and Alberta poured and passed him a cup of tea. "To what do we owe this pleasure?"

Gathering his thoughts, he told a condensed version of the events of the past thirty-six hours.

"Oh, my. Of course Lady Pepperdon and Miss Tuttle may stay here. And her kitten. What is another animal about the place, right, Jonas?"

"I like kittens," he replied as he slurped his tea.

"Thank you," Julian said. "I do not expect it to be more than a couple of days. I believe my son and Lady Pepperdon will come through this."

"I cannot imagine a father selling his daughter. Isn't it against the law? The man is a monster. He deserves debtor's prison, or worse," Alberta remarked.

"Is it where men go when they can't pay their butcher's bill?" Jonas asked.

It occurred to Julian that Jonas was not as simpleminded as he'd first surmised. It was as if he stood between childhood and manhood, a foot planted firmly in each aspect, stuck there for the rest of his days. It was clear the young man followed their conversation and was able to understand it.

"You're correct, Jonas. But he would have to owe many people, with no way of paying them all. The court will make a ruling, and the baron will be sent there to either work off his debt or stay until he is able to pay it."

"The baron should go to a prison. He's a bad man," Jonas stated.

"Just so. I completely agree," Julian replied.

"My dear," Alberta said to Jonas, "why not take some fruit out to your hedgehogs?"

"Wearing my suit?"

"Yes. Be careful not to get it dirty."

Jonas smiled, grabbed a napkin, and placed pieces of apple in it. He scurried from the room.

"I admit, in our first encounter, I believed Jonas more…psychologically impaired, intellectually speaking," Julian said.

Alberta laughed. It was as husky and sensual as her voice, and it caused a blast of heat to tear through him. "How diplomatically put." She sobered. "My husband said Jonas was slow developing, didn't speak his first word until nearly four years of age. When Reese passed, Jonas was nineteen, and is as you see him now."

"A man-child?" Julian asked gently.

"Yes, I suppose he is. I fear he will never marry, which is a tragedy, as Jonas has a great capacity to love. It would take a woman of immense compassion and understanding to take him on."

Julian took her hand. "Not many widows would take their late husband's brother under their wing, especially one with the challenges Jonas faces. Many would have shipped him off to an institution, one of those wretched asylums. But not you." He lifted her hand to his lips and kissed it.

"Tensbridge…"

Jonas burst into the room. "Tens! Come see the hedgehogs, and bring more apple."

Julian welcomed the interruption. The room had become hot, the air close, the emotions powerful. He was not looking for this, or anything remotely close to it. He stood and gathered his greatcoat from the nearby chair. "Good afternoon, Mrs. Eaton."

"Good afternoon, my lord."

He grabbed a handful of sliced apple and left the room. *Damn it all. Never should have come here. Should have sent a damned footman instead.* His safe, staid world has been thrown off its axis, and it annoyed him to no end. But a part of him was intrigued.

Chapter 27

"Thank you, Mrs. Eaton, for taking us in for a couple days." Sabrina, Mary, and Alberta sat in the front parlor, drinking fresh lemonade in the early evening.

"Please, do call me Alberta, Lady Pepperdon."

"Only if you call me Sabrina. I no longer use the courtesy title."

Alberta passed a plate of ginger biscuits to Mary. "And may I call you Mary?"

"I insist on it," she replied as she took a couple of biscuits and laid them on her napkin.

"I do apologize for the state of this small manor house. My late uncle was a hermit and an eccentric, and in his final years allowed the place to go to ruin. We are slowly putting the place to rights. Our generous neighbors, the Wollstonecrafts, have been a great assistance, especially Garrett." She smiled. "They are generous to a fault. I've never met such indomitable men." Alberta stood. "I will leave you two to catch up while I check on Jonas and Mittens. He adores animals." Alberta smiled and exited the room.

Mary blew out a cleansing breath. "Good Lord, what drama we find ourselves in."

"I'm relieved you are here; I've been feeling rather adrift." Sabrina placed her empty glass on the tray. "I don't know where to begin."

"My dear, you have a decision to make. It is not for me to make it for you," Mary said, her voice kind. "Do you still love him?"

A loud sob escaped her. "Yes. Oh, yes. It's what makes this difficult. You've heard the particulars?"

Mary nodded. "The earl filled me in. I understand why Riordan used the name Black; it is his middle name, his mother's maiden name, and he wanted no distractions, to be treated as an equal, not a man from the peerage."

"Yes, I understand it as well, but why did he not tell me as we grew closer? The other night we…well, he told me he loved me, and he showed me how much. Apparently he could not trust me with the information."

Mary's eyes widened. "That is the explanation he gave you?"

"No. He claims he wished to use the false name as grounds to obtain the annulment." Sabrina paused and bit on her lower lip. "It makes sense. He did tell me he was keeping it hush-hush so I would act appropriately surprised before the court and would not be lying when the truth was revealed."

"Again, sounds reasonable. And the settlement?"

"Riordan put up the money. Can you imagine? He knew about my father selling me and said nothing." Sabrina thought to when they were leaving Durning House. She'd asked him if he had the settlement and he'd patted his pocket, claiming he had it well in hand. He hadn't actually lied, but he wasn't truthful either.

She waved her arm as Mary was about to speak. "I know. Generous to a fault. He kept the revelation to himself to protect me. But it is as if he were controlling my life, as Pepperdon and my father were." Sabrina sighed. "I sound irrational to my own ears. I'm still coming to terms over the vile acts my father and the marquess perpetrated. I'm finding it difficult to sort through my feelings."

Mary patted her hand. "Take as much time as you need. No one is pressing you for a decision. You have a choice, which is what you've always wanted, isn't it, my dear? To be able to steer your own destiny? Here is the opportunity to do it."

"If I decide to leave, what will we do for money?"

"As I told you, I have a nice sum. There are your jewels…we will manage. Do not let money influence your decision. I should tell you that Riordan has been dismissed from his position."

Sabrina gasped. "What?"

"When I informed him you were missing, he left the school, and though he asked me to stay, the board was quite put out. However, his grandfather, the earl, spoke to the board member in question. I'm not sure of the outcome; Riordan will tell you." She patted Sabrina's hand, then reached for a biscuit. "The earl did state Riordan would have to decide what to do. I would guess the earl managed to get him reinstated, if he should wish to continue to teach."

Sabrina mulled over the information. There were many paths to take for both of them. “The marriage is not a real one, even if I decide to stay with Riordan. He used a false name.”

Nodding, Mary nibbled thoughtfully on her biscuit. “Another ceremony will be needed.”

A long, frustrating sigh left her. “I acted like such a ninny earlier today. Riordan walked into the room and I became overwhelmed by his words, his very presence. Even being under the same roof as him drives me to distraction.”

Mary laughed. “Any of those men would drive a woman to distraction. You’ve met his grandfather? Good Lord, what a fine specimen of a mature man. How old is he?”

For the first time in the past forty-eight hours, Sabrina smiled. “Why, Mary! Does the earl interest you?”

Mary cleared her throat. “He’s fascinating to be sure, and handsome, with all that white hair and those large, expressive blue eyes.”

“Helen, the maid who attended me, said that the earl is sixty-four, the viscount forty-five, and Garrett thirty-two. Riordan and his paternal twin, Aidan, are twenty-six.”

“Twin? And where is he during all this?” Mary asked.

“He is away, apparently.” Sabrina stared out the large window in front of her. “I do love Riordan most desperately, but I want to be sure of my decision.”

“You’ve been through a terrible ordeal. No one will force you to decide anything until you are good and ready. I’ll stand guard and keep everyone away until you are.”

Sabrina impulsively hugged Mary tight. It *had* been a terrible ordeal. Honestly, she would be a stubborn, arrogant fool to turn from love. From passion. From a friend turned lover. From a man who was honorable. Decent. Sensual and alluring.

They could have it all. Now to find the courage to grab life with both hands. *Make a choice.*

* * * *

Three days had passed since he and Sabrina met in the guest room. Riordan had stayed well clear, as she’d requested. It had been utter agony. But now he’d been summoned, and the final verdict would be rendered. Whatever she decided, he would honor her wishes.

But first, she would have to hear him out. Even the lowliest criminal was given a chance to speak at trial. As he strode toward the Eaton residence, the cold November wind chilled him to his bones. He held firmly to the brim of his hat, lest it be carried away. The sky was overcast, which matched his mood, not only due to this situation with his wife, but upon hearing he'd been dismissed. It gave him little comfort to learn the blacksmith had acted on his own, and that the rest of the board had overridden him once the earl brought it to their attention.

He was reoffered the position, but his grandfather stated they would have to find another educator until the first week in January, as Riordan was dealing with a family emergency. If Riordan even wished to return to the post. Though initially angry for the curt dismissal, he did miss his students. It was not in him to quit, he should at least finish out the school year.

How Sabrina felt about it—or anything—was a complete mystery. When he first met her, she'd been aloof, self-contained, sad, and lonely. Slowly, he'd peeled away the layers of her protective shell to find a woman of deep feeling and passion. But trust did not come easily to her. He should have known this and told her the truth regardless. A major misstep. Because of it, she'd retreated behind her wall once again.

The incident with her evil father did not help matters. Damn it, it never crossed his mind Sutherhorne and Durning would perpetrate such a malevolent crime. The baron was in dire straits financially, but to sell Sabrina *again*? All Riordan wanted was to protect her, and he'd failed miserably.

Arriving at the Eaton home, he exhaled as he used the brass knocker. An attractive blonde woman answered the door.

"There is no mistaking you're Tensbridge's son." She smiled warmly and held out her hand. "I'm Mrs. Alberta Eaton."

Ah, the widow. He could see why his father's interest had been sparked. Taking her hand, he bowed over it. "Riordan Wollstonecraft. A pleasure, Mrs. Eaton."

"Do come in. I will take your coat and hat. Sabrina is through to the parlor. Help yourself to whiskey from the decanter. There is tea as well."

He entered the room, where Sabrina stood by the window once again. No doubt she'd watched him all the way to the door. She turned, her expression impassive, her manner guarded and cool. He would need that whiskey. Glancing about the sparse room, he located it. Without hesitating, he strode to the sideboard, picked up the decanter, and motioned it toward her.

"No, thank you," she replied tonelessly.

There was only a threadbare armchair and a sofa in the room, and Riordan would bet a sack full of gold guineas that she would sit in the chair, which was farthest away from him. Sure enough, she stepped toward the chair.

"Will you join me on the sofa?" he asked, keeping his voice gentle, as if approaching a skittish horse.

"Yes." She sat on the edge, primly clasping her hands on her lap.

Riordan took a long swig before he joined her. "I regret that I failed to protect you from your father and Sutherhorne."

She met his gaze. "You were not to know. How could you?"

"I found out from Durning there was no dowry. He took great delight in informing me of Sutherhorne and his pact with him. Garrett and I headed directly for the inn and made certain threats, demanding Sutherhorne leave town immediately. I fear we angered and humiliated him, hence it became the motivation for his plan of abduction." He took another long drink, the burn sizzling down his throat. "I'm heartily sorry we set this in motion. Were you harmed in any way?"

Sabrina shook her head. "No, not physically. The baron made me swallow laudanum or he would have killed Mittens. When I awoke, I was in that horrible room."

Jesus. He placed the glass on the small table, struggling to control his fury. "I've news of the baron; do you wish to hear it?"

"No." She sighed. "Yes."

"His creditors are circling him as we speak. Sutherhorne has refused to assist him. Grandfather has it on good authority that your father owes more than twenty thousand pounds. Even selling Durning House and all its possessions will not see him free and clear from this crushing debt."

She shook her head. "He claimed it was a railway scheme."

"There have been quite a few investments that have fallen through and ruined all those attached to them. What these men, including your father, are doing is referred to as speculation, and it is heading for complete collapse. Again, improper regulation leads to utter greed and—you don't want to hear this. Your father's hearing is in early January. Durning is heading for debtor's prison, I've no doubt. It's over for him." Riordan frowned. "Sutherhorne is another thing entirely."

"Why?" she asked.

"He's a marquess. Untouchable. I will not bring charges of abduction and the buying and selling of a human against him if it means involving you in public conjecture, especially when nothing will come if it. Unless you wish to see him brought up on charges?"

"No. It would come to nothing, as you say. I want to put it behind me."

"We will keep an eye out, as I did not like the way Sutherhorne glared at us, Garrett in particular."

She clasped his hand, a worried look on her face, the first show of emotion since he'd arrived. "Are you and your family in danger?"

He would not lie. Not ever again. "Perhaps. But if the marquess is smart, he will let this pass."

"My father told me the marquess would seek vengeance, and he did. I fear this is not over. I should have told you that I came across my father the day I sold the jewels. It appears we both kept secrets."

"We will never do so again. As for the family, we will remain vigilant, I promise." Riordan threaded his fingers through hers. "Speaking of danger, I must tell you of the curse."

She allowed his touch for a moment, then pulled her hand away. "What curse? Oh, the one tied to your family, about how women who love Wollstonecraft men don't live long?"

"I suppose another reason I was reluctant to mention my real name is because I do not wish to place any woman I care for at risk." She gave him a dubious look. "It is part of my family. Our legacy. Not easily dismissed."

"Do you believe in it?" she asked, her voice soft.

"Yes...and no. Not enough to deny love. But I would understand if any woman turned from me because of it." Sabrina's eyebrows furrowed, and she didn't reply. He might as well soldier on. "Again, allow me to apologize for lying to you. About my name, the settlement, not informing you of your father—"

"It hurts. Deeply. I understand the motivation, but after what we shared, you should have told me," she whispered.

"I agree. I'm not perfect. Far from it, it turns out, as I've made many mistakes. I arrogantly thought I was protecting you from hurt, because you've been hurt enough. But I failed in all ways." He reached in his suit coat pocket. "Allow me to make amends. Allow me to give you what you desire most...your freedom."

Her brows knotted in puzzlement as she reached for the paper. As she read it the furrow between her brows deepened. "What does this mean?"

"A week from today, we appear at the ecclesiastical court. The annulment is all but guaranteed. My father pulled various strings. You will be free. It is what you desire most."

She shook her head as she folded the paper with trembling hands. "No. It is *not* what I desire most."

"The money will be yours—"

"I don't want your money! I want you!" she cried. "*You* are what I desire most. I love you, you stubborn, glorious man. When you told me you loved me the night I lay in your arms, I was too frightened to say it in return. For you see, I'm not perfect either." Sabrina choked back a sob. "Once, long ago, I dreamed of having a father who would spoil me, read me stories, and teach me how to dance. One who would share the last piece of cake with me. Bring me a gift when I least expected it, like you did with Mittens."

Shaking her head sadly, she continued. "How I yearned for it, but never experienced any of it." She caught his gaze, her eyes shimmered with emotion. "But I have found a different version of it—love—with you, haven't I?"

"My darling, I will spoil you just enough, and when you least expect it. I will continue to read to you every night, share my cake, and lavish you with small gifts. Dance with you whenever you wish. I love you to absolute distraction. I would do anything to see you smile, laugh, and enjoy life."

"I do, with you," she whispered.

Riordan gathered her in his embrace, burying his face in her neck, his eyes wet. Sabrina held him tight, stroking his hair. Lifting his head, he kissed her. As always, it turned fierce for the both of them. He pulled away. "Do you forgive me?" He leaned his forehead against hers.

"Yes. How can I not?"

"We will stay married?"

Sabrina laughed. "We'll need to arrange another ceremony."

He laughed in return, joy filling his heart. "I will obtain a special license. I come from a powerful family, you know. As for your freedom? You will have it with me. I pledge this with my life. I will never treat you as property. We will be equal partners."

"What of your teaching position?"

He kissed her again. "We will decide together. I would like to finish out the academic year."

Sabrina stroked his cheek. "And after?"

"I'd hoped to start my own progressive board school here in Kent. I've decided to set myself as headmaster, as I wish to stay in teaching. But we will discuss it at length. After all, I have money and a powerful family—or did I tell you already?"

She smiled, then sobered. "On the subject of children, the earl blamed me, but the doctor did say the problem, as it were, lay with Pepperdon. I do hope that is the case."

Riordan kissed her hand. "My love, it is no matter. I'll have more children than I can count for many years to come. And different ones each school year. We will take what comes."

She laughed, clutching his hand tight.

"All I need, or desire, is you. Until the end of my days. My partner, my friend, my passionate lover." He cupped her face and kissed her tenderly, with every raw emotion swelling his heart until it nearly burst.

Their story was not over—nor was it for the rest of the men of Wollstonecraft Hall. Riordan had found his soul mate, the lady of his heart. Curse be damned.

He fervently wished the rest of his family to find love and happiness. To not allow the curse to deny their hearts.

Especially Garrett.

Author's Note

Obviously the Wollstonecraft men are fictitious, but the progressive causes they supported were not. The 1840s were the beginning of many changes for the decades that followed: reforms to improve the quality of life for all, especially for women and the poor.

Wife-and children-selling was prevalent in England until the mid-Victorian age. Prosecutions started around the 1820s, which was the reason the baron wished to keep his auction of Sabrina a secret and demanded that everyone involved do the same.

Wuthering Heights was published in 1847, almost two years after this story takes place. I took a little artistic license to distort the time frame to fit my narrative.

Meet the Author

Karyn Gerrard, born and raised in the Maritime Provinces of Eastern Canada, now makes her home in a small town in Northwestern Ontario. When she's not cheering on the Red Sox or travelling in the summer with her teacher husband, she writes, reads romance, and drinks copious amounts of Earl Grey tea.

Even at a young age, Karyn's storytelling skills were apparent, thrilling her fellow Girl Guides with off-the-cuff horror stories around the campfire. A multi-published author, she loves to write sensual historicals and contemporaries. Tortured heroes are an absolute must.

As long as she can avoid being hit by a runaway moose in her wilderness paradise, she assumes everything is golden. Karyn's been happily married for a long time to her own hero. His encouragement and loving support keeps her moving forward.

To learn more about Karyn and her books, visit www.karyngerrard.com.